TO MISSY

Shifting Sands: The Lost Town

Emma Palova

Emma Palova
Aug. 18, 2024
Paradise

DEDICATION

To my fans and followers from around the world.

WORKS BY EMMA PALOVA

Shifting Sands: Short Stories
Shifting Sands: Secrets
Greenwich Meridian Memoir
Shifting Sands: The Lost Town

Upcoming
Shifting Sands: Steel Jewels

SCREENPLAY

Riddleyville Clowns

PODCAST

For the Love of Books Podcast

For Ida

A Chicagoan by birth, a Michiganian by heart and marriage,
an entrepreneur and a teacher,
My beloved Ida touched everyone like the breeze coming
from the lake,
Like the ferocious waves, she swept the shores of Singapore,
Turning lumbering souls into unforgotten heroes,
The wild savage into a gentle friend,
Diving into the blue waters of Lake Michigan,
She found treasures lying at the bottom,
Forbidden love, painful love, encompassing love,
Emerging anew, a white dove,
Buried at the foot of the sand hill,
Ida conquered the hearts of Singapore forever.

A bleeding heart between two men,
Lost in a sea of waves,
Picking grains of sand,
That through her fingers fell,
Trapped in a heart-shaped box,
With feathers and wings that only laudanum gives,
Rising like the moon in the afternoon.

Contents

EMMA PALOVA

ACKNOWLEDGMENTS

I would like to thank editor Carol Briggs, Lowell Person of the Year, 2019 for her ongoing impeccable editing of my body of work.

A big thank you goes to my friend and former editor of Lowell Ledger, Jeanne Boss of Rockford for the stylish cover that eloquently captures the content of the book.

Special thanks to Randy DiRosa, board member of the Saugatuck Douglas Historical Society (SDHS).

Thanks to my hometown newspaper, the Lowell Ledger, for publicity, inspiration and ongoing support of my author's work and other creative endeavors such as my new podcast show For the Love of Books Podcast.

Special thanks to the Fallasburg Historical Society for hosting my author's book signings at the signature one-room schoolhouse.

And mainly, I would like to express my gratitude to all my fans around the world; you are the reason I write.

1

Ida

Anxious, Ida smoothed her blue conic skirt and touched her bonnet as she boarded the steamer "Anthony Wayne" headed to St. Joseph across the big lake. She has never traveled on a ship before but was eager to move out from the growing city. Chicago was choking her, much like her growing family. She didn't even have her own room, and her younger siblings were all over the small house. She watched the raindrops fall on the windows as she held on tight to her luggage that ma bought for her.

"Now, you be careful girl," ma said. "We don't know what's on the other side of the lake. I've heard tales of savages attacking white men."

The word savage was still ringing in her ears when she made herself comfortable and took off her coat. Ma said it was a 70-mile ride across the big lake. She took out of her luggage a book of poems, and an instructional booklet, but kept on looking for the invitation letter. However, Ida was too nervous to find it, because she heard the whistle and the hissing sound of steam signaling, they were on their way. Ida looked behind her at the disappearing city in the distance. The waves swayed the boat and the wind from the west was pushing it forward out on the lake. Instead of the letter, Ida found the "Chicago Weekly Democrat" newspaper rolled in her bag. Dad, who was supportive of Ida's ventures, must have put it in there.

"Do you have to go, Ida?" he asked her on their way to the docks.

"Yes, daddy," she said. "I got this invitation."

She showed daddy the letter with a stamp from New York, but with an invitation to come to a place called "Singapore."

"But what if there are savages?" he said.

True, she read about Indians in some instructional booklets for her training, and in the "Legends of Michigan" book, that daddy had bought for her.

"They're Indians, not savages, daddy," she said. "Goodbye. Take care."

Ida smiled at the thought of that last goodbye at the docks; daddy was in a hurry to get to the meatpacking plant.

"If you don't like it, you can always come back," he waved at her.

She looked around the passenger steamboat at fellow travelers; they were mostly well-dressed men in search of business on the other side of the big lake. Ida packed her own food--some salt pork from daddy's work--but noticed that people were going toward the bow of the ship or on the deck. She ate her sandwich and opened the newspaper to read mostly about politics. Ida turned 23 on the first day of fall, ready to explore the world beyond the Chicago she had known. And when the invite arrived with the postage stamp from the Allegan Post Office, she was overwhelmed with joy.

"Look, daddy, Mr. Bosch is inviting me to this new town," she showed the letter to daddy.

"How do you know Mr. Bosch is an honest man?" daddy asked.

"Mr. Bosch must be a fine gentleman," she said. "Look at the stationery."

The steamer leaned to one side in a big wave causing her luggage to shift and slide. A big wave splashed on the windows, and Ida couldn't see anything. Daddy had warned her that travel on these steamers could be wild and dangerous, mainly because of the lake. She reached for the luggage and pulled it closer toward herself. The rocking in the waves continued until the cloudy sky started to clear up with the sun peeking out, as the wind slowed down. Ida pulled out another piece of paper with information about the port of call, St. Joseph.

St. Joe at the time was an important point of American travel and commerce, as it lay along a key water route between the Great Lakes and the Mississippi River. Both the Miami and Potawatomi used this route and would use the area as a camp. The St. Joseph River also allowed for connection with the Sauk Trail, which was the major land trail through Michigan.

The St. Joseph River mouth was straightened through a channel and piers were added. The first lighthouse on Lake Michigan was built here, and St. Joseph was incorporated in 1834.

The first water route across Lake Michigan between St. Joseph and Chicago began as a mail route in 1825, but service was sporadic until 1842 when Samuel and Eber Ward began a permanent service.

Ida stayed overnight in a hotel, and the next morning headed out in a horse-drawn carriage to Ganges Township, according to Mr. Bosch's instructions in the invite. There was a boarding house for the lumber mill hands, with room for her to stay. The woman at the boarding house known as Mrs. Wilkinson was kind and friendly, in spite of her strict appearance with slick black hair parted in the middle.

"Mr. Bosch is expecting you tomorrow," she said. "Come on in."

They sat down in the small dining room with a library and a stove. Mrs. Wilkinson made pork and potatoes, and also an apple pie.

"What can you tell me about this town," Ida asked as she pulled out the letter from Mr. Bosch. "I think it's called Singapore."

"A bunch of investors from New York want to turn it into another Chicago or Milwaukee," smirked Mrs. Wilkinson.

"I don't understand the town's name, Singapore," said Ida. "That's in Asia, not here. We're here in the wilderness of Michigan where Indians abound."

The name of the lumbering town located half-a-mile from them was indeed Singapore. It was founded by a dreamer, Oshea Wilder, president of the New York and Michigan Company in 1837. Ida glanced at the letter on pretty stationery again, and the words resonated in her head like they did the first time she read it in Chicago.

"The town of Singapore will rival both Chicago and Milwaukee, and its counterpart in Asia," Mr. Bosch wrote in his letter to Ida.

"How did Mr. Bosch find me in Chicago?" Ida asked.

Mrs. Wilkinson gave Ida another piece of pie.

"That's men's business, but I know that O. Wilder traveled out West to find a suitable place for Singapore, and found it here on the shores of Lake Michigan," she said.

It was most likely that Wilder found her in the list of the early settlers of Chicago, and listed among teachers.

"You must have been involved in some women's

associations," Mrs. Wilkinson took a wild guess. "He wanted someone educated."

Daddy insisted for Ida to be active after she finished her teacher's training, and she was a member of several women's area associations.

"You probably also had good recommendations," Mrs. Wilkinson said.

The next day, with the cloudy sky hanging over, Mrs. Wilkinson handed the lines to the horses to Ida standing ready in front of the boarding house with her luggage.

"My child, do you know how to use these, may I ask?" she said.

"I do, my daddy taught me how to use these before we moved to Chicago from the coast," she said. "What are their names?"

"Arion and Argo," Mrs. Wilkinson said. "They're good fast horses. They will take you anywhere you wish. And they know the road to Singapore."

Ida took the lines to the horses into her hands and threw the luggage on the seat in the buggy. She shivered in the fall chill, but continued to Dugout Road. The road, squeezed between the river and the big dune, curved along the northernmost bend of the Kalamazoo River and the sides were overgrown with brush. An occasional sprinkle brushed her blue dress with a conic skirt. The buggy bumped up and down on the dugway, and she could hear the rattle of the luggage in the buggy. She drove past the oak openings further down the dugway until she saw the lake in the distance and the town below her. It sat in a cove shaped by the big lake and the erosion of the rocks.

As Ida entered the town, she could hear the sawmills at the far end. She arrived at the Big House, which was a boarding house for six families. Mrs. Fisch was waiting for her at the main entrance.

"Welcome, we've been waiting for you," Mrs. Fisch said. "How was your trip on the steamer from Chicago, were the seas calm?"

Ida glanced around and then turned back to Mrs. Fisch.

"Could I go and change before I meet Mr. Bosch," she said. "I dare say that the trip on the steamer was better than the carriage ride from St. Joe and now the horse and buggy shook me up on the road."

It was muddy on the Dugout Road, and mud was all over her skirt and shoes. Mrs. Fisch took Ida to her quarters on the third floor, where a special corner room was designated for this lady from Chicago. Pleased to see shelves for her books, a desk and a wooden wardrobe closet, Ida ran to the window to see the great town of Singapore. The main street unfolded in front of her eyes. Although she had driven the buggy through the town, she did not pay attention to the buildings, but was fully engaged in steering the horses away from the oncoming traffic that was heavy at that time of the day. But the other window uncovered vast mounds of sand hiding the lake from her view. The mounds of sand formed mountains around the town.

The traffic consisted of horse-drawn carriages, buggies and dray cargo carriage bearing the sign "Draw" instead of "Dray." From the third floor, she could see the store, the sawmills and a big building with a sign, the "Astor Hotel." Ida was genuinely surprised as she thought that Astor Hotel was only in New York. She made a note to ask Mr. Bosch about the hotel. She changed into her best dark green dress with a matching hat and descended down the steps into the main room.

Mr. Bosch stood up to greet the young lady from Chicago. He laid his eyes on this young blonde with blue eyes, and a body tied into a corset and covered with a pretty dress. He took his hat and nodded to Ida and extended out his hand. Surprised Ida looked at the handsome man in his thirties; dark hair parted to the left, and a mustache graced his face. He was tall and slim and had warm, brown eyes.

"Welcome, Miss Ida," he smiled. "How was your trip on the steamer? I've heard bad things about them."

"It wasn't as much as the steamer, but the curving road into the town," Ida said. "It bumped the soul out of me, but I was a little nauseated on the steamer and almost threw up."

They both sat down in the empire salon suite overlooking the main street. Mr. Bosch couldn't take his eyes off the young beautiful woman from Chicago.

"I want to know everything about this town," she said eagerly.

Mr. Bosch lit a cigar and spoke of his own dream of the

future metropolis of Singapore on the east shore of Lake Michigan. He was one of the investors together with Oshea who founded the New York and Michigan Co., that built the sawmills, the Big House aka the boarding house, and the Astor Hotel modeled after the famous hotel to attract visitors, much like the name of the town, that had nothing in common with the port in Asia.

"I see in front of my eyes a thriving metropolis visited by tourists and business people from all over the world, and from Chicago," he said. "That's why I picked you because you are from Chicago, and you will attract more people like you to this beautiful treasure amidst the sand hills."

Mr. Bosch painted his vision of the future resort of Singapore as a bustling, prospering city that never sleeps with all its vices and flashy nightlife.

However, Ida saw the town for what it was--a typical pioneer settlement with rough buildings and sawmills.

"Come with me," he said. "I will show you the plat of my city."

They both entered his gentleman's business quarters on the other side of the house guarded from the noise of the main street. The big plat map was hanging on the wall. Ida stepped up to look closely at map. The plat was laid on the north bank of the Kalamazoo River at the horseshoe bend in section 4, and was about a half-mile wide, and block 27 contained three acres owned by the company. The streets had names, such as: Beach, Walnut, Chestnut, Pine, Oak, River, Cedar, Cherry, Detroit and Broad, and the C.R. Calkins Hotel.

"We built the mill, opened the company store and the Astor House," Mr. Bosch gloated with pride. "It's the finest hotel by far."

The 40 x 60 feet Astor House had a large dining hall and it was three stories high, while the bread-and-butter of the town was the sawmill, and its green fuel--the endless white pines growing on the surrounding dunes reaching up to the sky.

"Miss Ida, I see this port town as the next financial capital of the world," he said. "But let's walk down the street, so I can show you around, and we can stop at the Astor."

Mr. Bosch helped Ida into her coat, since the first snowflakes fluttered like a bird in the wind coming from the lake. They walked on the boardwalk made from the local lumber, so Ida wouldn't get her dress and shoes dirty. They stopped at the store owned by the New York & Michigan company. It was here where people did their trading, not always honest. It was more like a hardware store that sold cut iron nails, plain iron cook stoves and heaters, most of them for burning wood. There were no plumbing goods except for hand water pumps and some pipe, as all the plumbing in the village was primitive. The store sold wooden wash tubs and water pails, tin and copper wash boilers, tinware, axes and saws, oil lamps and lanterns, candle mold, gun powder and shot, cast iron pots and pans, house carpenter's tools and tools for ship builders.

"We build ships here in Singapore, Miss Ida," Mr. Bosch said. "We will visit the harbor too so you get a better idea."

The store traded with French Canadian ship builders from the Dutch colony further up north, but it also got its first hard coal heaters.

2

Big House and Astor

Ida was shivering as they approached the Astor House located at the corner of Broad and Oak streets near the port of Singapore. It was modeled after the famous Astor House in New York, and built only one year later after its N.Y. counterpart in 1837. Many building materials like granite were brought in by a ship, much like the machinery for the sawmill. Ida gasped at the beauty of the "Astor," as Mr. Bosch helped her with the coat in the cloak room. Clerk H.H. Stimson met them in the lobby and escorted them to the dining room. Many tables were taken, and a lot of the gentlemen seated in different clusters greeted Mr. Bosch with respect and dignity. Stimson seated them by the window overlooking the port at the company table.

"You have the best view in the house," said the clerk as he pulled the chair for Ida.

Ida looked around the interior of the dining room with all the important people, as she assumed they were important. Pictures hanging on the wall were images from the "Astor House" in New

York, much higher and more ornate than the one in Singapore. She glanced at Mr. Bosch, who commanded respect of all those present. Her heart fluttered, as she recalled ma's words: "Beware of the savages and white ambitious men."

But, on the walls, all the paintings only depicted the high-class life of the wealthy and the powerful in New York, no Indians. Stimson himself brought them the menus, not allowing the waiter to take care of Mr. Bosch and his new pretty companion from Chicago. The town was well informed about all the newcomers.

Ida shuffled her feet deep underneath the table, not sure whether her shoes were still not muddy from that horrible trip along the river on the Dugout Road. She touched her right cheek, that was glowing from the walk in the streets in the cold weather, and from being surrounded by such luxury and attention. She noticed the clusters of all the fine gentlemen tightening together, and their voices grew softer. But there was music playing that saved Ida from impeding silence she had created by being by the side of Mr. Bosch.

"Stimson, bring us the best bottle of wine that you have," he said.

"I will have tea, Mr. Bosch," she said. "A good strong English or Russian tea."

"But, Miss Ida, it is dinner time, and Mrs. Fisch is not expecting us for dinner this evening," he said. "It's to welcome you to this great town."

"I am not used to drinking wine," she said. "I will have tea."

"Alright Stimson, bring me some good whiskey, if you can find an aged one," Mr. Bosch said. "Russian tea for Miss Ida."

Most of the fine products were delivered on ships since land transportation was difficult. As the ship traffic from the Great Lakes increased via the Mackinac Straits and the Erie Canal, so did the hopes and dreams of the investors in the New York and Michigan Co. founded by Oshea. The land was cheap and immigrants were attracted to the area earning Singapore its nickname, "Ellis Island." The boarding houses in Singapore flourished serving as homes for the immigrants and the mill hands.

Labor was cheap at $16 a month plus board. Prosperity was on the horizon for land speculators from New York. Nothing could stop them from turning this port town into a metropolis. They had deep pockets and wide vision encompassing greatness much bigger than the Great Lakes. With the growing town, there was a growing need for more labor; both for the sawmills, shipbuilding, the upcoming bank and for the boarding houses.

Ida pulled out of her purse the invitation letter she had been searching for so long on the steamer.

"Mr. Bosch, may I ask what will be my role at the Big House?" she said feeling the heat rise into her cheeks. "I don't see it in the letter except you mentioning that I will be in charge of the operations at the Big House. What does that entail?"

Ida recalled once seeing in the "Chicago Weekly Democrat" an ad for Mistresses; she wasn't quite sure what the title meant. Mr. Bosch sipped on his whiskey watching Ida's cheeks turn from pink to red. The pretty woman from Chicago appeared to be educated and knowledgeable, and brave to question his intentions. As the major investor in the New York and Michigan Co., and the upcoming bank, he wasn't used to being questioned.

"Will you excuse me, Miss Ida," he said and walked toward the cluster of gentlemen, who started talking again, when they saw the tall investor from New York approach them.

In the meantime, Stimson refilled her tea from the ornate tea pot. Ida could hear the voices getting louder, and more boisterous, as they greeted the well-respected man. In a few minutes, Mr. Bosch was back at the table with a leather-bound black book that he opened and searched for something, and then he closed it, somewhat relieved.

"Just like I've stated in the letter, you will be in charge of the operations at the Big House; that title is sometimes referred to as "Mistress," he said closely watching the young woman.

Ida couldn't shake off her suspicions about mistresses, despite Mr. Bosch's vague explanation. The Big House was not a brothel, or a saloon from the Wild West. It was a boarding house for up to six families, as Mrs. Fisch stated while giving her quick tour for the lack of time. She noticed the sleeping apartments in the right wing of the house on the east side, while the bar-room was located on the west side, facing the river.

However, the view of the lake was obstructed by a mound of sand, which upset Ida, who was used to seeing the lake in Chicago. Mr. Bosch kept studying the menu as if it was one of his books, afraid to look at Ida again.

"Stimson, I will have your best fish or lobster," he said.

Along with the building materials, the ships delivered lobster and other fine products from New England. Ida wasn't used to fine food or any delicacies. Ma usually bought food from the street peddlers and hucksters or she went to small shops operated from private homes. Ida didn't even know if there was a restaurant at that time in Chicago.

"I will have the braised duck," she said.

Mr. Bosch looked Ida directly into her eyes, as Ida also raised her head from the menu to look at Stimson, and handed him the menu. The music played louder, and the gentlemen's talk resonated in the big dining room. She regretted not knowing how to behave in a fancy place by the side of an important man. Ma didn't give her any instructions, neither did the training school. Ida longed to be respectful and proper in front of her new boss.

"I personally will give you a tour of the Big House tomorrow, since we had no time for that today," he said. "I would like to clear up any suspicions that I can see in your eyes."

Ida was shaking as she sipped on the hot tea. She was tired from the long trip on the steamer and in the horse-drawn carriage, with the bonus ride in the buggy, that got her all muddy. She searched the crowd again looking for women. There were a few well-dressed women accompanied by men. As if he was reading her mind, Mr. Bosch spoke out again.

"Miss Ida, as you can see, these are places of good reputation," he assured. "I know most of these people. I know them from New England. I went to school with some of them; the women are the wives of the gentlemen. You spoke with Mrs. Fisch."

Mr. Bosch was right. At the time of the influx of the land speculators from the East Coast, it was a custom that men would come first to scout the land, and then go back to bring their wives and children, thus men outnumbered women in the general population. The town's sawmills employed men, as well as the shipbuilding and other industries. Women stayed at home and took care of the children, since a school hadn't been established yet, in Singapore.

When they reached the Big House, Mr. Bosch retired to his private quarters in the southeast chamber. Mrs. Fisch took Ida's coat and climbed up the flight of stairs with her to the third story apartments. They passed the other rooms occupied by the Hollanders and the French, speaking their own languages. Ida fell straight on her bed, and stared at the ceiling where she could see the shadow of the flickering candle. The noise on Main Street had died down, and the restless clashing of the waves had taken over. Ida longed to see the waves she was so used to seeing from Chicago, if it wasn't for that enormous mound of sand. She put on a different coat and sneaked out of the house through the back door as the view in front of her opened up to the infinite sands blocking off the strong wind. Only timbers laid between the house and the port dipped in the dark of the late fall evening. Ida walked on the timber planks that abutted to the back of the house and grabbed one of the six oil lamps used by all the occupants of the house.

Walking toward the port, Ida pulled her coat tighter, holding the oil lamp so she could see in front of her. There were some lights flickering from the port. As she came closer, the lights grew brighter, and she could make out the silhouettes of boats in the harbor. There had to be a harbor master to guide in the ships, as the lighthouse hasn't been built yet. She could hear the distinct sounds coming from the harbor; sailors who had just arrived on a ship. Ida remembered hearing the hollow sound of the whistle announcing the entrance of a vessel earlier in the evening. It was brighter in the docks, and she approached the harbormaster's shack by the docks, lit by an oil lamp. She could finally feel and see the lake even in the dark. Cold mist chilled her blushed cheeks still hot from the evening with Mr. Bosch at the "Astor." She lifted her conic skirt as she took a few steps to the shack and knocked on the door.

"Enter," said a deep voice.

Ida slowly opened the door leading into a small room. An old man was sitting behind a desk in the corner by the window overlooking the lake. He was cross writing with a quill to save on pages and postage. Paper and postage were expensive, whilst the closest post office to Singapore was in Flats, south of Singapore. As a former teacher, Ida never used cross writing, neither did Mr. Bosch in his invite letter on the fancy stationery. When Ida showed the letter to ma, her mother exclaimed:

"This must be a rich man, Ida."

"Ma, how can you tell?" she said.

"He didn't cross write to save on postage or on the fancy stationery," ma said.

Now, watching the harbormaster cross write, she understood how ma came to the conclusion about the status of Mr. Bosch. The old harbormaster kept writing without looking up at her, but drew closer to him the oil lamp, then he looked at the wick, and turned his head to Ida. His long gray hair was disheveled, just like his beard. His baggy brown shirt and pants looked like they were sewn from a flour sack from the ships. He had a rope tied around his waist instead of a belt. He pointed to a chair, and nodded motioning her to sit down. The light in the oil lamp was flickering because the wick was getting shorter. Ida could hear the waves crashing against the docks and the blowing wind was rocking the docked boats.

"What do you want?" the harbormaster asked with a scratchy voice. "You have no business being here at this time of the night."

"I got lost," Ida said. "I don't know the town."

"Then why are you wondering around in the dark," he said. "You can't sleep, hm?"

He turned the page again to cross write on the edge of the paper and held it up against the light adjusting the wick. Ida could see the writing, but couldn't make out the letters or were they numbers? She couldn't tell. The paper was yellow and looked greasy from the oil lamp. The harbormaster hid the paper from her and instead, shoved across the table a torn journal nodding his head again toward Ida and the journal. She opened it slowly and saw the endless numbers with some words.

"What is this?" she asked looking at the old man.

"First, I want to know who are you?" the harbormaster said.

Ida held tight onto the journal as if her life depended on these numbers, which most of them she couldn't decipher. She leafed through the journal, as some pages fell out on the floor. As she bent down to the floor to pick them up, the old man grabbed her by the shoulder, and tightened his grip.

"Let go of me," she grabbed his hand.

"Not, until you tell me who are you, and what are you doing in this cursed town?" he said.

As the old man loosened his grip, Ida wrestled out and ran off as the door banged behind her in the wind. She could hear the old man shouting, but the wind carried his voice out on the lake. Holding her skirt in her hands, she jumped across the timbers now floating in the mud, as the first snowflakes dusted her coat. All muddy and scared Ida tore through the back entrance of the house and up the three flights to her corner room. She slammed the door behind her and locked it carefully. The town was quiet now, with the exception of an occasional clopping and the neighing of a horse. The lights at the harbor were still flickering. While stripping off her dress and corset, she could feel something in her pocket, and Ida pulled out the loose papers from the harbormaster's journal. Exhausted, she threw the papers on her desk, and fell asleep on the bed. The papers fell behind the headboard and seemed to have disappeared forever.

3

The New York & Michigan Company, 1836

John Bosch was born in Massachusetts, and he graduated from Harvard University in 1820. He worked as a teacher and authored an arithmetic textbook. Bosch met up with his distant cousin, Oshea, and other investors in New York in 1836 to discuss investment in land in the states of Michigan, Illinois, Wisconsin Territory and in Indiana. Bosch invested $15,000 in this western venture to acquire land entrusting his cousin with the hard work of going by water to explore the territory where the Ottawa Indians used to roam in what was known as the Black Lake Region between the Kalamazoo and Black Rivers.

The investors formed the New York and Michigan Co. on April 7, 1836, and Bosch remained the contact person for Oshea, who wrote to him about his adventures from Phil to Pittsburg, and on to Cleveland.

"My route was a most tedious and fatiguing one; the press of the travelers was so great on the route that no rest could be obtained or room to write a letter," he wrote. "Your letter of credit on the Bank of Michigan was duly and fully honored."

Travel in those early pioneering and settling days was

treacherous whether by water or by land. That's why Bosch stayed in New York, and sought out more investors for the company. He became the vice-president of the company, because Oshea was constantly away traveling either on a boat or on horseback between Marshall, Chicago and New York City. Bosch was well connected through Harvard and supported by his family in his financial ventures. Through his vast network of business and political connections, he became friends with William Astor Sr., the son of John Jacob Astor, the New York real estate mogul, who founded the Astor Hotel in 1836. Bosch captured Astor's attention when he spoke of the company and its western exploits of the territories by the Great Lakes.

"I am waiting for news from my cousin Oshea," he said. "We would like to start a settlement around the Black Lake Region."

With the fortune inherited from his dad, Johann Jacob Astor, William favored the proposed investments out west, but was careful to commit to anything before seeing more concrete plans and the plat for the future dream city. Bosch was anxiously awaiting more news from Oshea that arrived later in a letter. It was a rough draft of the proposed town at the mouth of the Kalamazoo River that covered nearly 80 acres, including the surrounding country. The plot was on an elevated sand bank and free from marshes, and the government surveyed the harbor increasing its importance along with an already erected warehouse.

But Bosch balked at the price of $100,000 for the land in cash and drafts, and thus didn't respond to Oshea for a while. The company was founded as a land speculation firm, and here Oshea was proposing a town and a sawmill in the subsequent letters to the company.

"There is no place for a town at the Kalamazoo, besides the plat I sent you," Oshea wrote. "The plot is an elevated sand hill but not so high to be seriously objectionable. I think our main operation will be most conducive to the interests of all concerned to chiefly confine it to the mouth of the river."

The investors held a meeting in New York in the fall of 1836 to decide on the purchase of the land and to name the new settlement. They've heard of the island Singapore near the tip of the Malaysian Peninsula in Asia, which at the time was a fledgling town originally acquired by the British. As the president of the company, and the only one to explore the actual site, Oshea proposed the name "Singapore."

"I walked the sand hills and the sand was squeaking and singing," he said.

The rest of the investors looked at him in sheer disbelief including John Bosch, who was well versed in finances, business and geography.

"Why do you want to use the name of an island in Asia?" he asked. "We have nothing to do with them. The British own them."

"I wasn't thinking about the island but about the sands, the singing sands when I walked on them," said Oshea.

"You walked on the sands of this place?" Bosch raised his eyebrows looking at the other investors, and back at Oshea.

Oshea, a pioneer from Massachusetts, who lived near Marshall, indeed explored the land of the future settlement on his own. He borrowed a canoe from the Indians upstream on the Kalamazoo River, and paddled toward its mouth, where Oshea disembarked with a survey of the harbor. It was summer on the lake and hot, so he took off his shoes and walked in the sand along the shore to the cove of the future Singapore. The sunrays reflected in the river and on the lake. The light breeze lifted the grains of sand from the sand hills surrounding him, and the constant movement of the grains bouncing off each other sounded like music to his ears. He saw Comstock's warehouse further up on the bank, but his interest remained in that cove. Even though, the warehouse was the seedling that would sprout into a prosperous business in the area based on the fact that the arriving settlers needed to store their household items, since the captains of vessels did not venture into the stream of the river. So, the warehouse was used for the reshipment of flour from the incoming ships.

"We can make money on selling the lots," Bosch concluded, "and Singapore is an exotic name deserving our attention."

So, the fate of Singapore was sealed in that fall conference held at the ornate Astor House on the corner of Broadway and Vesey streets in New York. The company paid for Oshea's stay in one of the 309 rooms of the hotel, which had its own gas plant. The business chamber was lit by gaslights, and the gentlemen inspected the surveys and the plat. At that point, Bosch was sold on Singapore in Michigan. In his head, he was weaving plans of building a boarding house to accommodate the incoming settlers coming by the sea and by land. Bosch retired to his room on the fifth story and sat at the desk by the window looking at the plat. He trusted Oshea in his judgment that the location would serve well the vessels and the labor for the sawmill. The town was planned to cover two tracts of land on the northernmost bend of the Kalamazoo River, and a sawmill that would need labor and millhands, who would need a place to stay, such as Bosch's boarding house.

In the months following the meeting, Oshea kept Bosch informed about the dealings via letters. Oshea had spent $10,000 on one of the two parcels that made up Singapore. He was frantic to make all the applications on time and he had made contracts for a scow and boats to be built early in the spring. He made contracts for timber for the mill, shingles and building a small house for workmen among the pines.

"I have put things in trim agreeably to the general understanding in New York," he said.

Oshea was feeling good about the new town, as he kept sharing his enthusiasm with the N.Y. & Michigan Co. that procured the funds. He loved the land which he described "as a handsome plain inclining to the river. The east part is hill and covered with timber. The point in the Oxbow is a marsh." He was ready to go to Singapore in the spring to build it out. Oshea invested in the vessel, *Trowbridge*, launched in October of 1838.

In the meantime, Bosch was preparing to leave New York for Singapore by land. He heard news about people getting seasick on the vessels, and preferred a horse carriage ride. The preparations for the long trip ahead of him were endless. He knew the dangers of travel by land but disregarded them. Oshea warned in several letters that he should take a steamboat, but Bosch remembered his descriptions of the maiden voyage to Detroit.

"I am not going to subject myself to the crowds on the deck," he wrote to Oshea who was busy with the construction of his own house for the family and the sawmill.

"It's more dangerous on land than by sea," Oshea wrote back.

"I will wait until you have the sawmill done," Bosch said.

Bosch reconsidered based on the family's successful history of coming from England on a boat. However, the cabins on the Great

Lakes steamboats were expensive, and he also needed money for his new boarding house in Singapore, and he had to find staff while he was in New York. Although Bosch was well off, he wasn't ready to invest all of his money into the unknown; a part yes, but not all of it. He could make drafts on behalf of N.Y. & Michigan Co. for all the company needs, and Oshea needed a lot of money for the machinery at the sawmill: mainly boilers with steam power sufficient to carry six saws, fixtures to float pine logs down the Kalamazoo River, and general expenditures to build the wharf and storehouse.

The company banked with the Bank of Michigan, and Bosch made several drafts to Oshea for the mill equipment, the engine, the timber; among these he made one for general expenses in Oshea's name and signed it as Oshea. In two weeks, Bosch was holding onto his luggage and a ticket to the Port of Detroit aboard the steamboat *United States*, its decks filled with passengers. The *United States* steamship had two smokestacks, two boilers, and two gaff-rigged sails. He secured a costly ticket inside the steamship to avoid the elements and smoke from the stacks.

4

Singapore & Oshea

When Bosch arrived in Singapore in early spring of 1837 just before the onset of the Financial Panic in May, Oshea was surprised to see his New York business partner standing in front of his own eyes on the land they had purchased together as the principals of the company. On the other hand, Bosch too was surprised that the first sawmill had been built as promised, and the town, even though in raw state had five buildings standing. They walked to the wharf near the sawmill that would be working eight months of the year, due to Michigan winters, at $25,000 per day with a gain of $15 per thousand. And the Big House to serve as a boarding house for incoming settlers had been built. Wily Oshea was more than optimistic with his progress.

"Money is rather scarce but real estate continues to advance," he said. "It is the opinion of all well-informed men that

Singapore will not be second to any place on the east side of the lakeshore."

Bosch was convinced about their sound investment as the westbound migration of settlers continued in search of land and prosperity. The wharf already had docks for ships and the house for the harbormaster. It looked more like a shack to Bosch who was used to the luxury of New York.

"Hey, Oshea, what is that shack for on that pier to the right?" he was pointing to the big sand hill on the north side of Singapore. "And what's on top of that hill, may I ask?"

Wily Oshea wasn't about to reveal all his shady plans for Singapore and its expansion, not even to his business partner of the same wiles.

"That's for the harbormaster, if I can find one," said Oshea, leaving open the question about the warehouse, and what's in it.

Bosch looked at the lake in the setting sun, and the fresh wind blowing from it breathed new life into him. He turned around to look at the surrounding sand hills and the river, the pines on the hills and back to the wharf. He extended a handshake to Oshea looking directly into his eyes. That handshake sealed the Singapore deal forever and into eternity.

"Oh, you did well," Bosch said. "I doubted you at first, and I doubted you more and more with all your grandiose plans. How the heck did you do it?"

Oshea sporting his buckskin outfit made from the deer he had shot stamped his feet on the ground as to shake off the early spring chill coming from the lake. They walked back into town and to the Big House that housed the company's office located on Broad Street. Timbers lay in the mud after the first thaw. They entered through the main entrance and Oshea walked with Bosch into his office. It was a big room with windows facing River Street and Broad. Oshea gave Bosch a quick tour of the three-story Big House, but paused to stop by the kitchen. A robust young woman with black hair meticulously parted in the middle, and tied in a bun, was standing by the large stove making dinner for the visitors, since Oshea let her know via a messenger from the sawmill by the wharf. Bosch took off his hat and nodded to this firm woman.

"This is Mrs. Fisch," Oshea introduced them. "And this is my partner from New York, John Bosch."

Mrs. Fisch was overwhelmed to see a visitor in the loneliness of the settlement counting five houses including the big house, the wharf and the sawmill. She discounted the warehouse on top of the sand hill. Like Oshea, she came from Boston to assist the adventurer in the exploration and settling of this town of Singapore. She occupied two front rooms in the basement, and was in charge of everything from housekeeping to cooking, and boarding. The kitchen with the long dining room was located in the right wing on the east side behind the main building with an entrance through a wide porch. More additions were to be constructed with the influx of new settlers. She escorted the two into the dining room with views of the river on one side, and the sand hill on the other. It was an ambitious structure, but timber was plentiful and made right here in Singapore.

"How was your trip, Mr. Bosch?" she said.

In this house trapped between the sand hills, but decorated by the river bow known as Oxbow and the thunder of the waves from the lake, Bosch immediately felt at home, far from the bustling streets and intrigues of New York. Mrs. Fisch wondered what this handsome young New Yorker was doing in this sandy cove hiding behind the lake. He was well dressed in a tailcoat jacket, unlike Oshea in his buckskin, and left his winter coat in the cloakroom at the entrance. They sat in the dining room overlooking the rushing river raised by early spring flooding. These new sounds to Mr. Bosch's ears were heaven on earth, after the long trip on the Buffalo-Chicago steamship route, the rough landing in the Port of Detroit, and then the land trip through the wilderness of the country.

"It was daunting and fatiguing," he said. "I even rode on a horse-drawn train part of the trip."

"Oh no, Mr. Bosch, I've never heard of a horse-drawn train," she said in awe.

"We had horsecars in New York going from the Madison Depot," he smiled at the friendly woman. "What are you making for dinner? I hardly had anything to eat on this bumpy trip."

Mrs. Fisch made salted pork with beans, potatoes, and an apple pie as dessert. She had a large pantry in the basement of the big house, and a store room. Oshea made sure it was well stocked with imported flour, beans, salted pork, salted fish, maple sugar, dried apples and rice.

"If I had known you were coming Mr. Bosch, I would have made something fancier, but Oshea kept this a secret from me—well, kind of," she paused.

Oshea laughed looking at his distant relative from Boston, whom he had known since childhood. They grew up together in Gardner, Massachusetts before moving to Rochester, New York.

"It was a surprise for me too," he said.

After a good dinner, they moved to the corner office of the company, but decided not to conduct any business until tomorrow, as Oshea left. Mr. Bosch unpacked his luggage in his private room adjacent to the company office. He sat at the desk and unfolded the plat map of the town of Singapore in front of him, and the list of lands purchased by Oshea. The second part of the list showed plots conveyed to N.Y. & Michigan Co. by the Boston Co., which had founded Allegan. From the plat map, it was clear that the shipbuilding company will be located by the saw mill and the wharf.

The next morning, sipping on fresh brewed coffee, Bosch met with Oshea who confirmed that major construction was well under way, and scow and boats were being built under the signed contracts, timber was in and a boarding house for the mill hands had been completed on Cedar Street near the saw mill. That was everything Oshea had promised in his letter to the company.

"Where did you find the labor for the saw mill?" Bosch said.

Wily pioneer Oshea was well connected in Calhoun County near Marshall where he moved his family in 1832 from New York. He wasted no time, and built his own sawmill and house "Wilder's Creek", a blacksmith shop, a wagon and chair factory, and a tavern. The two partners had another thing in common: a keen interest in politics. Oshea was appointed by the territorial governor as one member of a three-man commission to locate a county seat for the new Allegan County being formed in 1834. He was also the first postmaster of the settlement of Eckford.

"I have my ways," he said. "I rented out my own sawmill so I could come here to build the glory of Singapore and our own glory."

The early spring morning brought in the roar of the waves crashing against the pier. Oshea took Bosch to the industrial part of town on the north side where the shipbuilding plant was under construction, while the saw mill was already running and spitting out lumber for the buildings. The hum of the engine was music to their ears. Back at the company office inside the big house, the two men well-versed in business and finances, were avoiding the obvious, as Mrs. Fisch rushed into the house and burst into their office with big news.

"I heard talk of a lighthouse at the mouth of the river," she waved off the sentence like a fly. "It's just talk at the store."

Oshea and Bosch stood up in delight that a lighthouse would bring in more business to Singapore guiding ships in.

"Come on in," Bosch said. "We want to hear more. We need a lighthouse for the harbor."

"Well, you know the ships in the upper lakes had a season of hard luck, and politicians like Lyon are riding it like a wave," she shrugged her shoulders. "I got work to do."

However, when Michigan attained statehood in 1838, U.S. Senator Lucius Lyon ordered the lighthouse to be built near the mouth of the river. But the first stone and wood lighthouse was built too close to the water and was undercut during high water in the spring and had to be replaced by a new one with brick foundation in 1859.

5

Mistress Ida & Ellis Island

Ida assumed her role of the Mistress of the Big House with the elegance of a true lady. She had her own reception office at the main entry to the big house. With more ships coming into the harbor as the steamship navigation on the Great Lakes increased, there was an influx of immigrants from Europe who came on steamboats via the Erie Channel. Ida boarded the Hollanders, who landed at Singapore against their will on boats trapped by the slushed ice accumulated at the mouth of the river. They found work at the sawmill and stayed for a few months or years.

In the evening, Ida liked to watch the Hollander men in the

sitting room knit as well as the women. On Sundays, she heard them sing and worship together from their basement room in an unknown language. They trekked the Atlantic waters from Amsterdam to New York, boarded a steamship to Milwaukee and a scow back to Flats or Saugatuck. In her free time, Ida read books, as she was hoping a school would open in Singapore soon.

Once while looking for a teaching book, she found the papers from the harbormaster's journal. The yellow papers had both cross writing on them and nautical symbols and lines. Ida sat down at her desk and tried to decipher the various symbols. She moved on to the pages with cross writing and scribbling of all sorts. It could have been written in the language of the Hollanders, but the light was dim.

She knocked on Mr. Bosch's office door and entered with the yellow papers in her hand. Ida took a seat across from Mr. Bosch who appeared busy leaning over the desk looking into some books. He glanced at the young woman, and looked back down into the books. Then, he straightened up and leaned back into his chair, and closed the books. Outside the waves were roaring, and they both could hear the clip clop of the dray horses bringing in freight from the harbor.

"A busy day out there, Miss Ida?" he said.

Ida blushed as always when Mr. Bosch spoke to her. It could have been from the trip to the store in the winter chill and the wind coming around the sand hill.

"Have I been neglecting you for my company affairs?" he said with a slight smile and a twinkle in his deep brown eyes. Mr. Bosch also straightened his jacket and touched the buttons. "I deeply apologize for that."

He rang the bell to get Mrs. Fisch's attention. To his surprise, she immediately opened the door, as she was standing right behind it. What a coincidence.

"We will have tea and coffee in here," he said. "Tea for the lady, strong coffee for me. Do not disturb us; no one is allowed in, not even Oshea."

The smell of fresh-brewed raspberry tea filled this gentleman's office. The full tea pot was on the nearby hutch close to Mr. Bosch. Ida watched the snowflakes outside, not knowing what to say or why she came here in the first place.

"I trust that Mrs. Fisch took good care of you and taught you the business of being a mistress," he said. "We have a full house and money coming in. I am very happy with your work, Miss Ida."

Mrs. Fisch was standing behind the door eavesdropping on the conversation, but she was disturbed by someone entering the hallway.

"Darn," she whispered.

"I need room and board," a young man was standing in front of the reception desk.

"I will get you the mistress," she said.

She went back and knocked on the door despite the warning of no disturbing. Mr. Bosch got up and opened the door and stepped out into Mrs. Fisch's face.

"I said no disturbing, not even Oshea," he raised his voice. "What does he want?"

Mrs. Fisch's hands were sweating even though it was cold in the hallway.

"It's not Oshea," she said scared.

"Well, then send whoever it is away," he said in a high-pitched tone. "We have a full house. There's no room in here for any more bodies, alive or dead. Send them away."

Ida could hear the rushed steps and a loud exchange in the hallway between the two; then a slam of the door and shouting. Mr. Bosch sat back at the desk and straightened his jacket again and ran his right hand through his thick almost black hair.

"Sorry about that, I thought it was Oshea," he said. "We're in the midst of important company business. What is on your mind?"

Ida paused a bit and then handed the yellow papers to Bosch. He looked at the cross writing and the nautical symbols and shrugged his shoulders.

"I have no idea what this is," he handed the papers back to Ida. "Where did you get that?"

"I found it in the library in my room," she lied.

Mr. Bosch smiled at the young woman all blushing as she took the yellow papers back and stuck them in the pocket of her yellow house dress.

"We'll go for a ride tomorrow, it's Saturday," he said. "We've been working hard both of us. I will ask Mrs. Fisch to fill in for you. I want to show you a few things around here. I want you to feel comfortable and at home in Singapore."

6

Comstock's Warehouse

Mr. Bosch owned a stagecoach custom-built for him, with golden engraving N.Y. & Michigan Co. Mr. Fisch, who maintained the Big House, became his own stagecoach driver, while a regular carriage route to the Flats, later Saugatuck and Allegan, were in the planning stages.

On a wintery morning, Ida and Mr. Bosch rode the nicely appointed stage to the foot of the sandhill and around it to the warehouse on the top bought out by the company from Horace Comstock. As they entered the warehouse, so did the chill with them. Mr. Fisch waited outside with the horses. The warehouse was filled to the rafters with stock: re-shipped flour from the river upstream and settlers' belongings.

"Comstock and Nichols left this here," Mr. Bosch said. "I want you to make good use of it. You will be in charge now. Oshea and I have many other dealings."

Bosch looked at Ida, touched her glowing cheeks and kissed her. He took her hand and led Ida through the side entrance outside. Ida gasped at the vastness of the lake with the swelling waves in the western wind covered with white flakes. Bosch squeezed her hand and looked at her beautiful face with perfect features.

In the distance far away was her hometown Chicago, but the lake roared its own story of eternity and all-encompassing love. Stunned, Ida couldn't move away from the view. She could feel the warmth of Mr. Bosch's body drawing closer to her and kissing her on the lips. She gave in to his soft, firm touch and returned the passionate kiss filling it with promises of love.

Then, they heard the neighing of the horses, and Mr. Fisch consoling them. Freeing herself from Bosch's hug, Ida turned her head to the lake, took off her glove, and bent down to pick a handful of sand. The cold sand grains soothed her hot skin.

"Let's go," he said locking up the warehouse. "They're waiting for us. We can come back anytime when it warms up."

Ida was surprised at Mr. Bosch's proper behavior despite his advances; she wished they had stayed longer at the warehouse. She wanted to see the settlers' belongings that she would be handling as part of her growing responsibilities.

The descent around the sand hill was steep, but Ida marveled at the surrounding sand hills with white pines and the blue river flowing at the foothills. The grains of sand sparkled in the morning sun turning into hues of gold, brown and orange. The sands were shifting, as the wind molded them into different mounds in front of her eyes. The landscape into the distance, with an occasional juniper bush, looked like the Sahara Desert, except it had the life-saving lake and the river.

"Take us to the harbor," Bosch said.

The harbor area bustled with action and movement coming from the wharf. Oshea was running around contributing to the chaos, but he stopped when he saw the two coming from the stagecoach. The sun was over the lake now, and the couple's figures silhouetted in the winter sun.

"I have a request, Oshea," said Bosch.

Oshea looked at his unpredictable partner from New York, who was more unpredictable than Oshea himself. Dressed in buckskin, Oshea unlike the two was warm, but the two were shaking in the cold morning. All three of them walked to the harbormaster's house to take shelter from the cold. The old man inside was boiling water in the kettle on the stove. It felt warm and cozy away from the freezing wind. At the sight of Ida, the old man paused a bit, but went about his business.

"Can you make us some coffee and tea," Oshea said. "It's freezing cold outside."

"Yes, sir," said the old man. "What would the lady like?"

"Tea, please," Ida said blushing.

"Any particular tea, ma'am?" the old man pierced her with his squinting eyes in the wrinkly face.

"Do you have a selection?" she smirked blushing more.

"I do. Russian or English tea?" the old man snapped.

"Russian, please," she said.

The three sat down at the old man's table, as Oshea chatted about the harbor and the growing town of Singapore with the waves beating on the docks and the pier. The old man set the cup of tea in front of the lady and coffee for the gentlemen. He sat down with them. Ida noticed he was pouring something into his coffee, and she could smell something from her Chicago past, when daddy came home from hard work at the meatpackers plant. Ma was never happy when he planted a smelly kiss on her cheek after work.

"We're expecting more ships docking here," said Oshea to the nodding of the old man.

"They've already announced their arrival in about three weeks," replied the old man. "An Indian brought me the letter from New York."

Bosch looked at Oshea somewhat reluctant to say the unexpected.

"Oshea, will you marry us in the spring?" he asked.

Oshea stood up in surprise fearing the investment in the company, but he was married too, with six children and built a house in Singapore. The old man hid his surprise under the hood and walked to the window to watch the scows swaying in the wind from the lake. Ida's cheeks changed color from pink to deep blush, and her hands were shaking, as Bosch took her hand in front of the two men unapologetically.

"I love Ida," he said. "Ever since I laid my eyes on her photograph."

A thousand thoughts ran through Ida's hot head at the unexpected proposal inside the old man's harbor shack. The marriage to this rich New Yorker would pull her forever out of the Chicago poverty of a meatworker's family. Did this fine gentleman search her out with the intention to marry her? Was she involved in some kind of a mail order or picture bride scam? But she didn't remember having her photograph taken except when she became a member of the women's associations.

"Why so fast?" she voiced her worries about the abrupt proposal. "I am not even sure if I want to stay in Singapore."

"Oh, I agree," Oshea jumped right at Ida's hesitation for the fear of his own investments. "The lady needs to experience what it is like living in a pioneer lumberjack village. This is no Chicago."

Well, at the time Chicago, although growing, wasn't exactly a metropolis either. Then, there was no church in Singapore, only sheds were people got married by either Rev. Taylor who came in from the older fledgling settlement of Flats, a mile upstream on the river, or Oshea himself, who was a justice of the peace and former postmaster of Eckford. Versatile Oshea never stopped at an opportunity when it presented itself in front of his own eyes.

"We could have a church built by then," Bosch said in high hopes.

"I doubt it," Oshea had a better judgment of the situation in the growing settlement. "Life is rough here, you know. We need a post office more than we need a church."

However, post office was an elusive subject in Singapore much like the church. Wilder petitioned Lucius Lyon, the State of Michigan's first U.S. Senator, with a request to establish a post office in Singapore. The town was using Allegan's post office, which was 28 miles away, and presented difficulties of its own. According to Oshea's letter to the senator, the town was two-to-three weeks behind in receiving a paper or letter. Oshea requested the authority to have the mail carried between Allegan & Singapore twice a week. The post office politics were stalled.

Seeing Ida's hesitancy, Bosch quickly turned to the other subject of the day, and that was appointing Miss Ida as the manager of Comstock's warehouse along with her mistress duties at the Big House on Broad Street, with Mrs. Fisch serving as her assistant. Oshea, who was too busy with his own dealings, agreed to the proposal; he wasn't against women in business other than the household. The old man looked at Ida with a smile under his hood, and nodded toward her. The private stagecoach was waiting and only Ida boarded it at the harbor, leaving the two partners behind to discuss the company business, being comfortable at the harbormaster's shack.

Mrs. Fisch must have overheard some conversations, as she was all smiles in the hallway. She took Ida's coat and put it in the cloakroom. They went to the spacious sitting room to chat about their advancements in the company unusual for women. And then, there was the proposal to marry Mr. Bosch to ponder. Ida wasn't sure if Mrs. Fisch knew about his intentions.

"I wish there was a church in Singapore," Mrs. Fisch said as Ida blushed. Mrs. Fisch must have been reading her mind about Bosch's proposal or he confided in her.

"I have good news for us," Ida said. "I am the new manager

of Comstock's warehouse, and you are my dear assistant with our many upcoming duties. What do you have to say to that?"

It was time for Mrs. Fisch to blush with a wave of happiness rising inside her.

"You will be spending more time now at the warehouse," she said. "Do I understand correctly?"

Ida wasn't sure if she was going to be spending more time up on that sand hill rather than in the Big House which was congested with six immigrant families. The house was now fully occupied by Hollander John Loukes in the northwest basement room, by the Norwegian blacksmith Ola Peter Johnson with wife and two children on the first floor above the basement, and another family. In turn, these families boarded more families coming from Holland in Europe.

"I will need your assistance for sure in handling all these matters that are more than I can take," Ida said. "I have always appreciated your warm friendship."

"Mr. Bosch seems to like you," Mrs. Fisch ventured out into the unknown territory based on gossip around the town and the company shop.

Ida paused to respond weighing her answer by the pound, just like the store clerk down the street weighed the flour not to cheat the company or himself. As a teacher, Ida knew numbers well. The job at the warehouse will be all about numbers; how many pounds of flour are coming in and going out. Flour was like gold in this settlement in the wilderness first roamed by the Indians who left an Indian trail and Indian fields. She would also have to inventory the immigrants' belongings.

A fur trader from the Astor's American Fur Co. made a cache at the mouth of the Kalamazoo River and came back on a canoe to get his valuables. The other pioneer who made a stop in this wilderness was William G. Butler and his family; they took a small boat from a schooner anchored off the beach by the mouth of the Kalamazoo River. According to the tradition, the vessel was a small fore-and-aft sailing ship called *Madison*. The Butlers were originally from Connecticut and lived in Elkhart, Indiana and at St. Joseph before they made a shelter at the mouth of the river. However, after a few harsh months, they constructed a raft and poled upstream to their new home, a flat area on a wide spot on the

Kalamazoo River, which would later become the village of
Saugatuck.

7

The "wildcat" bank scheme, 1837

Still concerned about the sound investments in the company
in face of his partner's marriage proposal, Oshea pursued the
company's and Singapore's interests with the passion of a hunter,
which he was. He often headed into the nearby woods to hunt to get
a break from the company and the politics and took his hides to the
tannery upstream. But, his first love remained the glory of
Singapore. Coming from the woods with fresh ideas, bold Oshea
laid the financial scheme out in front of Bosch, after he had
contacted the rest of the investors in New York, who had shown no
interest in his latest financial whim.

However, Bosch was inclined to grow the company's
existing investments to support his upcoming
plans of establishing a stagecoach line to Allegan, 28 miles away
and beyond, a new hotel, along with a new wife. The new state of
Michigan had just recently passed a General Bank Law
that permitted 10 or more individuals of any county to organize
themselves into a corporation for banking business transactions with
a capital of not less than $50,000 and not more than $300,000. These
free banks without any federal oversight could issue their own
money with the backing of a 30 percent "specie" or hard money.

"Oshea, we need to find eight more investors," Bosch said.
"New York doesn't want to have anything to do with this."

Oshea acted surprised, but he was determined to find the
other investors among his friends and other companies with
individuals tied to Allegan, such as The Allegan Co., The Boston
Co., and the Singapore City Co. At that time, firm bonds between
the two villages, Allegan and Singapore, were formed due to the
postal   connection.

"You find the investors, Oshea, and I will secure a building
for the bank," Bosch said.

But a few large buildings had already been constructed as

tenements or boarding houses, so the two partners just upgraded the purpose of the two-story building located on Broad Street to a bank status. A new bank was formed in Singapore as of Oct. 5, 1837, when the Allegan County Clerk scribbled on a piece of paper notice that the books for the subscription of capital stock will be open for viewing at Field's Tavern in Allegan Village on the 7th, 8th, 9th, and 10th of November, 1837, between 2 and 4 p.m. On the morning of November 7th, the two partners took Bosch's stagecoach to Allegan for the first time. Mr. Fisch took the lines into his hands and guided the horses on the old dugway. The books were at the tavern, and members of the three companies were listed in them. Later in the evening, all the bank members celebrated the formation of the new bank at the tavern. Oshea's son Dan became the president, and Rob Hill of New York City served as the cashier. The expensive vault of the bank was made of pressed brick that was shipped to Michigan from Boston.

Ida, worried about Mr. Bosch's absence for the night, sought Mrs. Fisch's company in her basement apartment of the Big House. However, she had to find an excuse for going to the basement, so she grabbed vegetables from the kitchen to store them in the basement next to Mrs. Fisch's quarters. She knocked on her door. Mrs. Fisch already in her night gown and cap opened the door surprised to see Ida in her house dress. She invited her into her humble apartment with basic furniture while glancing at the clock that showed five minutes before midnight.

"Are you not sleeping yet, Miss Ida?" she said. "It's almost midnight. And what a night it is."

"They're not back yet," Ida said.

Mrs. Fisch put on a sweater in the chill of the night and motioned to Ida to sit by the fireplace as she threw in a few logs. Flames licked the wood and warmth spread from the fireplace.

"I don't want to waste any oil in the lamps," she said. "We have light from the fireplace."

The two women sat long into the night in front of the fireplace until they fell asleep. It was the early morning chill that woke them up, since it was still dark outside. They both ran to the stables behind the Big House, but the stables and shed for the coach were empty. Not even a trace of a human being or a horse remained from yesterday, just some horse dung. The daylight trickled in through the cracks between the boards, as the town was waking up to a new day. They could hear horses on Broad and the sawmill with its engines starting up a long shift ahead. Back inside the house, Mrs. Fisch made breakfast, as Ida decided to go to the company store to find out about the happenings of the day. The clerk was surprised at her early visit; he had hardly opened the store for the day, but Ida was confident that an occasional trader would come in. She looked around the store with new eyes, and saw the notice signed by the Allegan County Clerk on the counter and picked it up.

"What is this?" she demanded holding up the notice against the light of the day.

The clerk, a company employee, shrugged his shoulders, as Ida looked into his eyes and he turned his head. Ida shoved the piece of paper directly into his face.

"You don't know anything about a bank in Singapore?" she asked.

A trader with frost on his eyebrows and beard with bags over his shoulders walked into the store and collapsed into a chair with exhaustion; his bags fell on the floor. They both stared at the half-frozen man unable to make any sense of his words.

"I will come later in the afternoon," Ida said.

"Give me back that notice," the clerk demanded.

Knowing she wouldn't get away with it, Ida handed the clerk back the notice about the bank. The clerk put the notice back on the counter by the register for all to see and tended to the exhausted traveler. Ida walked on the timbers hoping the men would have returned by now to the big house. When the stagecoach left the house yesterday to pick up Oshea, Mr. Bosch only mentioned they had to take care of business and would be back as time allowed. Ida bumped into other people walking the Broad Street, as she was light-headed from the lack of sleep and from fear of what may have happened with the men. Ida sat in her registration boarding office looking at the clock as it struck 5 p.m. This time she thrusted the door open to the company store, with the clerk standing behind the counter, and the store full of strangers, not town people. The folks' interests were redirected to this well-dressed woman with apparent bad manners.

Standing in the doorway Ida yelled at the top of her lungs:

"Has anyone heard of a bank in town and its subscribers and their whereabouts?" she stumbled into the store with a vengeance.

"Miss Ida, would you please calm down," the clerk begged. "I am tending to my customers."

Silence spread around the store shutting down the lively chatter. Most people were local farmers or workers at the sawmill and shipbuilding factory. They looked puzzled at the desperate young lady, who walked up to the counter and grabbed the notice to show it to the townsfolk. However, most of them couldn't read, so Ida read it aloud word for word.

"Notice is hereby given that application has been made to the subscribers, according to the provisions of the act entitled "An Act to organize and regulate banking associations" passed by the Michigan Legislature March 15, 1837; and that the books for the subscription of the capital stock of an institution to be located at Singapore, Allegan County with a capital stock of $50,000 will be open at the Tavern Field in the village of Allegan on the 7, 8, 9 & 10th days of November. They will remain open between the hours of 2 o'clock & 4 o'clock p.m. of each day."

The silence was broken by enthusiastic chatter of the crowd packed in the store, like flour in the sacks.

"The notice is dated Oct. 5th," she continued. "Who has subscribed their capital to the new bank?"

The clerk interrupted Ida's brave speech taking the notice away from her. The news spread around every corner of the town and out on the lake. At the Big House, it was another restless night without their men for Ida and Mrs. Fisch. Ida repeated the same action from yesterday, this time bursting into the store right when it opened.

"Miss Ida, if you don't stop, I will have to take you outside myself," the clerk said. "I represent the company whose interests you are hurting. Please leave the store now."

"Let the lady speak her mind and heart," a deep voice from behind said.

In vain, Ida searched the crowd for the person who defended her in what was to become a "wildcat city" on the banks of Lake Michigan, one of the first ones in the Union and the first one in the newly-formed state of Michigan as of January 26, 1837.

8

Old man Jack

Restless, Ida crawled out of the bed, changed into her yellow house dress and sneaked out of the big house into the black night. The lights were flickering in the harbor, and a new schooner must have arrived, since a live chatter was coming from the docks. Holding tightly onto her oil lamp, all muddy and exhausted from often slipping on the timbers laid for the future boardwalk, she made it to the harbor shack. She could see the old man behind his desk writing in his journal as she knocked on the door.

"Come in," the scratchy voice uttered.

Upon her entrance into the room, the old man didn't even raise his head and kept on writing in his journal. Ida sat down across from him and gazed through the window to watch the lively docks.

"I was expecting you," the old man raised his head from his journal. "Did you forget to bring my pages?"

"I didn't, they're here," she handed them to him. "That's why I came to return them."

"No, that's not why you came here," said the old man looking directly into her sad blue eyes. "You're looking for someone. And it's not me."

"I am looking for my future husband," she whispered. "He left two days ago, and I haven't heard from him since. I am afraid he got lost in the woods."

The old man gazed at the beautiful young woman with sad blue eyes that turned gray like the waters of Lake Michigan, all breathless and tired.

"Who is your future husband, may I ask?" the old man said.

"I don't even know your name?" she said.

"What does it matter," the old man snapped. "Do you need my help or not?"

"Mr. Bosch, the vice-president of the New York and Singapore Company," she rushed the words. "We've been here together before with his partner Oshea and the driver. This is where he proposed to me. They all disappeared."

"I remember you; you took my pages and ran off with them into the night," the old man laughed, "but you couldn't decipher them, neither could Mr. Bosch, or could he tell you what was written on the pages?"

Ida wept cold tears that rolled down her cold cheeks from the winter chill clinging onto her dress. The old man turned to the missing pages with symbols and graphs from his journal. He looked again at the other navigation charts hanging in his main room.

"How did you end up here in the harbor shack in the town of Singapore?" she asked.

"You have all these questions for me, don't you?" he snapped. "You're nosy. Didn't they tell you that's rude."

Old man Jack scouted the woods after his schooner crashed on the lakeshore in a squall.

"Our schooner crashed in a squall, most died or drowned," Jack said. "Oshea saved me by giving me the job of the harbor master in Singapore when he found me moved into this place. He needed one anyways."

Ida was amazed at the seafarer's life story of survival.

"How did you make it alive out of the woods?" Ida persisted in questioning the old man. "Ma and daddy told me that savages live out here, and wildcats."

"I have my ways, dear," Jack said.

"Tell me your story, Jack," she begged to hear the whole seafarer's story.

Jack told Ida everything about his adventurers from stealing the navigation charts and the captain's log from the captain's cabin in the schooner. He hid the precious maps in the little cabin that he built in the woods and kept a careful eye on them.

One day as he scouted the woods for food, he came across the warehouse stocked with settlers' supplies, flour and salted pork. He helped himself to some supplies. And often came back to fetch more supplies to survive. He lived like a hermit and almost forgot to talk.

Once, standing on the sand hill, he noticed activity at the foot of the sandhill and at the river mouth. From then on, he came every day to the warehouse to watch canoes come down the river and unload their households and food. His heart skipped a beat when he saw a pier being constructed and five more buildings erected. He still dared not venture into the settlement at his feet, because he was all disheveled from living in the woods.

On one wintery morning, he almost clashed with Horace Comstock who was shutting down the warehouse, leaving everything behind. In a few months, Jack ran out of the supplies he had taken from the warehouse and transported on a sled into the woods to his dwelling in the woods. He walked the Indian trail that cut through the land until he reached the river, where he waited for the night to settle in. In the dark, he dragged himself to the wharf, and found the harbor shack filled with bags and sacks that sailors had left behind.

There were no lights yet, so he lit one of the candles he had stolen at the warehouse and looked around the shack. Jack stayed overnight and woke up to the sound of the steam boiler engines at the nearby sawmill, but he dared not venture into town during daylight, and he waited until the night to bring in his belongings from the woods. He made a raft from timbers, floated his belongings down the river to the wharf, and moved into the harbor shack. He kept his own diary and often read in the captain's log, until that morning when Oshea found him in the harbor shack and let him stay as the new harbormaster of the port of Singapore. When not writing or reading, Jack carved wood and first made his own sign by burning the letters in the white pine wooden planks, plentiful at the sawmill. The sign read:

"Harbormaster Jack."

Jack dragged into the shanty all sorts of wood from the sawmill, and he made his own bed and desk so he could write. He insisted on a guiding light for the scows and the schooners from the big lake, and petitioned Oshea several times. After a few weeks, Jack got his light; it was an oil lantern that he set on a nearby post on the dock. Jack had one oil lamp for his reading and writing, but he wasn't going to give that up. Oshea, favorable to navigation, promised an oil streetlamp for the harbor and a lighthouse for the seafarer. Oshea bought land from Comstock to secure a lighthouse site near the mouth of the river.

"You will get your lighthouse, Jack," Oshea promised, "in due time."

Jack often scouted the shore for treasures drifted ashore from schooner wreckages as far as the Upper Lakes. He decked his harbor shack with maps and the drifted treasures. Looking back at Ida, fully awake from his dream of the past, he noticed the young woman was shaking, and he gave her his shabby coat, which she accepted. He poured her hot tea from the kettle on the stove.

"You didn't come here looking for Mr. Bosch, you want to know what's in those books," harbormaster Jack concluded. "I can't tell you that, you will find out on your own. All I know is there was another great shipwreck on one of the lakes, and only a few survived the wreckage."

Ida paused for a while still not sure why she came to the harbormaster's shack. However, there was a storm approaching and the wind was howling from the lake as the waves hit the pier, so Jack let Ida sleep in his shack overnight. When she returned in the morning, Mr. Bosch was back and steaming over Ida's absence. As she entered the hallway, she heard him shouting at Mrs. Fisch.

"Where the hell, did she go?" he turned red seeing Ida enter the sitting room.

"How come you let her go anywhere at night?" he screamed at Mrs. Fisch.

Ida looked all gray from the cold and sleeping in the cold shanty. She was shivering and dusted off the snowflakes from her coat, and without a word flew up the stairs into her room and locked it. She didn't come down, not even to eat or for her shift to board visitors to Singapore. Ida sat down behind the desk ignoring the numerous knockings on her door throughout the day. In the evening someone knocked softly three times.

"I have some food for you," whispered Mrs. Fisch as she handed a basket through the door left ajar. "Don't come down. I will be back to get the basket."

Ida took the basket and devoured the bread, ham and cheese. She sat behind her desk, lit the oil lamp, and grabbed the quill and dipped it in ink. She brought in her luggage some fine stationery from Chicago that she hadn't used yet.

"Dear Mrs. Fisch,

I will be leaving for Chicago as soon I can find a liner and a coach out of this wilderness between the sand hills. Although I haven't encountered any savages on the Indian trail or on my walks to the harbor, I have come to understand that I cannot live under the same roof with Mr. Bosch. You have been more than kind to me. If you could assist me in finding a way out of this town, I will reward you many times, again and again. I will not come out of this room until this matter finds resolution. Please don't say a word to Mr. Bosch.

   Kindly,
   Ida

She sealed the note in an envelope and put it in the basket under the plate, and covered it with a fine cloth. Mrs. Fisch tired from the day's events grabbed the basket from behind the door and left it in the storeroom for the morning. She only locked the door to her basement apartment, since the storeroom always remained open for all to use. Around midnight, Mr. Bosch sneaked inside the storeroom and took the basket. Earlier he saw the housemaid go up the stairs with the basket.

In his company office, he set the basket in front of him on the desk and watched it in the flickering light of the oil lamp, afraid to take the cloth off the top as if there was an exotic animal inside, perhaps a cobra.

Still angry, he reached under the basket and read the note from Ida to Mrs. Fisch. He walked to the window and back, pacing between the windows and the door, cursing and promising eternal fire of hell to all, including Oshea, who didn't want to leave the damn tavern and was delaying the marriage for his own selfish reasons. It was a dark night, but he couldn't sleep, so he climbed the three flights of stairs and pounded on Ida's door.

"Open the door or I will kick it open," he yelled.

Ida hid in the corner of the room behind the green floral drapes. His shouting woke the entire house, and the Hollanders had to drag Bosch away from the door, down the stairs and into his room. One of the Hollanders offered him some jenever that came from Holland on the same boat as Loukes did. He had more in the storeroom and fetched a jug of jenever. The Hollanders left before dawn as Bosch finally fell asleep. Mrs. Fisch helped Ida pack and took her to the other stagecoach in town.

"Did you get me the ticket to Chicago?" Ida asked. "You know I am leaving Singapore for good. I never want to hear about this place again in my life."

"No, I had no idea you wanted to leave," Mrs. Fisch said. "Mr. Bosch found the note in the basket in the storeroom and threw it on the floor in his office, and I found it in the morning. We have to hurry before he wakes up. He won't remember anything; the Hollanders gave him some jenever."

The two women hurried down the timbers on Broad Street to the store that also sold tickets for stagecoaches and boats to Chicago. The clerk recognized Ida from her bold expose over the past few days.

"I need a coach ticket and a boat ticket to Chicago, as soon as you can get me out of here," she said.

The clerk raising his eyebrows looked at Ida and pulled out boat and coach schedules bound in hard black covers from underneath the counter.

"The next boat to Chicago doesn't leave for four days," he said. "You can wait here in town."

The two women said goodbyes, as Ida ran toward the harbor to catch Jack before his rounds.

"You have to help me get out of this town," she begged Jack.

Seafarer Jack watched the distraught woman thinking how could he be of help.

"You're getting married to Mr. Bosch, why do you want to leave Singapore?" he asked.

"I don't want him, he's rude," she said. "He forced me into this."

9

Cabin in the woods

Jack rented the horse and the buggy from the other stagecoach in town, took the lines in his hands, followed part of the Indian trail and drove Ida to his old cabin in the woods. It was still there, just like he left it before he found home in the harbor shanty in Singapore.

"You have to stay here," Jack said. "Bosch would find you in the warehouse. I will get you food for four days before the coach and the boat leave. Don't leave my hideout no matter what."

Bosch woke up in the middle of the day with a headache and fresh anger, flew up the stairs and kicked open the door to Ida's room. The room was empty with clothes scattered over the bed and the floor. Her books laid open on the desk, where he found another letter. He ripped it open in hopes of an apology, instead it confirmed his fears.

"Dear Ma and Pa,

It is with a broken heart that I write this letter. I will be leaving Singapore as soon as I can find a liner to Chicago. The vast wilderness and the unwelcoming behavior of Mr. Bosch made it difficult for me to stay amidst the scheming of a new bank here, and my upcoming employment at a warehouse........"

Bosch ran to the store where the clerk confirmed Ida was trying to buy a ticket to leave the town.

"Where did she go?" he yelled at the company clerk.

"I don't know," the clerk said backing away from the counter until he hit the shelves behind him with goods that fell on the floor.

"Well, next time, you better know, because this is your business," Bosch quipped. "Miss Ida is our company business. Do you understand that? I want her back."

Bosch jumped on his horse and rode to the warehouse on top of the sand hill and tore in, fuming with anger. It was musty with old smells, full of other people's furniture and belongings stuck in the back. Up front, there were big sacks of flour that had recently arrived on the steamer from upstream villages, waiting for Ida to count the pounds for distribution. He noticed that one sack of flour had been opened and tied back up again. Bosch prowled through the warehouse in search of Ida and the robber who was stealing his goods. Comstock left behind old Swiss and German cuckoo clocks that people took with them aboard the ocean steamboats from Europe, paintings of family members and lush landscapes, mountains and animals grazing in the fields. Bosch took two the elaborate Black Forest cuckoo clocks from the warehouse and placed one in his office at the Big House and the other one in the big dining room. He loved the engineering precision of the cuckoo clocks and studied them intensely.

Outside the wind was lifting grains of sand that pierced his face, combined with snowflakes blowing from the lake. Bosch pulled his coat tighter and jumped on his horse for a wild gallop down the trail around the sandhill that crossed the Indian trail.

Breathless, he arrived at the Big House, where he found Mrs. Fisch making an early dinner for the entire boarding house.

Everyone pitched into the monthly boarding house dinner once a month on Saturdays. The dining room was already full with the Hollanders, the Norwegian and the Germans. As Bosch walked in, dead silence spread around the room. Oshea was already seated behind the main long table in the front with other subscribers from the Bank of Singapore. It was the board of the required 10 people, with Bosch's chair empty and one other left unoccupied.

The company used the lovely dining room for major announcements rather than using the Astor, which not everyone could afford. Among the bank subscribers were, Rob Hill, Joe Fisk, D. B. Stout, S.D. Nichols, D. S. Wilder, B. Eager, Dan Emerson, Noah Briggs, L. Loomis, D. Jewett, O. D. Goodrich, John Jewett, J. L. Shearer and Artemas Wallace from New York. The board agreed that the bank would be housed first at one of the boarding houses, before the other frame building was ready.

"Today is a big day for the subscribers of the Bank of Singapore," Oshea gloated as he pointed to the board members. "These fine gentlemen represent three companies: Allegan, Boston and Singapore plus an investor from New York, who has yet to arrive."

A loud applause followed from the guests. Together the subscribers invested $15,000 in specie or capital stock that would be kept in the pressed brick vault at the new building; right now, it was in a nail keg in the basement. The board agreed to print ornate banknotes in one-, two-, three- and five-dollar denominations at Rawdon, Wright & Hatch, a New York engraving firm. They were printed on a single sheet on one side only and cut apart and signed by the cashier and president before they were put in circulation. The board members stood up and shook hands to congratulate each other. Oshea and the board members paid for the expensive wild game dinner for all present, and the house guests contributed with their jenever or juniper brandy, predecessor of English gin. The celebration extended into the evening and surpassed the sailors' binges at the harbor.

In the meantime, Jack borrowed a horse from Oshea, and came back to the hideout cabin in the woods with a bag of food, blankets and made a fire in the pit that he left uncovered, not far from the dwelling. As he was approaching the pit, a bobcat jumped out of there. Before he pulled his gun, the wildcat was gone. Freezing Ida refused to come out of the shack.

"I got to get you out of here," Jack said. "It's too dangerous. I know Bosch well. He won't go back to the warehouse, but he will look for you at a new place, and he won't give up until he finds you."

Once Jack spotted a coal stove in the warehouse among other settlers' belongings on his regular trip for flour. He packed Ida's bags, and they rode horseback together to the warehouse. They were crossing the Dugout Road when a stagecoach coming from the east halted right in front of them and Oshea's horse stopped dead, refusing to move. A young tall man stepped out of the coach and walked up to them nodding to the lady.

"We're lost, we've been on the road since this morning," said the young man with a deep voice. "Can you direct us to Singapore?"

Jack looked at the well-dressed man in a tight jacket and a tall hat, then he pointed to the setting sun on the horizon before it dipped below the sand hill.

"Just follow this road," Jack said. "It's the only road to Singapore."

Jack turned away, but the horse from Oshea's stables didn't want to move, and neither did the young man. He set his eyes on the beauty with big blue eyes seated behind the old man.

"Does the lady need a ride?" the young man said. "There's plenty of room in the stagecoach. Your horse seems tired."

"No, the young lady has a ride on this horse," cautious Jack said. "You best be on your way before the night sets in. There are wild boar and wildcats in these woods, and Indians."

They continued uphill on the trail as the stagecoach disappeared on the dugway into the dusk. The stagecoach stopped at the Big House, and Mr. Fisch took over the horses. The lamplighter had just started lighting the street oil lamps, since dusk came early in the winter month, and the wind had been picking up all day, signifying another storm coming from the lake. The stagecoach also brought in some much-needed oil and candles in the box behind the coach. Mrs. Fisch answered the door upon a loud ring. She took the young man's coat and hat and placed it in the cloakroom. They could hear the loud conversation coming from the house.

"Who should I announce, sir," asked Mrs. Fisch. "They're all in the dining room. You missed the board meeting, and the announcement, sir."

"I am one of the shareholders from New York," he said. "Artemas Wallace."

Mrs. Fisch ushered Artemas into the dining room and announced the young elegant man.

"This is Artemas Wallace from New York, ladies and gentlemen," she said.

Artemas took a bow in front of the board.

10

Artemas Wallace

Artemas was dressed in his best black tailcoat and a golden chain adorned his embroidered vest. He sat down in the last empty chair at the large wooden board table after shaking hands with all the present board members. The company clerk from the store recognized Artemas as soon as he saw him in the doorway. Slick Artemas quickly caught on to the conversation that was all about the new bank.

"I must say gentlemen there was great resistance in New York to approve this, but I convinced them," Artemas smiled. "Only a fool wouldn't invest in this opportunity."

With Artemas' and the rest of the N.Y. Co. investment, the specie grew to the required $50,000 per organization by the General Banking Act. Oshea nodded at Artemas, pleased with the fine gentleman's late arrival. The board appointed the cashier, Mr. Rob Hill, who came from New York City to Singapore, to assist with the bank formation. Jenever was flowing freely, and Artemas was no stranger to it. After the party, he left for the Astor House where accommodations had been made for him to stay.

"You were in my store," the clerk said upon his departure.

"I was," said Artemas. "I was looking for a place to a stay.

I don't see the lady orator here. I thought she was involved in the company business, the way she talked, like she was the head honcho."

"Miss Ida left for Chicago four days ago to visit her parents," the clerk lied.

"You can then introduce us when the lady comes back," Artemas said.

"No, but I can introduce her," Bosch's voice thundered behind Artemas' back. "She is my fiancée, and we are getting married soon. She is visiting with her parents in Chicago. We will get married when she comes back home to Singapore. This is our home. Once your business is done here, you will be on your way back to New York."

Artemas' face turned red.

"Excuse me, sir," he said. "No one directs me what to do."

Back at the cold warehouse on the sand hill, Jack set up the coal stove for Ida to survive the next two long days before the stage and the boat depart. Among the settlers' belongings, he found blankets and more coats.

"I have to get back to the harbor house. A ship is coming in." Jack said. "You stay warm, I will be back tomorrow."

It was a crispy morning when Artemas headed out into the woods and searched for the trail where the two on horseback had crossed his path. He followed the trail around the sand hill as it looped up the hill overgrown with juniper brush and white pine. The horse neighed and stopped in front of the warehouse as it recognized Ida who was outside bathing in the morning sun that turned her blonde hair into gold blending with the sand hills. Artemas rubbed his eyes to make sure he wasn't dreaming a dream spiced with juniper berries from the jenever from yesterday. At the neighing of the horse, she turned around.

"Good morning," Artemas tipped his hat and gave a slight bow to the lady.

Startled Ida recognized the voice from last night trying to find his way to Singapore. The morning full of promises was young and crisp like their desires.

"I thought you were on a boat to Chicago for a visit," he said with a smile on his face.

"You're the man with the deep voice from the trail and from the store," she said. "Who are you? What are you doing in Singapore?"

Ida hesitated to invite him inside the warehouse and stood outside in the morning chill as Artemas got off the horse and tied him to a post by the warehouse.

"I am leaving for Chicago in two days," she blushed. "I am just waiting here."

"I am Artemas from New York on company business here in Singapore," he bowed slightly. "Pleased to meet you."

"I am Ida from Chicago, on my way back to Chicago," she quipped. "And you sir, should be on your way back to New York. There's nothing but wilderness here, and wild men and savages abound. You could get hurt staying in Singapore."

This was the second time that Artemas was being told that he should be on his way back to New York, but he liked the solitude of the woods, the sand hills, the lake, and mainly the pretty feisty lady. They both watched the town in its bustle below and boats coming down the river. The river sparkled through the woods and joined the lake in a unison of blues and greens.

"You're getting married soon," Artemas said. "That is after you get back from Chicago, right?"

Ida stood strong in the morning wind from the lake whipping grains of sand into their faces. The grains of sand were dancing in front of their eyes on the magnificent blue backdrop of the lake and the sky, as they touched on the horizon. They were singing a love song. Both Ida and Artemas grew up in cities that weren't cities yet but had already ports, horsecars and stations. This vast wilderness reminiscent of Sahara showed new opportunities, new lands, new hopes and new unfulfilled desires.

"When is the boat leaving?" asked Artemas.

"In two days," she answered. "I am not coming back to Singapore."

"Why are you hiding in this warehouse?" he said.

"I am not hiding, I am waiting," she said. "I can't stay down in town."

Ida didn't understand why she was explaining herself to

this handsome fair-haired New Yorker with a mustache.

"Aren't you going to invite me inside," Artemas said shivering. "It is cold out here."

Ida looked into his eyes, turned around, walked into the warehouse, and shut the door behind her.

Artemas remained, standing speechless outside, as he spotted amidst the sandhills a man on a horse leading a second one by his side. They were making their way up around the sand hill on the road that crossed the Indian trail. Jack got off the horse and tied the horses to the other post. He brushed off his duster covered with sand and looked up and down tall Artemas, dressed in a fashionable black cloak. Artemas extended his hand to Jack and said with his deep voice, "We met yesterday on the trail."

"It was dark, but yes," Jack said. "I recognize your voice. You're the New Yorker, the new banker?"

Jack invited Artemas inside the warehouse where they found a table and chairs to sit close to the coal stove. Ida made some Russian tea and coffee for all of them.

"You should be on your way back to New York, Sir," Jack said.

Ok, this was the third person telling Artemas he should be going back to New York. At this point, Artemas had no intentions of going back to the city, where he had no family and no past.

"I am in no particular hurry to go back to New York," he said. "Nothing draws me back. On the contrary, everything is telling me to stay here where the opportunities abound. Plus, this beautiful unhappy young lady will make me stay for sure."

He glanced at blushing Ida; even her ears turned red.

"If you stay you will die," said Jack. "I know Bosch, killing has never stopped him before. In all his rudeness, he loves this young lady."

11

Of squandered dreams and esquires

The warehouse with other people's belongings whispered stories of vanished dreams, lost lives and squandered opportunities, some at sea, others in the wilderness. But there were also stories of success, like that of William G. Butler who sailed in on a fore-and-aft small sailing ship, the "Madison," built a shack and left the wilderness to start a new village upstream, then known as "Flats." All there was left of him was the shack on the shore, but Butler left a lasting legacy of future Saugatuck near Singapore.

However, before any white man set foot on the lands near the mouth of the Kalamazoo River, the Potawattomi and Ottawas had lived in the area and established trails to major hubs: Mackinac Island, Detroit, Ann Arbor and Chicago. The trails were first roamed by the migrating bison, and well established by the Indians, as single path trails, later turned by the state into roads and highways. The intricate network of Indian trails crisscrossed the state and connected the major hubs.

Fur traders from John Jacob Astor's American Fur Trading Co. like G. Hubbard made his way up from the mouth of the Kalamazoo River to establish future Kalamazoo. And then, there were paper settlements like Naples and Breese, that never materialized and remained on paper and in historical records, only of what could have been, only if.

A squandered dream of the engineers of 1837 was the proposed Kalamazoo-Clinton canal that was to bring prosperity to Singapore, to Oshea and the Company, by connecting the Kalamazoo and the Clinton rivers. The waterway would run from Fredericks, near Mt. Clemens on Lake St. Clair, to Naples, a proposed settlement upstream from Singapore, and enter the Kalamazoo River.

Due to its coinciding with the financial panic of 1837, which left the government without funds, the project ended at Rochester on the east side of the state. But that didn't stop wily Oshea or the company in their Singapore ventures.

It wasn't just Oshea and the company, but also other pioneers like C.C. Trowbridge of the Boston Co. who set their eyes on the Singapore dream. It was Trowbridge, a pioneer from Detroit, who suggested that a steamboat should be secured to ensure traffic on the Kalamazoo River, but he backed away from the Singapore project.

The dream steamboat, *"C.C Trowbridge"* built by William Wilkes, was the first steamboat built in Singapore, and it became a reality in the fall of 1838, as it plied the river between its mouth to Allegan. It was to carry wheat coming from the west to the settlements upstream. Adventurer Oshea believed in this dream come true, just like in everything he touched, that it would turn into gold like King Midas. In reality, the riverboat made only two trips on the river before it was deemed as unsuitable because of its size and the tricky configuration of the Kalamazoo River, with its twists and bends like the Oxbow, making it too difficult for the captains to navigate. But Oshea contended that the steamboat could cross Lake Michigan, which it did, and return back to Singapore before being sold to new owners in Milwaukee.

However, what the riverboat did accomplished, was strong bonding between Singapore and Allegan further upstream on the river. Allegan too established its own "wildcat bank." Whenever the Allegan State Bank received warning from nearby towns that the state bank examiner was coming through, the two banks would pool all the money from the Singapore State Bank and Allegan State Bank at Allegan. After the inspection, the banker in Allegan would make sure to get the bank examiner drunk. While he slept, they would get a head start on him and take all the money from Allegan to the Singapore State Bank in time to pass the inspection there.

Singapore founder Oshea was an esquire in its true sense; he was justice of peace and a knight disguised in buckskin, but he wasn't naïve. He let his own daughter sail aboard *Trowbridge* to prove his strong belief in the shipbuilding industry in Singapore. That morning, when old Jack came to him to borrow two horses, Oshea wondered why he needed the second horse.

"Jack, what are you hiding from me?" he said eyeing the old man closely. "Who is the other horse for? Why do you need two horses?"

Old Jack trusted this esquire in buckskin disguise since he made him the harbormaster of the best harbor in the world. He gave him light and promised a lighthouse and the lightkeeper's post, which was much sought after by Will Butler himself. Even though Oshea was crooked, he was a man of his word.

"Sir, swear to secrecy," Jack looked into Oshea's eyes.

When he saw Oshea's eyes flickering with little flames, Jack changed his mind about trusting this man.

"My partner Bosch has been searching for Miss Ida," said Oshea. "I am supposed to wed them as soon as she appears. You wouldn't happen to have anything to do with that, Jack?"

"I only met her once when you and Mr. Bosch came over," Jack lied into Oshea's eyes. "That was it. I barely know her name."

"Why the two horses, and where is Miss Ida?" Oshea asked.

"The store clerk said the lady left on a boat to Chicago," Jack continued to lie.

"My partner and I checked the schedule, the boat doesn't leave until Friday," Oshea said.

Then Oshea handed the lines to the horses to Jack.

"If I find out you had anything to do with Miss Ida's disappearance, I will make sure that you won't leave this town alive," Oshea said. "Now go. I have work to do, and you do too. New ships are coming in. I want the horses back soon, and Bosch will want his Ida."

12

Escape from Singapore

The stagecoach was rocking from side to side as the driver skillfully guided the horses around the bends on the Dugout Road, copying the Kalamazoo River and further upstream, then taking a swing down south to St. Joseph. Without stopping anywhere after St. Joseph, the coach followed the old Indian St. Joe Trail to Detroit to catch an earlier steamboat to Chicago from Buffalo. The wild ride with the horses galloping ahead moved the two on the seat closer together. As the coach leaned to the right, Ida slid on the seat toward Artemas, who held her so she wouldn't hit the window with her head.

Once the driver regained balance, Ida slid back to her seat on the left. The woods were covered with fresh snow, and the coach slowed down in the trenches made by other stagecoaches and horses. They stopped at the trail crossing on a ridgeline at Ann Arbor. Since the trail ended there, they bid farewell to the driver and continued on a riverboat on Huron River to Detroit. They barely made it, since the steamer was departing at noon, and they had traveled all night and morning.

"Goodbye, Ida," said Artemas. "I will be waiting for you here in a month. I know you will come back."

Heartbroken, Artemas watched the smoke from the stacks, as the steamer disappeared on the horizon, when a hand from behind squeezed his shoulder. He turned around, and Bosch was in his face pulling him up in the air by his cloak. Bosch caught up with the two at the transfer station in Ann Arbor and was on the same riverboat.

"This way you can't have her, and neither can I," Bosch barked at Artemas. "She's not coming back to Singapore. Chicago will take her into its arms, but you won't, you sly bastard. You go back where you came from. I don't ever want to see your face around here, and if you come to Singapore, I will kill you. You can board the next steamer to New York, and I will make sure you do."

Artemas felt the barrel of a gun poke under his left shoulder blade as it buried deeper into his clothes and skin. Bosch took Artemas to the ticket booth and purchased a ticket for him to New York. The steamboat was departing soon, according to the busy schedule en route between Buffalo-Detroit-Chicago.

"This poor soul needs me to get him on the boat; he's very sick," he said to the naval officer. "I will take him to his cabin."

Bosch forced Artemas into his first-class cabin to New York, as he motioned to the officer.

"He needs to be tied down and locked in the cabin, so he doesn't escape," said Bosch. "His mother will be waiting for him in Buffalo to take him to a mental hospital."

Bosch handed to the officer fake papers about Artemas' mental health condition. Artemas couldn't talk because he had a gag in his mouth and a scarf was tied around it, while his hands were tied behind his back.

"If he gets loose, he could hurt someone; the boat then will be liable," Bosch said.

He handed $100 to the officer to make sure tied Artemas did

not escape from the boat. Then he handed another $100 to the officer to have Artemas watched all the time until they reached Buffalo. In vain, did Artemas struggle to free himself, as he was pushed into the cabin, and he heard the key turn in the lock.

"I expect your report to the New York & Michigan Co. in New York, that Artemas made it to Buffalo," said Bosch, "or you will cease to be an officer on this steamer, understood? You will be sued for letting this nut loose."

"Yes, sir, I will make sure this poor gentleman makes it safe in his cabin to Buffalo, where I will hand him over to his mother or the authorities in charge, if she is not there," said the officer as he saluted.

Bosch had already notified the authorities in Buffalo with a letter that a sick person was arriving on the boat, and that he should be taken to the local hospital, so he doesn't hurt anyone.

"I would like the key to the cabin," said Bosch. "You can pry the door open in Buffalo. Here's another $100 for the damage."

The officer saluted Bosch, handed him the key and left.

13

Financial Panic of 1837

Oshea and Bosch met in the new bank building on Broad Street with the new vault made from press brick shipped from New York and a shipment of ornate banknotes. All had arrived in December despite the news of the Financial Panic of 1837. The Michigan Legislature, in a special session on June 12, 1837, following the lead of the big banks in New York, Philadelphia, Boston, and Baltimore, suspended the specie redemption requirement, leaving the general banking law in force. Rob Hill was eager to take on his cashier duties as required by the subscribers' agreement. The new two-story frame building had rooms on the second story for boarding. Hill occupied one room.

Earlier, Oshea paid a visit to Jack and requested a large sign be made for the bank building, "The Bank of Singapore." Oshea paid Jack in advance, trusting the old man, except for the disappearance of Miss Ida and his heartbroken partner Bosch. As justice of peace, Oshea was looking to prove that Jack was involved. And then, there was the unexpected disappearance of board member Artemas.

Oshea read the fake letter signed by Artemas Wallace, Esq. of New York:

"Dear partners,

I regret to inform you that I must hurry back to New York to tend to my mother who had fallen ill to a strange disease. I will keep you abreast of her health. I will come back to Singapore, as soon as she gets well.

Duly noted,

Artemas Wallace, Esq.

Hill gave them a tour of the bank building with the fancy money cage upfront made of plated steel and iron with golden and silver engravings and the press brick vault in the back.

"How much money do we have in the vault, Rob?" asked Oshea.

"We have the required $15,000 and we will be circulating $35,000 as soon as tomorrow," said Hill. "We will start with our company store. The New York office printed some extras for their use in the city, mostly small bills that would fill the gap left by big banks such the Bank of New York, founded by Alexander Hamilton in 1784. The real banks of New York, so far away, lacked small denominations but were somewhat leery when they saw the ornate bills with the imprint "Bank of Singapore."

The people of Singapore flocked to the store to pay with the new bills; even Jack, the harbormaster, got carried away by this enthusiasm, and ran to the store. He was an employee of the N.Y. & Michigan Co. Bosch and Oshea sent him with mail on a raft upstream to "Flats," (later known as Saugatuck) to the first post office. Jack glanced at the letter addressed to Miss Ida and her parents in Chicago. He got off the raft at Oxbow, made a fire and burnt the letter without opening it, as a true esquire. He hiked to the old Indian trail and to his old dwelling in the woods, where he would stay until the evening. Then, he crawled into his harbor shanty on the dock and fell asleep until the sound of a steam whistle woke him up, signaling an incoming boat to Singapore. Jack walked outside to get the name of the lake vessel, when he recognized *Octavia* that was built in Singapore for transportation of lumber.

"Howdy, captain, how was your trip?" Jack was curious what the boat brought into Singapore, in its hull.

Octavia traveled with lumber made at the sawmill to Chicago and carried back lifesaving flour, meat and tools to the eastern part of the country. The captain first had to oversee the unloading of the goods from the ship before leaving for the tavern on River Street with Jack, who made a log note of the arrival of *Octavia* into the port that day. By noon, the town of Singapore bustled with stagecoaches arriving from "Flats" and the village of Allegan upstream. Constructed by the N.Y. & Michigan Co., the tavern enjoyed the business from the port and the sawmills.

"What's new in Chicago?" Jack asked.

The captain who had been plying the Great Lakes for the last 20 years, since the first *Walk-in-the-Water* pioneer steamboat in 1818 navigated the lakes, knew his trade and his passengers. He too was an employee of the company, since Oshea and Bosch invested money in the shipbuilding at Singapore. Both men had the Singapore banknotes on them. The tavern's talk was the new bank in town and the increased traffic on the lakes. The boisterous talk carried messages of hope for growing Singapore at the foot of the sand hills, with lumbering boon and a thundering lake in front of them. The captain brought in more news from one of the crew members. He looked at his sailing buddy from *Octavia* who didn't need to be asked twice to share a strange message amidst the joy and hope. The sailor stood up, which in itself commanded silence, waving the Chicago Democrat in his hands above his head with a bold headline:

"Financial panic strikes major banks."

The folks in Singapore were cut off from the rest of the world, with its only artery the Dugout Road leading in and out of the settlement. Very few could afford the travel on steamers, and no newspapers were available in the immediate area. Someone else stood up and waved a letter with a New York stamp dated May of 1837. He yelled at the top of his lungs as the crowd hurled up front to the sailor. The crowd tore the paper into pieces, refusing to believe the news.

"Ok, folks," Oshea walked into the tavern, "It's old news. We knew about the run-on banks in New York in the spring. It doesn't concern us here. The state allowed the banking here to continue. Our money is safe in the vault. Don't listen to sailors' stories or other tall tales from the ships' decks."

The crowd sank into whisper and people went back to their seats, as the tavern keeper sighed a sigh of relief seeing his whiskey bottles intact on the shelves below the counter. The tavern was a sheehan, which two-faced Oshea tolerated even though he didn't let his own tavern in Marshall sell liquor. It was called "Sandy Hill Tavern," and it took in guests for the night. The two paid with the brand-new banknotes, still fresh off the Rawdon, Wright & Hatch presses in New York. The tavern keeper put them in the register with great care. He already had a stash of the new banknotes hidden in the nail keg behind him. The N.Y. & Michigan Co., invested in the tavern as well.

The captain aka Cap and Jack walked back to the harbor house and sat at the table by the window overlooking the entire wharf, with the waves clashing against the pier and the docks. They watched *Octavia* sway in the wind uncertain about its future as well as the town's future under the reign of the New York land speculators- turned businessmen. The captain admitted to hearing about the financial panic at the large banks in New York and the preceding flour riot.

"Is our money safe here in Singapore?" asked Jack.

"No, Jack, there is no such thing as safe money anywhere in this world," the captain said. "I've heard stories from passengers coming from the old country across the Atlantic. They lost all their money and came here."

Jack pulled out his nautical charts and showed them to the captain, pointing to a jutting out spot in Lake Superior.

"Can a boat get caught in a squall drift this far out?" he asked.

"Depends where she's coming from, but yes a boat can drift a long way," said the captain. "Why do you ask? You're stuck here with those New York crooks. They won't let you go anywhere."

Jack rolled back up the charts and maps and sat back in his

chair, reluctant to share his worries with this well-traveled man who spoke the language of French Canadians and the Hollanders.

"I will be promoted to a different line soon," Cap said. "Your company recommended me to the Chicago-Buffalo line."

"Will you ever come back to Singapore?" Jack said, worrying about his Cap friend.

"I might drift ashore one day when this becomes another New York," Cap laughed at the thought of Singapore turning into New York at the foot of the sand hills.

They walked the docks to the sawmill to oversee the loading of lumber headed back for Chicago and Milwaukee on "Octavia." The millhands floated the lumber on the river to the docks to be loaded aboard the ships headed west across Lake Michigan.

"When are you leaving, Cap?" Jack asked. "There's a storm from the lake this evening. You best wait 'till tomorrow."

"Don't have time to wait, as soon as we load her, we're on our way to Milwaukee," said Cap. "That is after dinner tonight here in Singapore."

Cooking on the first steamers was just as treacherous as the waters of the Great Lakes. The crew often fell sick from the spoiled food and its stink. It was difficult to find sailors who would cook on the freight steamers such as *Octavia.* The sailors suffered from pellagra and other diseases, like cholera and yellow fever, spread easily on the packed steamers, both among the crew and the passengers.

The sailors ate tack, biscuits made of flour and water, while the captains and the officers feasted on meat.

"We'll eat at the Astor tonight before I leave," Cap said. "It's my final trip before I go on the Chicago line. I will pay with this money."

Cap held the ornate banknotes against the window light, nodding his head at the fanciness of the money with depictions of galleons, steamboats, and mythical women signed by Oshea Wilder and cashier Robert Hill. The Astor accepted the local banknotes from the Bank of Singapore without flinching when they saw Oshea's signature, who was a major investor, together with Bosch, in the Astor as well. Upon their entrance into the main room, just as ornate as the banknotes, they spotted Oshea and Bosch seated at their designated company table. Unlike Jack and Cap, the two partners were regulars at the Astor; they were always waited on by Stimson, not the other wait staff. Soon they were joined by the other company members.

"I wonder what happened to Esquire Artemas Wallace?" Jack spilled out the obvious thought for Cap to ponder, while looking at the company board members.

"Who is Artemas," said Cap. "I've never heard of him. He's not from Singapore, right?"

"Who is from Singapore?" laughed Jack. "I don't think we've had a first baby born here yet or a dead body buried at the platted cemetery, unless you're talking about the Asian island far east. You will only find settlers, mill hands, pioneers, speculators and immigrants from the old country here in this town."

"He's a bank board member from New York," said Jack. "The last time I saw Artemas was by the warehouse with Miss Ida."

Jack covered his mouth, when he saw the surprise on Cap's face.

"I know Miss Ida Brown," he said.

Jack couldn't believe his ears and eyes watching Cap's every move; how could this sea dog possibly know Miss Ida from Chicago?

"I read about her in the Democrat," said Cap. "She received an outstanding award for her teaching, and she is active in the Women's Club of Chicago. Are we talking about the same lady?"

At the time, Chicago had a population of 4,170; how many Misses Ida could have traveled on a steamer to Michigan and work for Mr. Bosch? And teachers were stretched thin across the country.

"Are the gentlemen talking about Miss Ida of Chicago," asked Bosch behind their backs breathing down their necks. Jack turned around startled to see the robust tall man. Jack rushed to answer.

"No, we were talking about Miss Ada," Jack quipped at Bosch.

Bosch pulled a chair to join the two men, leaving the company of the board members behind to solve the problems of the day.

"Does the captain know of the whereabouts of Miss Ida, who recently left Singapore?" he asked breathing into his face.

The worldly captain sensed something was terribly rotten in the state of affairs in Singapore, as he looked at angry Bosch who turned all red. He had heard gossip about his angst and fury among the sailing crew who feared his anger, that had grown in recent weeks. Often, Bosch would unleash on the unsuspecting crew if he ran into them on his daily rounds through town.

"No, but I've heard of Miss Ada, who will be traveling on my next line," he said. "I already have the schedule of passengers from Chicago to Buffalo."

Bosch grabbed the captain by his uniform jacket and lifted him off his chair, fuming with anger and exhaustion over the two lying bastards from the port. He shook him and slammed him back in his chair.

"Your next line will be here working at the sawmill," Bosch said. "We need millhands like you. There is no need for more captains."

The two seafarers stared at angry Bosch, who walked away to the board members' table and called out loud on Stimson, so the entire room could hear.

"Throw those two out of here, and never let them set their feet inside the Astor again," he fumed.

"But sir, they're guests, they're not unruly," argued Stimson, "I cannot just throw them out."

Bosch stood up, face-to-face with Stimson, with a mean glare in his eyes.

"You will do what I told you to do, otherwise you're going with them out the door," said Bosch, still standing and staring down Stimson who panicked.

But Jack and Cap got up and left on their own and walked to the Sandy Hill Tavern instead and drank whiskey at the bar. The tavern keeper couldn't keep up with them, as he poured an endless string of shots, which the seafarers downed with the ease of a summer walk on the sandy beach near Singapore. And they drank late into the night, as the lake thundered against the pier and the docks with *Octavia* swinging in the wind from the lake.

"No more whiskey for them," a voice thundered from the door.

It was Bosch who followed the two sea dogs to the tavern by the river. He felt for the cold gun in the deep pocket of his cloak, as he swung the tavern door wide open into the chill of the night to face the tavern keeper. Assisted by Mr. Fisch and a millhand, they grabbed the two seafarers by their collars and dragged them out on River Street and toward the river rushing into the lake. There, they pushed them into the river and left without turning around.

"That's what they get for knowing Miss Ida," said Bosch. "That's what anyone will get for knowing Miss Ida."

14

In search of Ida

Bosch embarked on his search of Ida, following the address he found back in New York in the Morning Herald for the Association of Teachers & Women's Club in Chicago. He reluctantly boarded a steamer to Chicago and was seasick all the way.

Chicago was a little bigger than Singapore, but he found the family cottage and knocked on the door. A middle-aged man opened the door, surprised at the elegant but robust gentleman.

"How may I be of help?" he asked.

Bosch took off his tall hat and introduced himself as the president of the New York & Michigan Co. based in New York.

"May I come in sir?" he said.

Bosch sat down at the family table along with Mr. & Mrs. Brown.

"Ida is not here," Mrs. Brown uttered. "We don't know where she is. She left a few months ago for Singapore and never came back, nor has she written a letter. We have no way of locating her."

Bosch looked around the humble belongings of the family and heard children play in the other room. Mrs. Brown took him to Ida's room, after getting the children out of there. Ida shared this room with her siblings. Ida left some of her things behind, hoping one day she may return back to teach at the Chicago schools.

"Do you know where she could be?" Mrs. Brown asked with tears in her eyes.

"No, I don't. That's why I am here," Bosch said. "Did she have any friends or lovers?"

"She had a few friends from the Women's Club," Mrs. Brown said. "Sometimes they would have tea here in our dining room."

"Do you remember any names from the club?" Bosch asked.

Mrs. Brown went into the kids' room, opened the desk drawer and pulled out a handmade card with flowers and butterflies signed by the members of the Women's Club. The names scribbled at the bottom were barely legible, but Mrs. Brown recognized one name; Ellura, who lived in one of the cottages down the road.

"You might want to see Ellura," Mrs. Brown said. "She was her good friend and a teacher as well."

Innocent Ellura let Bosch in once he mentioned knowing Ida from a trip aboard a riverboat together on the Huron River from Ann Arbor to the Port of Detroit.

"All I know is that she went to Singapore to manage a big boarding house," Ellura said. "I had my thoughts about her title of being a "Mistress" of the house, but I didn't say anything, and we all wished her good luck. She was in good spirits and health but didn't want us to come to the docks. She's always been very independent. I assume she is still in Singapore. She was invited to Singapore by an honest gentleman from New York City.

Bosch's anger was burning inside his body as he hit another obstacle with Ellura.

"Did you go to school together?" he persisted.

"Well sort of, and we had friends there too," Ellura said.

"Where did you go to school?" Bosch asked.

At the time preceding the establishment of Normal Schools for teachers, public schools were not mandatory, nor established. Later, teachers got certificates at their high school and taught kids only a few years younger. But some communities established their own schools in sheds or in basements of apartments in the cities.

"It was more like a basement inside of a building," said Ellura shaking her head.

Bosch noticed the woman in front of him was nervous from his presence. He took his hat and cloak and turned to the door to leave. He walked toward the port not knowing what to do next, as the steamboat wasn't leaving until the next morning. Bosch found a store in the basement of a house and bought the Chicago Democrat paper. He would have to sleep at a boarding house near the port. He found one that was willing to let him a room in the basement for the night. Bosch couldn't sleep all night long; silhouettes of drowned men emerged out of the darkness of the wet basement. One silhouette even touched him and laughed into the night and talked to him:

"Jack knows where Ida is, but you threw him in the water, and dead men don't talk," laughed the silhouette. "You will never find your fiancée."

Bosch woke up from the nightmare to the howling of the waves. He paid for the night with the Singapore fake "wildcat" banknotes and left for the steamboat, where he ordered coffee and a biscuit. That voice from the nightmare was back again whispering into his ears:

"Dead men can't talk," the voice said. "You will never find Ida. She has a lover, who is better than you are."

He waved off the voice like a fly, as an officer stopped by the distraught nauseated gentleman seated all alone by the window.

"Are you ok, sir?" the officer asked. "You seem a little pale."

"Mind your own business," he barked at the officer.

Now, Bosch remembered he had bought a newspaper and hadn't read it yet, because there was no light at that darn port boarding house. On the third page next to the ads section, he found an article about a local club in a rural area outside of Chicago looking for more members. There were no names mentioned or addresses, just a local club in the rural area outside of Chicago. But it was a vague clue.

15

Long John Wentworth

With a determined mind to find Ida, Bosch stepped out of his coach by the Big House in Singapore with Mrs. Fisch running outside to greet him. Bosch handed her his tall hat and cloak and went inside his office without uttering a word of greeting. He must contact the publisher to find out who put the article about the women's club in the paper. He grabbed the quill, dipped it in ink and wrote a letter to publisher Long John Wentworth:

"Dear Mr. Wentworth,

It is with extreme urgency that I am contacting you in regards to an article in the Chicago Democrat, about a club in the rural area of Chicago. You may know the club members as they may be associated with the paper. I am looking for a witness to a murder that happened near the Kalamazoo River, close to Singapore. The club members may know what happened, as some of them were from the Singapore area before they moved to Chicago. If you would be so kind as to forward to me an address for the club and their president, so I can proceed with the investigation, together with Justice of the Peace, Oshea Wilder.

Kindly,

John Bosch, Esq., Bank of Singapore, vice-president
Singapore

Time went by in Singapore, and the mail was slow coming from "Flats" aka Saugatuck or from the village of Allegan, from a distance of 28 miles. The mail often got lost, as the bags fell off the raft or from the stagecoach since it was transported inside a chest tied to the back of the coach, not to take up any space inside the coach for travelers.

Meanwhile in Chicago, well-known publisher, Long John Wentworth, had received the mysterious letter about a murder in Singapore. Being a true newspaper man thirsting for justice, the letter about a murder stirred his interest. Since he was also the editor of the Chicago Democrat, Wentworth decided to investigate the case himself, so he could run an article about what had happened across the lake in Singapore. Wentworth called his reporter Max, who was also a newsboy, delivering newspapers, and showed him the letter on beautiful stationery with the "New York & Singapore Co." letterhead.

"Hey, Max, have you heard of this company or a town called Singapore?" Long John asked curious and breathless Max.

"Sir, are you talking about the island of Singapore in Asia?" curious Max asked. "A murder on the island? How in the world would we investigate that?" Nobody cares about Singapore here in Chicago."

Long John leaned into his chair smiling at young Max. The newspaper office was located at the corner of Clark and South Water streets at the lower level with the steam printers located above them. They could hear the noise of papers being printed.

"When you're on your newspaper routes, ask around about Singapore," Wentworth said. "I will check our ad files and make a few contacts."

Wentworth re-read the letter, and this time what caught his eye was Bosch's title, the vice-president of the Bank of Singapore. He went to a business meeting at the nearby Sherman House to chat with his business and political friends. The talk of the day was the financial panic and "wildcat banking" in America, with Michigan being the first state to embark on the dangerous venture of free banking without a charter, where any individual could organize into a bank. One of his agile political friends and a store owner pulled out an ornate banknote with the engraving of the "Bank of Singapore," signed by Oshea Wilder and cashier Rob Hill. Wentworth pulled out the letter and showed it to his business friends with the banknote. They compared the two: the letter and the banknote.

"It's the same Oshea Wilder," Wentworth gasped for air. "I'll be darned. Can I have the banknote? I will give you the Bank of Philadelphia money in exchange, not to shorten you."

Running down Randolph Street, breathless he entered the office of the Chicago Democrat, being the sole proprietor, writer and editor. He studied the Singapore banknote, before Max returned from his rounds of delivering the weekly paper to the Chicago businesses in downtown. He took the magnifying glass and clearly saw the signatures on the banknote of Oshea Wilder and Rob Hill. When Max entered later in the afternoon, Wentworth showed him the banknote.

"Not only is Singapore a prospering town in Michigan, but it has its own bank," Wentworth said. "Why does Bosch want the names of the Women's Club members?"

"He writes in the letter, they had witnessed a crime," said Max. "What club is he talking about? Definitely not in town."

"Max, could you find me that article about the Women's Club, so we know what Bosch is talking about," Wentworth requested. "Where is he going with this?"

Times during the financial panic of 1837 were chaotic enough, with or without Singapore.

True, the society and the just-incorporated city of Chicago were getting polarized due to the rising tensions, the one-day flour riot in New York, and now the financial panic and the run-on banks. Many clubs were emerging in the area, and they were looking for more members. However, the Singapore connection seemed wild even to worldly Wentworth. Max brought the paper with the club article he had written a few months ago. The headline read:

"Women's Club seeks members."

The Women's Club of Rural Chicago is seeking members to grow the organization with more fine women."

"Who brought me the information about this?" Long John asked Max. "Was it you?"

"I have to read it first, sir," Max said.

The city of Chicago, now counting 4,000, was growing so fast that it was hard for Max to keep tabs on everything. There were 29 dry goods stores, five hardware stores, 45 grocery and provision establishments, 10 taverns, 19 lawyers' offices. Chicago was the seat of Cook County and home to a federal land office and branch of the State Bank. It was also a trading center for those residing as far as 200 miles inland, and the canal was under construction.

16

Women's Club near Chicago

Upon her escape to Chicago, Ida Brown started the club

outside of Chicago, knowing Bosch would come after her if she visited Ma and Pa. Together with Ellura, they traveled by stage west of Chicago, in search of a hideout for Ida. They came across the town of Aurora, where Ida decided to settle and organize a women's club. She sent a letter to the major Chicago newspaper, the Chicago Democrat, in search of more members, stating the purpose of the club to unify women and teachers, somehow managing to hide the name of Aurora behind a riddle about the Goddess of Dawn riding from east to west in the sky. Then, she left a different address with the newspaper, asking for anonymity, except if requested by women interested in being club members.

"Sir, I found this," said Max. "The writer of the letter is requesting anonymity to protect herself."

"Yet, she's looking for women to join her and using our paper to do it," said Wentworth angrily.

"Sir, we don't know her reasons," said Max.

"What if she was the one who witnessed a crime in Singapore, that we now know exists on the other side of the lake," said Wentworth scratching his head.

Wentworth sank deep into a dilemma about his next action.

"Max, you're not helping any," Wentworth said. "I am going home. We'll see what tomorrow brings."

Ida stayed in touch with Ellura, who came for an occasional visit on a stage to Aurora. One day as they walked through the small town, Ellura announced she was getting married soon and asked if Ida would come to the wedding in Chicago next month. Ida remembered her own botched wedding plans with Bosch in Singapore. She too wanted to get married because Ida was struggling as a single woman. The times were not favorable for single women making it through life on their own.

"You have a teaching certificate. Maybe you could go to New York and find yourself a husband," said Ellura.

"I've never told you about Mr. Bosch from Singapore," said Ida.

Ellura stopped and gasped in surprise.

"Do you know Mr. Bosch?" she persisted.

"Yes, I ran away from him in Singapore and his banking schemes," Ida cried in desperation. "That's why I am here in Aurora and not in Chicago, because I am hiding from him, for heaven's sake."

"He came over to my place looking for you," Ellura said. "I had a strange feeling about his visit. He was all angry."

Ida thought of Artemas Wallace who helped her escape from Singapore.

"Have you ever been in love?" asked Ellura.

"Of course, at first, I loved him and wanted to marry him, but then the banking scheme, his lies and wrath," Ida said, "and his raw partnerships."

Ida's brief memories of Singapore consisted of hard work at the Big House, worries about counting flour at the warehouse, and the marriage proposal in the wilderness of Singapore. But then came old man Jack and Esquire Artemas Wallace of New York.

"I was in love twice and made a friend in Singapore that I left behind," she said. "I don't know what happened to Artemas, because Bosch caught up with him."

"Who is Artemas?" Ellura was curious about the esquire from New York.

The thought of Artemas sent a warm wave through Ida's body, longing for a man who would be kind and gentle. But Mr. Bosch was a gentleman too, except that wild outing to celebrate the wildcat bank in the village of Allegan that lasted three days. Ida has been waiting for a letter of apology, but refused to release her whereabouts, except for the letter to the Chicago Democrat about the club, and even then, she asked for anonymity.

"If you want a man, let's go to the paper in Chicago," said Ellura. "They will know. They know everything and everyone on this side of the lake. And you should see your parents."

They arrived by stage in downtown Chicago in the late afternoon hours, when the city bustled with a jam on Lake Street of arriving wagons with produce from the farmlands west of Chicago, stages and pedestrians. The stage dropped them off, and they continued on foot to the Brown's humble, small cottage.

"Oh my," Ma screamed and held her head at the sight of Ida and Ellura.

Ma ushered them inside the house, as Ida looked around to find Pa.

"Is Pa still at work?" asked Ida.

"Your father has been very sick," Ma led them to the bedroom with drawn curtains.

Pa lightened up at the sight of his daughter but was pale and couldn't breathe. Ida ran to his bedside to hug Pa, but Ma stopped her.

"The doctor doesn't know what's wrong with him," she said. "He's been coughing, and he can't go to work."

Ida felt Ma's struggle, lacking the money to take care of Pa in the growing city that needed labor like Pa but had little space for women workers. Ida decided to stay with her parents and help out as much as she could.

"I will get a job and help out," she said.

But at the time, there was not a lot that a woman was allowed to do; public schools didn't exist. But Ida managed to find a local women's club to would help her. She taught in a school in the basement of a big building that was also a boarding house. She again took on the duties of a housemaid and registering guests, while she put off her newspaper visit to the Chicago Democrat to take care of her ma and pa. Long days turned into long nights marked by exhaustion of running the Brown household and working at the boarding house. There was never enough food for the entire family, sometimes they got by with only one meal a day. Then came the dreaded day; Pa died of whooping cough.

They buried him on the north side cemetery by the Lake Michigan shore north of Chicago Avenue in solemn silence, except for the wind from the lake and from the West.

Ida finally entered the lobby of the Chicago Democrat, and a newsboy took her to Mr. Wentworth's office, who acted as he had been expecting her, nodding toward a chair across from his desk. With pleasure, he looked at the young woman with the face of an angel and sad blue eyes, worn out by early mornings of daily tasks and the lack of sleep at night. She was dressed in black from head to toe in memory of Pa.

"I've been meaning to contact you, Miss Ida, even though I am not a woman," he laughed. "It's not about your club."

Ida, nervous, appreciated that Mr. Wentworth spoke first, relieving her of begging him for help. The 6'6'' tall man had a reputation greater than his height and had a long arm. He pulled out from the drawer of his desk the letter from Bosch and showed it to Ida, who read the letter, shaking from fear of what Long John had written to her former fiancée. As if he had been reading her mind, Wentworth waved his hand to dismiss a thought or two in his head.

"I haven't responded to Mr. Bosch," he said. "The mail is slow, and letters get lost. That's what we need right now, to gain time."

However, in the meantime, Long John received two more letters from Bosch explaining the murder near Kalamazoo River, and the importance of securing a witness from the rural club to proceed with the investigation. As Ida read the other two letters, Long John watched her closely, her every move, until she looked up from the letters with her sad blue eyes.

"Do you two know each other by any chance?" he asked. "Have you witnessed a murder in Singapore? Have you ever been to Singapore?"

Newsboy Max tore into the office breathless, still holding a few rolls of paper.

"The free banks have been shut down by the government," Max said. "They have to turn in their money, notes and everything."

He swallowed his last words, as he noticed the pretty blonde to his left and nodded his head toward Ida, acknowledging her presence in the office. Ida stood up surprised by the newsboy's statement of wildcat banks being shut down. That opened up a whole new different world for Ida who had thought of Mr. Bosch being a crook and a drunk. But he was neither. She saw him in the new light of being a victim of Oshea's wile and greed. She hurried with her response:

"I know Mr. Bosch, and I've served as the 'mistress' in his Big House in Singapore," she blushed.

Both Long John and newsboy Max stared at Ida in disbelief that she knew the man who was involved in both free banking and the investigation of a murder on the Kalamazoo River. The two men were used to receiving and presenting the hard news of the day--on a daily basis--but to see the witness in her physical flesh was another story.

This gentle woman dressed in black was admitting in front of an important man in Chicago that she knew Bosch, the banker, and one of the founders of Singapore in Michigan.

"It seems like you have answered all my questions," Long John said, amazed at the situation that had unfolded in front of his own eyes. He was here looking for you. Are you sure you will be safe with him? He sounds like an adventurer."

"May I borrow a piece of your stationery, I need to notify Mr. Bosch that I am in Chicago," she said. "I want to be with him. I am tired of living by myself."

She scribbled a quick letter to Bosch, lifted up her skirt and left the office, running down Clark Street to Bigelow Building to mail it to Singapore.

17

The Wedding

Justice of Peace Oshea married Ida and John Bosch in the summer of 1838 in a sanctuary made of branches on the shore of Lake Michigan. Ida assumed her Big House duties with grace and forgiveness, while the Singapore schoolhouse located a mile down the road was under construction. She was determined that she would teach at the new schoolhouse. Bosch agreed to please Ida who had returned to him like a migrating bird from the south. He continued his dealings in the Singapore Bank in strict secrecy, hiding behind Oshea and the government's order to suspend the General Banking Act. However, the bank reorganized and continued to escape the state injunctions brought by the commissioners, who couldn't reach Singapore because of its remoteness.

One of her first stops was at the harbor shack with a gift from Chicago for Jack. Instead, she found a strange sailor at Jack's desk.

"Where is Jack?" she asked.

"I don't know who Jack is, ma'am," the sailor said.

"He's the harbormaster," she said. "In the port of Singapore."

"Well, I don't know Jack, and I am only here until the boat leaves," he said.

Back at the Big House at the dinner table, Ida asked about Jack in front of everyone. It was one of those common dinners held on a Saturday night when everyone pitched in their share of food.

"Jack left the town shortly after you left," Mrs. Fisch hurried with an explanation.

Ida looked around the dining room at all the present faces from the past year. She recognized most of them: the Hollanders and the Norwegian. There was a handsome newcomer from England, who just shrugged his shoulders at Mrs. Fisch's response. According to Mrs. Fisch, he had arrived on one of the vessels transporting lumber to Chicago. His name was Cameron.

"I am Ida," she introduced herself blushing.

Gallant Cameron stood up and kissed her hand, which she quickly withdrew from his touch. She could still feel his warm lips on her hand as he stepped away and back to the dining table. She noticed he was wearing a plaid kilt, due to the occasion of having dinner with the owners, whom he had never met before. But everyone dressed up as well. Ida wore her favorite blue dress with the conic skirt.

For her birthday, she got a horse from John, a Mangalyaan Marchador, with shining brown hair and white spots. She called her beloved horse "Misty," and whenever she wasn't busy went horseback riding along the shore and into the woods on the old Indian trails. Once she came upon the old dwelling in the woods, where Jack had lived and provided a hideout for her. She tied Misty to the oak tree and walked inside the deserted shack in the woods. She noticed clothes thrown in the corner on a pile with a blanket on the top. In the heat of the summer, Ida sat down in front of the cabin thinking about the harbormaster, and what happened to him. When she asked John about Jack, the answer was always the same, that he had left town in search of more adventurers. She had her doubts. Jack was happy in Singapore, and Oshea had promised him the coveted lighthouse job.

Ida rode back into town on the Dugout Road by the river where kids were playing and down River Street into the harbor and the sawmill, where Oshea had his office. Ida entered through the open door that aired the summer heat out; no one was in. Ida took a seat by the window overlooking the harbor, but since Oshea wasn't anywhere to be found, she rode into the harbor. She paused to watch the swaying scows, schooners and lumbering vessels and listen to the waves splash on the docks and on the pier. She spotted Oshea coming from one of the lumbering vessels. Oshea looked like a sailor himself; tanned with long hair and beard, sporting baggy pants and a huge smile, Oshea came up close to Ida.

"Oh, Mrs. Bosch, what brings you here, my dear," he said flashing a look at the beautiful Marchador, who was the talk of the town, just like the Scottish newcomer Cameron.

"I was riding by," she said.

"I haven't seen you since the wedding," he said. "How have you been? Come into the harbor house."

She tied the horse and walked with Oshea to the harbor house that was all painted, and it looked all anew. They walked inside and sat down to chat. Ida noticed the harbor house was adorned with new treasures from the sea: shells and driftwood.

"The Scott brought those from the sea," said Oshea examining a big shell.

Scott Cameron came all the way from England on the vessel *Vermillion.*

"I've been thinking about naming him the next harbormaster," he said looking Ida directly into her eyes.

"But you can't do that," she said. "What if Jack comes back? It's his post and you promised a lighthouse to him."

"Mrs. Bosch is right," old Jack was standing in the door. "You promised me a lighthouse that's already standing, I've noticed."

Yes, the lighthouse at the mouth of the river had been built while Jack was gone.

Oshea, not knowing about the night incident on the river, had just given up on Jack, after a week-long search of the woods, thinking he may have been devoured by the wild animals in the woods. He was surprised to see the old man standing, all shabby and disheveled, but alive. Ida ran to Jack and hugged him.

"I knew you weren't lost," she said. "I didn't believe their stories about you leaving Singapore. You love Singapore."

Old Jack smiled at Ida and turned to Oshea, who regained his balance, as quickly as he had lost it. He promised a lot of things to a lot of people; most promises he kept; some promises were never meant to be fulfilled. But he didn't want any conflicts in the growing town, and the port needed a harbormaster and a lighthouse keeper.

"Welcome back, Jack," Oshea extended his right hand to the

old sea dog. "I missed you, and we searched the woods high and low."

Jack threw his old sailor's cap on the table and put coal in the coal stove, so he could make some coffee and tea for his visitors. Ida was gloating; her old friend Jack was back, and she had her beautiful Misty.

"What happened to you, Jack?" she wanted to know.

"Only the old man river knows, and I want to keep it that way, Miss Ida," he said.

"It's Mrs. Bosch, now," Oshea was quick to make the correction.

Jack leaned over the stove to hide his surprise; he noticed the beautiful Marchador tied to the post outside.

"Yes, Jack," Ida said. "I married John a few weeks ago."

"I see," Jack nodded, pouring hot water into the tin cups. "You never invited me to the wedding."

In the meantime, Oshea made a promise to Cameron that he would be the next harbormaster. But now Oshea had other business to deal with, such as the reorganizing of the wildcat bank, and he would let the two men wrestle it out between them, as was his wicked custom. And then there was that darn investigation of the murder on the river that the town had been talking about.

18

Chief Macsaube

A few weeks ago, the clerk from the store broke the news of a murder in the area to the dismay of all Singapore people. A trader at the store said the body of an Indian woman had been found down in the shrubs and grasses by the lakeshore, north of town. Everyone knew that Indians could swim, and the woman couldn't have drowned.

Oshea made friends with the natives during his first stay in the area in the 1830s; livid, they came to him for help, suspecting that a white man must have committed the murder. Oshea tried to cover up this bad news in front of the townsfolk as much as he could. Together with Bosch, they investigated it, with the murderer being still at large.

According to various accounts, depending on who you talked with, the murderer was still running loose along the lakeshore, trying to escape to Chicago on foot. Tracks with stains of tobacco were found on shore, signifying the chewing of tobacco, which the Indians didn't use. They scouted the lakeshore north of town and back until they hit the lighthouse in St. Joe at the mouth of Saint Joseph River. It consisted of a conical, rubblestone tower, topped by a four-inch-thick soapstone deck, an octagonal lantern room with patent lamps and reflectors. The keeper of the light resided in the stone dwelling next to it. They both rushed inside, and the lightkeeper greeted them, confirming their worst worries that the murderer was still at-large.

"A white man stopped here asking for some food," said the lightkeeper. "I fed him and offered him a bed. When I woke up the next morning, he was gone."

"What did he look like?" Oshea said.

"All disheveled from traveling and sleeping in the brush," said the light keeper. "I didn't know a murder was committed."

Upon their return to Singapore, the furious Indians paid a visit to Oshea again, demanding the whereabouts of the murderer. In the tricky situation, Oshea found his way out.

"They found his dead body by St. Joe," he said. "You were right. It was a white man on the run to Chicago, but he never made it that far."

The Indians never trusted the white man, no matter how long they've known Oshea, and they demanded proof. But Oshea pulled out a knife to please the Indians.

"He had this on him," said Oshea. "It was all stained with blood. I believe it belonged to one of your women. This is not a white man's knife."

Oshea had procured the short Indian knife that looked like a dagger made of bone and adorned with fur at one of the trading posts at Three Rivers during his first lonesome stay in the Kalamazoo River area. He outfitted himself with knives, bows, and guns. Chief Macsaube examined the short dagger with fur and leather, and took it from Oshea's hands, and they all left for their Indian camp near Oak Openings, where Oshea had previously visited with them. Chief Macsaube was friends with white settlers and pioneers like Oshea, but that bond had been broken by the murder.

Oshea, now busy with the construction of the new lighthouse that was to replace the stone, dilapidated old structure, tried to forget about that bothersome incident with the Indians who were his friends and traded with him. The new lighthouse and the school construction contracts took up all his time. Although he had promised the post to old Jack, pioneer Stephen Nichols became the first light keeper and held the job for the next 17 years.

The construction of the first schoolhouse, located at the end of the Dugout Road, angered Bosch, who was furious with Ida's plans to teach at the new school. Their fights flared up again with the looming construction of the small schoolhouse. After the first teacher, Mrs. Mary Peckham, married and left, the teaching post was open. But Ida had been involved with the warehouse and the reshipment of flour, which she liked doing as well, because of her horseback ride to the warehouse on the sand hill.

"My preference is you stay with the warehouse," Bosch said.

Bosch paid Ida well to work at the warehouse so she could send money to her family in Chicago, and she made extra money for registering the guests at the Big House. Ida often rode Misty to the nearby Flats, to the Morrison General Store, when she didn't want to shop at the company store in Singapore, due to the gossipy clerk. Twice a week, Ida ventured on the Dugout Road to "Flats" to see what's happening in the new promising town that had a post office unlike Singapore, even though the mail coming from Allegan was slow. She was good friends with store owner and postmaster, S.A. Morrison. Ida shopped at the store for perfumes, fragrances, and soaps, as well as for new clothes that she would need as the new teacher.

"I've heard that you will take Mrs. Peckham's place at the new school in Singapore," he said.

"That I will," she said determined not to back off despite Bosch's objections.

"You're still working at the warehouse and boarding guests at the Big House?" Morrison asked.

"I am right now, but I want to teach children in town," she said. "We have none of our own with John."

She bought a new dress, perfumes and soaps for the Big House, but she wasn't satisfied with the poor selection of goods.

"Where could I find more goods?" she asked and quickly added. "I need them for the school and the house."

Morrison who often traveled on horseback to get the mail from Allegan, suggested Allegan as the county seat, Detroit or St. Joe down south from them.

"Of course, you could go to your hometown of Chicago, but St. Joe is well stocked from the steamers arriving with goods from Chicago," Morrison said.

"I'll go to St. Joe," she quipped at Morrison's remark of her hometown of Chicago.

During dinner that night, Ida said she was going to St. Joe that week to do some shopping for the Big House and the warehouse, and that she was going to stay overnight due to the distance of 50 miles. John didn't mind since the shopping benefited his business and trade in Singapore. After wrapping up her work at the warehouse, Ida boarded the stage to St. Joe, that welcomed her with traffic, a few stores, and a trading post.

19

The Diary

Since there was nothing to her liking in St. Joe, she decided to go to Chicago after all and gave a letter for John to the mailman who was just heading out to deliver mail to Flats and the area.

Once she got off the steamer in Chicago, Ida visited Ma first and gave her money for the next year to survive in the booming city with a population of 120,000 people. The year was 1840, and the two went shopping together for Ida's teachers' clothes and wares for the business in downtown's main district. Then, Ida paid a visit to the Jackson Building where Long John conducted his publishing business. He had turned the thriving paper into a daily.

"It's good to see you, my dear," he smiled at the young lady. "What brings you to this side of the lake? I hope the murder business has been resolved."

"Yes, it has been resolved. The murderer was found dead," she said. "I would like to put an ad into your paper, and I have some shopping to do for the business."

Wentworth was so pleased to see Ida that he invited her for dinner. Ida gave Wentworth a written ad looking for help in the Singapore warehouse.

"The mail is still slow, and sometimes it gets lost," she said. "This is too important for me to leave it to the mailman."

"Is this just an ad for labor or are you looking for someone?" Long John raised his eyebrows. "It sounds to me like you're looking for a lost person."

Ida wasn't going to reveal her secret about Esquire Artemas Wallace from New York City, but Wentworth had been in business and politics long enough to see through the ad for help at the warehouse on top of the sand hill near Singapore. The ad even stated the opening hours and to apply for the job at the warehouse in person.

"Do you expect a person from Chicago to apply at your warehouse, Mrs. Bosch?" he asked. "That's more than far-fetched, that's crazy. There's not enough help here in Chicago. But I can also send it to my newspaper friends in New York. That might help. Does John Bosch know about this?"

"Of course," Ida lied. "I am in charge of hiring help. All help for the warehouse and the boarding house."

In a few days, Ida was back at home with bags filled with goods and a present for John, but she crawled into bed early, not wishing to discuss her trip or the letter. She gave him the present, a tall hat for his birthday.

"I got your letter," he said. "Did you visit your mother and gave her money?

"Yes, I took care of all business that needed my attention," she said blushing.

In the morning, Ida showed him all the goods purchased for their business and the company, as John hurried off to a meeting with Oshea, in regards to banking. So, John wasn't paying much attention to Ida's words. She rode Misty around the sand hill. Ida was the only person now with a key to the warehouse. The winter was coming, and John was busy with errands and the company affairs, so he would be late tonight. Ida unlocked the warehouse and stuck a bag from Chicago in a dark corner. Then she came across a chest that had engraved on it: Esquire Artemas Wallace. In the chest she found the family's belongings saved from a steamer that capsized in a squall. She sat down to go through all the treasures: a beautiful watch, a necklace, rings, several books, and a diary.

"I put that chest there," Jack was standing behind her back. "Artemas left it at the harbor house with me."

"But these can't be his things," Ida held up the diary. "It's his mother's diary. She was writing about the trip across the Atlantic to the New World."

"I don't know anything about the diary," said Jack. "Artemas started telling me his story, but then you two had to leave town."

Ida stood up, while Jack put coal in the stove to heat part of the warehouse and a kettle of water for tea and coffee.

"I got some British and Russian tea from Chicago, and coffee," Ida said content with her expedition out west.

She held up the diary bound in black leather cover with the engraving of a rampant red lion with a blue tongue on a shield bordered with fleur-des-lis. Ida sat down by the stove, and as soon as she opened the diary, she had to stop at the sound of another incoming vessel reminding her that she had to divide flour into smaller bags from the large sacks at the entrance.

The dray wagon brought in flour yesterday, and the C.C. *Trowbridge* riverboat would take it upstream to the villages of Flats, Richmond, Allegan, and Kalamazoo. She measured the flour by the pound, two pounds, five and ten pounds, lined up the sacks by the front entrance, as the dray would come back in the evening. Ida was surprised to see Cameron from the Big House in the seat of the dray owned by the Singapore City Co., that was organized to establish the Singapore settlement. Jack and Cameron loaded the flour on the wagon in a hurry.

"Cameron, you drive the dray now?" she asked.

"For a while, yes," the Englishman with reddish hair said, smiling at young Mrs. Bosch.

"You look mighty fine today," Cameron said.

Ida touched her hair all tousled from the bun by the wind, as it spread on the shoulders of her cloak in the setting sun sparkling on the blue waters of Lake Michigan. Glowing, Ida never looked more beautiful than that evening on the sand hill above the settlement of Singapore and the lake. The sun set sparks on her hair, turning it red. She held on tight to the diary, her only connection to Artemas. Rowdy Jack and Cameron left with the dray, and she locked up the warehouse to ride Misty down the path around the tall sand hill. Soon after dinner, Ida went into the sitting room to read the precious diary.

"We boarded Sirius in Bristol for the New World. It was a wild ride on the vast sea that lasted forever, and I got seasick. I was exhausted from fear as the paddleboat swayed in the waves, afraid we wouldn't make it. Artemas was with us to witness the new land at the dawn of the new day. Later, I was told we beat the Great Western steamer by a day. One less day at sea, means one more day to live on land. I will never return to sea; thus, I will never go back to Edinburgh."

She quickly closed the diary and put it underneath the small table, as John entered the sitting room and joined her for the evening tea. The Singapore schoolhouse at the end of the Dugout Road was now standing, and Ida applied for the teacher's job, following Mrs. Peckham's vacancy. John looked at his wife glowing that evening.

"Who will take your place at the warehouse?" he asked concerned. "You've been registering the guests and measuring the flour that needs to be distributed upstream. People will starve without it. Will you let them starve?"

Ida looked up at John and noticed his graying hair on the temples. The Singapore settlement had taken its toll on this strong, determined man, whom she in part admired and part feared. The operations of the Bank of Singapore were suspended, and the Bank of Michigan filed suit in Allegan County to get the money due from Singapore notes that it had redeemed. At the time, no one could distinguish between 'wildcat' fake banks and 'wildcat' honest banks like the one in Singapore, although with doubtful reputation reaching beyond the borders of Allegan County. The banknotes made its way to New York City, where they couldn't be redeemed.

But the Allegan and the Singapore banks banded together for common interest of all the investors from the companies involved. The Bank of Allegan and the Bank of Singapore pooled their specie to create sufficient funds to satisfy the inspector on his rounds between the two banks in the wilderness.

A legend has it that the pooled bag of specie from the Allegan and Singapore banks was traveling down the Kalamazoo River, after it had been viewed by the inspectors at the Bank of Allegan. But an Ottawa Indian paddling swiftly to beat the inspector, who was traveling by horseback, capsized, and the bag of gold sank to the bottom of the river. The Indian rushed to Singapore to tell the story, while the blacksmith devised a drag hook to get the gold from the bottom of the river. In the meantime, a word was sent to Richmond to intercept the inspector for the night, until the bag of gold could be retrieved from the bottom of the river. The next day, the inspector and the gold met at the Singapore Bank. So, everything was covered up for a while, but the eastern banks deemed the Singapore money worthless.

"What about your wildcat banking?" she quipped. "The lawsuit and all."

Brit Cameron interrupted the couple after watching them fight for a while, as he eavesdropped often on the two. He had just returned from the harbor loading the flour on the C.C. *Trowbridge* to take off upstream the next morning. Looking like a snowman, Cameron was all covered with flour, head to toe.

"I can distribute the flour at the warehouse," Cameron said. "Tobias has nothing to do with his dray during the day. He can't even spell dray correctly."

Ida stood up, all red in her face, looking directly at the flour-covered Cameron.

"You will continue to drive the dray," she uttered. "I will find help for the warehouse."

John stared at the two surprised that the fight had shifted from his wildcat banking to Cameron's dray and the warehouse business.

"Let the lady take care of it," said John. "She will not assume the duties of the teacher until she secures help for the warehouse. Cameron, you will continue to drive the dray for the company. Tobias is slow and lazy."

John left the two in the sitting room and went to bed yawning, but with a victorious smile. Amazed at the final decision, the two stared at each other. Neither one of them got what they wanted, locked in John's trap.

20

New York City

Seated in his New York office inside the Greek-revival Merchants Exchange Building three-stories high between William and Hanover streets, Artemas saw in front of him instead of the city traffic, the blue waves of Lake Michigan crashing against the pier and the docks. He felt the sun and the mist from the lake that cast a magic spell over him. He felt the moist forests and Ida's warm touch.

He looked through the letters that had piled up on his desk; one caught his attention with a nautical seal of a steamboat liner company.

"Dear Mr. Wallace,

We hope this letter finds you well. We apologize for the behavior of one of our captains on the regular route from Chicago to Buffalo. He was found dead at the mouth of the channel."

Artemas didn't finish reading the letter, tearing it apart and throwing it on the floor of his neat office on the third floor of the Merchants Building in Manhattan. With pain he recalled the obnoxious ordeal in Buffalo, when he had to explain to the authorities that he wasn't crazy or insane, and that madman Bosch in Detroit locked him in a cabin and took the key. The port authorities thought he was crazy and had him transported to a country hospital for the insane. The more Artemas tried to explain that he wasn't crazy, the more the nurses and the doctors believed he was out of his mind due to a physical sickness experienced in the past.

"I came on the Sirius boat from Bristol with my parents to settle in New York. I was born in Edinburgh." he explained. "I held a reputable job with the Singapore & New York Co. before I wound up in a scam in Singapore. You must have heard about the "wildcat" bank scam in Singapore, or don't you read the papers?"

The doctors and the nurses laughed hard at the notion that this nut with long hair and a beard was ever reputable and traveled back and forth between Bristol in England, Singapore and New York. When he insisted on being a partner in the New York company's ventures in Singapore, they extended his stay and ordered a strict regimen of purgatives for three weeks. Artemas was wasting after the purgatives, and the bloodletting. The hospital staff demanded a proof of Artemas' sanity and a token from his travels. But Artemas left everything in that trunk in the warehouse in Singapore, except for a Singapore banknote, he had crumpled up and stuck in the pocket of his jacket. He pulled out the ornate banknote in front of the amazed staff. He showed to them the signatures of the bank president, Oshea Wilder, and the bank cashier, Rob Hill, and pointed to the heading "State of Michigan" on the banknote.

"I know both of these men," he confirmed. "And Singapore is a settlement on the shore of Lake Michigan. I traveled there for business, look at the note."

The chief doctor took the banknote and held it against the faint daylight coming from the window, where he could clearly read the letters "State of Michigan" on the top. The medical staff held a consultation whether to let Artemas go or not.

"He could have stolen that," the head nurse said.

"Where?" barked the chief doctor.

The asylum was overflowing with physically sick patients, and they had no beds for them, while this nut with a banknote from Singapore was taking up space in the saturated hospital.

"He was locked in a cabin on a boat, and had an entourage all the way to Detroit," the doctor said. "The authorities questioned him about a crime in Buffalo, and then sent him to us, because they didn't know what else to do with him. They kept whatever belongings he had."

The next morning, the doctor signed the release papers with a note to the authorities to return the personal property, but Artemas had to travel on foot to Buffalo. He handed the doctor's note to the officials at the port station, and they gave him back a bag with his belongings including his wallet. Relieved, disheveled Artemas arrived in New York City on a stage exactly three years later since setting foot in Singapore in the fall of 1838.

The persistence of memory of his stay at the asylum in the countryside near Buffalo haunted Artemas in nightmares, and during most days.

"Doctor, please let me go back to Singapore," he woke up one morning naked, sweating and screaming. "There's a beautiful lady waiting for me."

That nightmare kept repeating and coming back to him like a boomerang. He contacted the land speculators from the parent New York Co., and with their fair recommendation and his promise not to release the information about the wildcat bank in Michigan, left for Merchants Exchange where he landed a top position bringing in stock from the family holdings in Edinburgh. As such, Artemas became one of the major shareholders.

At the bottom of the pile of letters, he found an older edition of the New York Tribune. A letter to the editor from the Chicago Democrat editor and publisher, Long John Wentworth, caught his attention, because it had a picture of the ornate Singapore five-dollar banknote. He recalled Ida saying she was from Chicago, and that she was involved in a women's club. Artemas locked the door to the office and read the full article.

Dear Editor,

I would like to bring to your attention to the "wildcat banks" in Michigan and their impact on the nation. Having witnessed the circulation of the fake banknotes that I obtained from an anonymous source, an article about this scam is in line for the Tribune readers to beware of the Singapore and similar scams. However, Singapore must be thriving since they're looking for help. Thank you, John Wentworth, Chicago. See classifieds p.11: Singapore Warehouse needs help. Please apply in person, respectfully signed, Ida Bosch.

Artemas lifted his head from the paper, looked outside the window, and re-read the letter three more times.

"Does this mean that Ida was involved in this bank scam or is Long John trying to tell the world something," Artemas asked himself.

He read to the end where it had a tag line to go to the classifieds p. 11 when it dawned on him: Ida was looking for him. She was relying on the paper to get the word out to the world, having no other means, and not knowing if Artemas was dead or alive. A second thought occurred in his head:

"Does Bosch know about this ad?"

It was snowing outside, and travel was increasingly difficult, inside and outside the city of New York. The article was a few weeks old. But Ida sounded desperate. In that article, Artemas sensed a cry for help coming from the settlement of Singapore washed by the waves of Lake Michigan. Artemas was busy at the exchange when a special request for an investment came from the Michigan Central Railroad to be extended from Detroit out west. A meeting of the investors was to be held in Detroit. After the meeting, Artemas traveled to St. Joe to set up an office and find a place to stay.

21

A Long Kiss Goodbye

Ida was weighing the flour when she heard a distant knock coming from the entrance. When she opened the door and no one was there, she picked up her cloak and walked outside. She heard Misty neighing. Artemas grabbed her by the shoulders and turned her toward him and kissed her a long, succulent kiss. She did not resist and stayed in his arms. Together they walked inside the warehouse and talked until sundown when Ida had to leave for Singapore.

"You're here, how did you find me?" Ida said blushing.

Artemas looked at the woman whom he loved and admired ever since he set his eyes on her that evening at the crossing of the old Indian trail coming to Singapore. He dreamt about Ida when he was locked up in the cabin on the boat to Buffalo and in the nuthouse.

"Help, help, she's drowning," he cried so long until the officer came to his cabin.

"No one's drowning," the officer said. "We will be docking soon."

He dreamt about Ida in the asylum outside of Buffalo, and screamed into the night, only to see the nurse's face above him, instead of his love Ida. The nurse shook him to wake him up from his nightmare and to give him a plunge treatment. Naked in front of the nurse, he had to plunge into a tub with cold water. Screaming and cold, Artemas went back to bed, only to wake up again.

"I want Ida, where is Ida," he yelled. "She's drowning, help her. Get her out of the water."

The head nurse shoved him back into his bed, and that regimen was repeated for months, until he lost track of time and Ida.

He dreamt about Ida back in New York, in his office and in his apartment. Thoughts of Ida tortured him and deprived him of energy and life, which he wanted to end at one point. It was on a dreary evening in November that he walked inside St. Pete's Church in downtown. Since it was the month of the dead, the church celebrated All Souls and All Saints days. He came twice to the church; first on All Saints Day, and then on All Souls Day. Artemas sat in the back by the flickering candles, remembering his parents who died of the cholera epidemic plaguing the country, and that his mother left him her diary with the Scotland royal arms on the cover, which she started in Edinburg before the big trip to the New World.

In those days, the church became his refuge. Immersed in the cold beauty of the Greek Revival temple to St. Peter, Artemas prayed to God for death.

"Dear God, please let me die. You spared me on the boat and in the hospital. You spared me from that evil man with evil fake money. My God, grant me eternity, I pray that you accept me into your hands."

"Artemas, you're not worthy of death," God spoke to him through his heart and mind. "You need to suffer."

His head was spinning, as he freely accepted death, only to realize that he wasn't dead and could hear the chants and see the candle lights flickering. Coming from a devout Catholic family, he participated in the ritual of the dead in the Mass of Burial when he buried his parents at the old Mulberry Street cemetery.

The "Book of the Dead," with the symbol omega on the cover and adorned by crimson red roses, was placed on a stand by the St. Joseph altar. He took the pen and wrote their names in the book filled with the names of the dead. He looked through the names of the dead to find the dead captain from the boat who had him locked up; he was from New York. In the Book of the Dead, naval officers had the naval seal behind their names; he was determined to find him, dead or alive, and he vowed vendetta to the evil man with evil money from Singapore. Artemas went back to his seat by the candelabra with the flickering candles.

The next evening on the night of All Souls Day, he returned to St. Pete's for commemoration of All the Faithful Departed. The temple to the Roman Catholic Saint on Barclay Street was close to his offices, and so he visited the church often to meditate. But that night, he couldn't find peace around him or in him. After the mass, he took a horsecar to the Mulberry Street cemetery where his parents were buried. Artemas had engraved on the tombstone that they came on the boat Sirius and died of cholera in the New World.

The candles on the graves were flickering in the November night, casting light over the entire cemetery. The memory of Ida and the evil man from Singapore came back to him. Back at home, he searched in old books with indexes of names of the naval officers of the past 20 years, since the *Walk-in-the-Water* passenger schooner touched the sea in 1821. Then he remembered the name Quinn, when Bosch commanded the officer to keep a tight watch over him. The current note in the book stated that officer Quinn was serving on the Buffalo-Detroit-Chicago steamboat line.

22

Burning of the bills, 1842

Ida handed Art his mother's diary with the Scottish royal arms engraving on the cover. The November chill, with fog coming in from the lake, drove them out of the warehouse, along with the fear of Bosch. They departed at the crossing of the old Indian trail and the Dugout Road, where they first met a few years ago. Ida took Misty to the stables behind the Big House and entered from the back through the porch and the West Wing of the house. Freezing from the warehouse and her cloak covered with flour, she joined the company in the dining room with Bosch, Oshea and Cameron already seated.

"Cameron, you can have the warehouse job, I insist," she

said. "I can't find a different replacement than you."

"Who's going to drive the dray?" quipped Cameron.

"Tobias will return to his work on the dray," Ida said. "You will pack the flour and make sure it gets on time to the Trowbridge riverboat."

Bosch, who was busy with bank and company's proceedings, disregarded their conversation, occupied by Oshea's explanations of the suspension of the bank. Wily Oshea was pulling out and handed the Singapore Co. to greedy Bosch, who had the majority of investments in it. The Michigan Legislature annulled the charter of the Bank of Singapore, along with charters of most of the other wildcat banks of Michigan, including the Bank of Allegan in 1842. The bank officers had to destroy the bills on hand at the bank at the time of suspension. Oshea and Bosch stood up and left the table before eating. They walked to the Bank of Singapore located on Broad Street and found a table covered with bills in packages stacked in piles. Swiping them from the table, they threw them in the stove and burned them. The fire fed by the unusable bills burned strong, and the bank officers boiled water in the kettle to make coffee from the coffee beans that Ida had brought on the boat with her from Chicago.

The bank officers did everything to save the bank. According to an article in the Allegan Journal, there was an incident of a man coming from a neighboring town with $5 of the Singapore money who presented it at the bank for specie redemption. Cashier Rob Hill went out into the street, and borrowing a few shillings from others, was able to redeem the bill and save the credit of the bank for a while. The bank was ready to redeem their notes in goods and anything they owned in property.

Bosch kept a few banknotes of each denomination for himself, so did Oshea and the cashier. However, in the meantime, the ornate banknotes were still circulating in New York.

"We can't do anything about that," said Oshea closing on the "wildcat bank" deal forever. "The panic and the run on the banks didn't help."

The next morning, since the warehouse needed supplies and the holidays were coming, Ida announced she was going shopping in St. Joe.

"I will return in two days," she said. "The trails are vicious.

I will have to stay overnight."

Upset, Bosch over the bank and company affairs didn't respond, put on his tall hat and cloak, and left the Big House to meet with Oshea at the Bank of Singapore building down the street.

"Just see to it that the flour makes it upstream," he said. "Don't let our people starve."

Cameron and Tobias were already at the dray wagon in the stables getting ready to pull out to go to the warehouse for the day's shift. The town was waking up to a dreary November day, with the cold wind blowing from the lake and lifting grains of sand to mix them with snow. The sandy mix stuck to coats and boots, and it was hard to scrape it off. With the frost hitting the lakeshore, the sandy mix froze and formed bulges on the walking boards, making it difficult to walk on them. The two got the stage ready for St. Joe, with Mr. Fisch holding the lines.

The stagecoach took the old Indian trail to St. Joe at the foot of the sand hills bordering the lake. As the sun came out from the clouds and the slush from the sky stopped falling, the wind died down late in the afternoon. They arrived with the setting sun in the port town, and the two settled at a boarding house in the port. In the middle of the night, Artemas on horseback whisked away Ida through the woods to Tisdel's Tavern near the Sauk trail between Chicago and Detroit. The loud tavern accommodated weary travelers, lovers, outlaws and prostitutes alike. Hidden in the woods, far away from the bustle of the port town of St. Joe, the proprietor welcomed people on their journey between the growing cities.

Art and Ida made love in one of the guest rooms and stayed for the entire two days, sending word to Mr. Fisch to wait for Ida until Friday morning. That morning with the rainbow rising above the treetops and the shimmering sunrise on the leaves, Art kissed Ida in the backyard of the large tavern and handed her a small box. Ida opened the box; it was a shell cameo brooch. He found it in his mother's trunk where she stored her memories and memorabilia from Scotland, along with a black hat, a gift from her grandmother, that she never wore. Art put the black hat on Ida's head and stepped back to look at her. Glowing and filled with newly-found love, Ida promised to come back to the tavern.

She bought coffee beans at the harbor store, and Mr. Fisch stopped at a trading post to stock up on goods and wares for the company's growing businesses. The company clerk also let him know what the store needed, since it was running low due to vessels not coming because of storms racing across the lake. The shelves were empty, and even the competition had nothing to offer anymore. People were starving and Cameron distributed the last 10-pound sack of flour to the store in Singapore. They searched for another store en route to Singapore but found nothing but wilderness.

Ida unpacked the few things they had purchased in St. Joe: coffee from the steamships and the life-saving flour for the store, along with hardware for the business.

23

Steamer Milwaukie

That year, the snow was several feet deep, and the horses could no longer go on the trails, and the wood in the sheds was running low. The Hollanders prayed in their northwest basement room for the snow and frost to stop. As the hard winter persisted without letting up, the Hollanders took their prayers to the sitting room, by the warmth of the bigger stove, and others joined them.

"Mrs. Fisch, why doesn't Singapore have a church to pray for this winter to go away?" Ida asked all bundled up shaking with cold.

Bosch raised his eyebrows as he looked up at his wife. She hasn't been the same ever since she's returned from that trip at the onset of the hard winter last month, bringing back coffee and tea from the steamboats. She talked less, blushed more and immersed herself in reading and writing all day.

"What do you need a church for?" he quipped at her. "You can pray here at the Big House. It's just as good as any other house of faith. We believe, and it doesn't matter where we pray. You wouldn't be able to get to it anyway."

Cameron, who was a believer from the old country, supported Ida and the Hollanders to have a church in Singapore. The Hollanders, mostly seceders from the Reformed

Church, escaped religious persecution and were looking to establish a new congregation and a new life in America. The Seceders emigrated from the old country in the first wave of emigration in the 1840s, forming Calvinist colonies in the new world, and they attracted members of the Reformed Church as well. They formed a strong presence in the future settlement of Holland, Michigan, north of Singapore.

"We're going to starve," said Cameron. "I am going to get Jack; it's cold in the harbor. We can share my room, plus we have some rooms left."

In the winter of 1842 to 1843, the town of Singapore and the villages upstream the Kalamazoo River shivered in the unrelentless snow, wind and ice. The vast gray lake was frozen with only a few water holes opened in its surface, as far as the eye could see. Jack and Cameron went ice fishing for bluegills so Singapore wouldn't starve, but the whipping wind drew them away back into the Big House.

"Steamers will arrive," Jack said, "and they will bring us flour."

"How are they going to make it through the ice?" asked Bosch. "And I heard from Butler, that they want our flour, what we have left of it."

Jack pulled out his navigation log book. He got the wind of a few months ago that the steamer *Milwaukie,* from Milwaukee, would make Singapore a port of call to load up flour on its way to Buffalo. They had loaded up 3,000 barrels of flour in St. Joseph. However, the crew was angry at the captain for setting sail on the treacherous waters from St. Joe.

"They can't have our flour," said Cameron. "We will starve."

Before the onset of the hard winter and frost, Bosch and Butler agreed to a shipment of flour to Buffalo, but things have changed and the town of Singapore was starving, and so were her sisters up stream except for Kalamazoo, where the W.S Walbridge mill provided the flour for the shipment to Singapore on flatboats. The flour arrived and instead of readying it for loading on the expected steamboat, Cameron and Jack stored it away at the back of the warehouse to keep it for Singapore to survive. When the ship arrived, the two said they only had a few sacks of flour to spare from the warehouse and loaded it onto *Milwaukie.*

In the evening, the captain set sail for Buffalo with the angry crew on board, due to the treacherous waters and the night ahead. Suddenly, the wind shifted to the west and northwest and the temperature kept falling below the freezing point. Two miles north of the Kalamazoo River, the ship crashed sideways onto the beach, and it was embedded in solid ice up to the main deck.

An investigation of the shipwreck north of Singapore ensued, after the surviving sailors told their story to Nichols, the light keeper. They appeared in front of him half frozen and covered with ice and flour, they were the only survivors from the ship that made a call at Singapore, only yesterday. Three days later, the investigators from St. Joseph, Buffalo and Allegan arrived in two feet deep snow, in light two-seated cutters, and headed out to the shipwreck.

The ship broke beneath the blows of the stormy lake, and the captain and the rest of the crew died from freezing on the wrecked boat. The investigation team with Jack and Cameron pulled the dead bodies out of the shipwreck. Terrified, Jack recognized his friend, Capt. Dan C. Whittemore, who after all, found his destiny near Singapore, even though Jack saved him earlier from drowning in the Kalamazoo River, when Bosch pushed them both in to drown.

"I knew this man, Cam," Jack's tears froze on his cheeks. "We were friends. It's my dead friend, Cap. Rest in peace, buddy."

It was their duty to lay the seamen to proper rest at Singapore where they found their final destination, unless the family would come to pick up their dead bodies. And that's how the cemetery started in Singapore with these seafarers' dead bodies being buried far from their hometowns. However, the investigation of the shipwreck uncovered lifesaving flour, tightly packed in barrels that had remained intact and protected from water. Later, some barrels were sent onto Buffalo, but most remained at the warehouse. The investigators concluded that the captain acted irresponsibly when the ship headed out into the storm, and charges were filed in Allegan County; however, the suit was settled without going to trial.

The Big House boarded the investigation team and offered them food. One agent, who loaded the flour in St. Joseph, seemed familiar to Bosch, but he kept out of his way. The flour from the shipwreck in the barrels had to be redistributed, due to its quantities, everyone had to help, so the investigation agents were on their own with their paperwork and inventory of what needed to be salvaged, other than the flour. The investigators talked to the surviving sailors in the sitting room, while the rest of the Big House residents were working to get the flour into the warehouse. One sailor told a story of rats leaving the ship in St. Joseph, confirming that they should have never left the port.

"It's an old superstition," said the agent from St. Joseph.

Ida, who was nearby, recognized the deep voice coming from the sitting room. Startled, she peeked in to see the team with the sailors seated at the table. The agent looked up from the table and nodded to her. She gasped for breath and ran into the kitchen, with Mrs. Fisch at the stove taking up most of the space.

"We have to make a lot of food," Ida said pointing to the sitting room. "They will be with us for a while because the snow is still falling."

The snow kept falling for the next 40 days when Singapore was cut off from the rest of the world, both by sea and by land, with four feet of snow. Most of the team had left, but the mysterious agent from St. Joseph stayed and moved to the other boarding house.

24

Hard Winter, 1842-1843

Ida was teaching at the schoolhouse with limited days due to deep snow of the hard winter of 1842--1843. The 40-day storm that marooned *Milwaukie* seemed to last into eternity. Ida met up with Art after school, which was out in the countryside, and they rode their horses on the old Indian trail that connected Fort Dearborn to Fort Michilimackinac. With the snow covering the oaks and laying the branches low over their heads, they rode to Pine Plains Tavern, the only house between Singapore and Allegan. The winter favored the coverup of the two lovers bundled up in woolen shawls and coats, as they sat by the fire at the tavern. Ida was wearing the cameo brooch from Art, who kissed her by the post with the tied horses. She stalled for a while before jumping on Misty but had to leave, since the evening was coming, and the days were short.

Mr. Fisch took Misty into the barn and looked with apprehension at the lady glowing from the cold air. He had noticed before the brooch on her dress, which reminded him of the time when he couldn't find Ida back in St. Joe before the onset of the hard winter. She told him that she was going shopping and wouldn't be back until later. The next day, Mr. Fisch received a note on a foolscap paper and written with skim milk. The letters couldn't be seen until heated.

"Where are you coming from, boy?" he asked.

The messenger boy looked around him worried that someone might see them. He was carrying a big sack full of letters and notes like the one he had just handed over. The messenger couldn't have known what the note said. The lady at Tisdel's Tavern who gave him the note reminded the messenger not to reveal to the receiver where he was coming from.

"From town," the boy said and left.

"Mrs. Bosch, did you get lost on the trails coming from school?" Mr. Fisch asked.

"No, I had to stay late to correct papers," she said. "The light was better at the school than here in my office, and we're running out of oil."

"The school will also run out of oil," Fisch took the horse away making a mental note to talk to his wife.

The winter evenings were long and with the shortage of lamp oil, to her distress, Ida couldn't read anymore in the evening, thus she had to put up with the company in the sitting room of the Big House seated at the large table.

"How was school today?" asked Cameron looking Ida directly into her eyes.

Cameron found the letters from Art to Ida, hidden in the trunk in the warehouse. Art upon his return to Singapore hid them in his old chest with his belongings; he never mailed the letters fearing that the receiver would reveal the secret love between the two.

"Dear Ida,

I've given up all hope of ever finding you. I am alive and back in New York after a horrible voyage from Detroit, where the

captain held me at gunpoint hidden in a cabin. I was deemed insane and locked inside an infirmary near Buffalo where I almost died from the bloodletting treatments. I didn't kill myself in New York, because I wanted to live for you. I hope you are safe somewhere in Chicago.
Loving Art."

Cameron pulled a few letters from the pile inside the chest and kept them in his room at the boarding house. He now had this particular one folded in his pocket. During the 40-day storm counting since *Milwaukie* was beached in the late fall of 1842, the settlers all ate together in the dining room to save on oil for the lamps and heating. Only the common rooms were now being heated with the little coal left. Men went into the woods to cut timbers for heating, and the business at the two sawmills had slowed down. Vessels could not travel anymore on the frozen lake. Life came to a stop.

Ida seated herself at her place, hungry after the cold rides on the trails and long walks by the Pine Plains Tavern and dismissed Cameron's question.

"The school must be taking up a lot of your time, Mrs. Bosch?" Cameron persisted in his questioning.

"They're busy now with more kids," said Mr. Fisch, fearing the worst. "But they will close with more snow coming."

Bosch was concerned about the sawmills not running due to the harsh winter and also the survival of the settlement; the school was the last on his mind.

"We will have to head into the woods for more wood and hunt," he said. "We're going to die if we don't. What's all this school business?"

Everyone was looking down into their plates fearing Bosch's wrath. Since they've been locked in by the snow from all sides, Bosch's anger often flared at the sight of all the hungry people residing at the Big House. They dragged the barrels with the flour from the shipwreck and stored them in the barn by the big house and in the basement. The flour would last a few more months before the spring thaw.

"The school is just taking up extra oil and wood that we all need here," Bosch said. "We will decide at the hall whether to close it down for the winter before we all freeze and starve to death in this ice trap."

From then on, Ida gathered the kids in the small sawmill shed, with a circular saw as the bell in town, cutting off Art's advances for the time being. However, with the first thaw she would head back to school.

"I missed you," Art kissed her. "It's been a long winter."

They were back on the trails, horseback riding to Pine Plains Tavern, determined nothing would stop them. Time apart drew them closer together and broke all obstacles to love manifesting itself all around. Art loaded up on food at Pine Plains and brought it into town, so people wouldn't starve, thus dodging any suspicion.

25

Schooner *Octavia*, 1849

The snow was still four feet deep in the spring of 1843, as the people went to the schoolhouse for the town meeting on snowshoes. Bosch led the meeting, announcing a complete takeover of all of Singapore Co., dealings and the town affairs, since Oshea had left the settlement after the suspension of the Bank of Singapore. Bosch already owned the store and the majority of interest in Singapore's sawmills, the Astor House and the other boarding houses. Ida seated in the corner listened to her husband's exaggerations of Singapore's future: his vision of Singapore's magnificence outshining the ports of Chicago and Milwaukee, attracting both settlers from the east coast, tourists and adventurers of Oshea's brand and magnitude. All she saw was a small company working camp with weary and hungry settlers after the long winter; the town was still unincorporated, it didn't have a church, and there was only one road in and out of town--the old dugway squeezed between the dunes and the river.

The Congress was not in favor of appropriating money for harbor improvements at the Kalamazoo River, and Senator Lucius Lyon suggested taxing public lands and selling them, which the people resisted. The first sawmill was destroyed by fire; it was thought to have been arson since the insurance money was more profitable than the milling business. However, as one friend left the

Singapore scene, another one showed up. Francis Browne Stockbridge from Maine appeared as the major investor in a lumber yard in Chicago that sold the products of the Singapore mill, while Bosch ran the business at Singapore. The two were made for each other.

The new Singapore sawmill, that replaced the burnt one, provided a steady supply to the growing town of Chicago. Life was good again as new immigrants sailed in on boats from Milwaukee. Between her job at the boarding house and teaching, Ida found time to visit with Art who worked for Stockbridge in the offices of the lumberyard in Chicago. With the onset of spring, Art had to leave for Chicago to escape growing suspicions of his love for Ida.

Ida covered up for her visits in Chicago using the same excuses as before-- getting supplies for the company, the town and visiting with her mother.

"You must leave him, now," Art begged her when she visited. "Don't force me to wait any longer than I have been."

One day midweek when Ida was in Chicago visiting with her mother, Cameron walked into Bosch's office in Singapore with a stack of letters and handed them to Bosch.

"What's this?" he said. "I don't have time now. Stockbridge is coming."

Stockbridge was at the door waiting for Cameron to leave. Bosch shoved the letters in his slush pile and nodded toward the door for Cameron to leave his office.

"We'll talk when I have more time," said Bosch.

The shipbuilding in Singapore was in full swing, as the partners needed a vessel to transport lumber to the lumber yard in Chicago. They began building the three-masted schooner, *Octavia,* that was first recorded at the port of Chicago with her first master, Capt. Alexander A. Johnson, an old saltwater sailor from Gloucester, Massachusetts, who came with Stockbridge to the area.

Ida visited with Art in his apartment where they talked about her leaving Bosch and their life together in Chicago. The city was growing, even though it suffered from the bouts of cholera in the late 1840s. Her ma died of cholera and was buried in a mass grave designated as Cholera Cemetery. Ida cried cold tears at the cemetery, regretting she had left Ma and Pa to die all alone in the city. She cried tears of remorse that she would no longer see Art.

Ida returned back to Singapore, dressed in black from head to toe and crying. She first went to see Jack, back in the harbor house shack, but there was no shack, only black ashes and circles in the wood where the shack used to stand. But the harbor was busy again, with higher demand for wood. Vessels leaving Singapore for Chicago and Milwaukee were piled high with lumber, shingles and other products of the West Michigan forests, but ships coming to Singapore traveled empty except for a few retail goods.

"Where is Jack? Where is his harbor shanty?" she rushed back to the Big House and to the stables.

She saddled Misty and rode up to the warehouse.

Cameron greeted her with a big smile, showing no signs of deceit or love for the lady. He was working on filling the barrels with flour and getting goods ready for reshipment.

"Where is Jack?" she asked without responding to Cameron's greetings.

Cameron took her back outside in the fresh air dipped in sunlight, and they both gazed across the deep blue waters of Lake Michigan marked with sailing schooners. The white dots on the horizon, where the water met the sky, were moving slowly. The spring air breathed new hope and expectations. Cameron was reluctant to answer and tried to engage Ida with town talk.

"The school is waiting for you, and the town of Singapore is doing good now," he said. "We're shipping out more lumber than ever and building more ships."

Upon her arrival in Singapore, Ida noticed changes while she was gone; another store was built, more houses, a large shipyard with three-mast schooners, and more mills. John Bosch too welcomed her with big news from the shipbuilding world. The 127-ton three-masted schooner, "*O.R. Johnson*," was under construction. He introduced her to his partner Stockbridge, who was delighted by the lady's presence.

"You must visit me when you're in Chicago," he said.

"I will be happy to," she said.

Ida's heart skipped a beat. She will be able to go to Chicago again, due to the lumber business with Stockbridge who ran the Chicago operations of the lumberyard that accepted lumber from

Singapore. Stockbridge invited them for dinner at the Astor House in Singapore, busy with guests, as Singapore's reputation grew as the Ellis Island for immigrants heading out west from New England. The transportation improved with more schooners crossing the Great Lakes, and the first railroads were built.

They were in good spirits at the Astor, but Ida was determined to tell her husband about her real love for Art when she settles back down in Singapore. She kept putting it off, even though she promised to Art in Chicago. But John Bosch flooded her with affection and gifts from the schooners docking in Singapore.

Back on the sand hill by the warehouse, Cameron played with the sand in his hand and then pointed to their horses.

"Let's go for a ride in the woods," he said.

They rode on the old Indian trail to the old cabin in the woods, where Jack offered her the dwelling when she was running away from John Bosch. Cameron helped her off the horse and led her behind the cabin and showed her a mound of dirt with a cross.

"He's here," said Cameron. "He got the germ from one of the sailors on the ship."

Cameron buried old Jack, who died of cholera, behind the old cabin in the woods because he couldn't be buried at the town cemetery. Brokenhearted, Ida cried more tears than all the tears combined before for her parents and all the dead. A lonely crocus was blooming on top of the grave. She could hear nature awakening to spring. Bosch, who knew about Jack's death, had the harbor shack burnt down to prevent the spread; only the charcoaled wood remained after a man who had saved her life.

Ida kneeled by the grave and prayed for the old man.

26

Secrets

They both lingered around the cabin where the old man still kept his belongings that he had forgotten to take to the harbor house or stored back in when he wasn't happy with Oshea and Bosch. They had threatened to tear down the harbor house, ever since the light house at the mouth of the Kalamazoo

River was built. They went through his treasures from the sea when he sailed the waters of the Great Lakes. Jack even dragged in the belongings of his deceased captain friend. Due to the hard winter, everything was well preserved. Jack had several silver bullions and ingots, a cross, and a compass. Sometimes he referred to these as his "nauticals."

Cameron packed Jack's things into a big sack to take to the warehouse to preserve it. He touched Ida's arm and looked at her with warm eyes and leaned forward to kiss her.

"Get away from me," she said as she pushed him away. "You are disgusting. Keep your hands to yourself. Don't touch me."

But there was a shortage of women in Singapore; some were leaving the wild town with its lumberjacks and new ones were not coming. A woman of Ida's caliber was just as desirable as the gold and silver ingots from Jack's nautical treasures.

Ida jumped on Misty and rode away to the Dugout Road leading back into town. Partners Stockbridge and Bosch were talking in the office about the growing shipyard business and the Chicago lumberyard.

"John, why did you burn down Jack's harbor shanty?" she said.

The two men looked at her with interest thinking she was teaching at the schoolhouse, but instead the lady was browsing around town for news and gossip. They looked at each other and back at Ida hesitant to answer. Stockbridge spoke up for John Bosch.

"My dear, cholera is plaguing our cities and towns," he said. "A sailor aboard *Octavia* brought the germ into the docks, and infected Jack and the shanty."

"I had to burn it down to protect the town," John said. "Have some tea with us."

Ida sat down in the office with the two partners. She was staring outside the window, looking over the mouth of the river that created a lake, sometimes called Kalamazoo Lake. High spring waters spilled out of the riverbed into the town streets, but boardwalks instead of timbers lined the streets of Singapore.

"You can travel to Chicago more to see to our operations at the lumber yard," John said to please his wife. "Mr. Stockbridge would love to show you around. Your home city is growing faster than Singapore, but it needs our lumber--tons of it."

"I will, when I am done with the school," she said.

Ida was determined to finish the school year at the schoolhouse before going to Chicago again, this time forever. The school had around 42 students from the area. Some of them were children of the immigrants who came to settle down in the area, or who had just stopped in for a while before moving on to further inland settlements like Holland. The schoolhouse was typical for the times, with all the grades combined within one school building. She encouraged writing and reading to her students, who often spoke one of the foreign languages of the settlers, including French Canadians and settlers from Europe. Having no children of her own, Ida loved the school, where she wrote letters on a regular basis to Art.

"Dear Art,

It is with a broken heart that I have to write that our friend Jack has died of cholera. He wasn't allowed to be buried at the town cemetery because of the germ, and John even burnt his harbor shanty. There is nothing left but charcoaled wood on the dock. I lost my only friend in town. The town is growing with shipbuilding at large and spreading to the Flats, a village upstream from Singapore. There's a post office in Flats, where I go often.

Our dream will soon come true. I will be able to travel to Chicago as I please. John Bosch and Mr. Stockbridge have partnered in the lumber trade, and the office is in the harbor of Chicago. Mr. Stockbridge has invited me on several occasions, but I have to finish the school year. So be patient with me. Love, Ida."

Ida rode on horseback to mail the letters to Art, not trusting any messenger boys with the precious mail. She placed the letter inside a wrapper written over with skim milk, so Art wouldn't have to pay for extra sheets. When placed under heat, the letters could be deciphered. The receiver paid postage of 25 cents per sheet of paper. Ida arranged with Flats postmaster, Morrison, to have letters from Art saved at the post office until she picked them up, to prevent the messenger boy from taking the letter to the Big House for Mrs. Fisch to scrutinize.

When she returned to the Big House, John was waiting for her in his office.

"The messenger boy said you had some letters from Chicago at the post in Flats," he quipped. "I spoke with Morrison. From now on, all the mail comes here to the Big House, and I will pay for it. No need for you to go to Flats."

Ida, flabbergasted by the bad news, turned around to leave the office as John stood up, walked to her and took her by the arm, seating her in the chair right across from his desk.

"Who is writing all these letters to you?" John was curious.

"It's Ellura, my friend from school," she lied. "I need to see her the next time I go to Chicago."

"I will think about the next time you go to Chicago," John snapped.

"You can't keep me a prisoner in Singapore," cried Ida. "I can pick up my mail in Flats."

"I will see to it that you don't," John said. "All the mail will go through me first. Morrison will tell me if you go to the post in Flats. We all have work to do with our new business with Stockbridge."

Ida had no way to let Art in Chicago know to stop writing to her. She dreaded the day when the next letter from Art would arrive in John's hands. From then on, she waited for the messenger boy, who didn't show up for days. Ida set up by the river where she used to see Jack fish and wait for the Indians to come with mail on a canoe or a raft. Later the messenger boy took over the tasks of floating the mail down the river. She was waiting at the bend in the river upstream. As the boy attempted to dock the raft, she jumped in the water and pulled it closer, grabbing the only bag with mail, and then she pushed away the raft into the current, carrying away the messenger boy to the river mouth. She tied the bag to the saddle and rode Misty until they reached Jack's cabin in the woods.

27

Mail fraud at Oxbow

The cabin was located in the woods by the Oxbow lagoon near the Indian trail, so she had to cross the river to get to the other side. Since it was spring and the riverbed was overflowing, she couldn't get to the other side without a raft or a canoe. Jack always had a canoe. Ida realized she would have to take the bag instead to the warehouse on top of the sandhill. She took off to the warehouse and went through the stack of letters until she found the one addressed to her. She shoved the rest of the letters in Art's old trunk that he had left behind in the warehouse. She took the sheets of paper out of the wrapper.

"Dear Ida,

I can't wait for you any longer. You must come to see me, otherwise I will die by my own hand. The torture is too much to take for one man trapped in his own mind. I can't work or live without you. I will meet you in heaven.

Love eternal, Art."

But Ida also wanted to read the wrapper, so she turned on the oil lamp, took off the cover and read the additional lettering in skim milk against the heat of the flame.

"I will be waiting for you on the last Friday in June at the harbor. Be there."

Ida was shaking wet from having to wade in the cold river when she arrived back at the Big House. Nosy Mrs. Fisch hurried to tell her that the messenger boy came all wet into town and that someone had attacked him by the river bend and had stolen the mail from him.

"Mr. Bosch assigned me to watch for the messenger boy to get the mail for the Big House, but the messenger boy came all wet and without the mail bag," she swallowed her words. "He feared for his life that it could have been one of the drunken Indians."

"It must have been one of the Indians," nodded Ida. "I saw them on canoes going down the river."

The word had it that the Indians have been stealing the "fire water" that was coming on the steamers and bottles of fine wine from the *Milwaukie* wreck hidden at one of the warehouses. Growing Singapore, with the ever-expanding shipbuilding industry, now had several warehouses. The keys to all the warehouses were kept inside the safe at the old Bank of Singapore building, which was now a boarding house. A new clerk had been named to keep an eye on things at the old bank building.

"How did they get inside the warehouses?" asked Ida without flinching.

Bosch stored several bottles of fine wine and whiskey in the basement, along with cigars, tobacco, coffee and tea. Everyone had access to the basement for storing their own goods.

"Now what?" asked scared Mrs. Fisch. "Mr. Bosch will demand the mail to be handed over to him."

The messenger boy explained to Mr. Bosch that it was a drunken Indian who had attacked him at the bend of the river. Ida wished the mail incident would go away. Stockbridge and Bosch were expecting a letter that day from the lumberyard in Chicago for a new shipment of lumber. They called on postmaster Morrison to come to Singapore to set things straight. Morrison swore he put the letter with the order from the Chicago lumberyard into the bag of mail.

"I saw it on the wrapper," he said. "Your competition upstream could have stolen the order and used it for their own business, they could have set up the Indian. They are friends; Oshea used to be friends with the Indians. They bribe them with your "fire water" and fine wines from the warehouses."

The partners looked at Morrison in disbelief as if he was a madman telling a tall tale.

"Morrison, are you trying to tell us that we were set up?" quipped Bosch. "And our friends upstream used an Indian to steal our order?"

Singapore had lumbering competition upstream in the villages of Richmond, Allegan and Kalamazoo. Anyone from the competition could have set up the Indian to steal the order from Chicago. The two took a stage around the sand hill to the warehouses, stopping first at the old bank to pick up the set of keys. To their shock, they found that several bottles of whiskey and fine wines were missing without a trace of anyone breaking in. It was a clean steal; the robber didn't leave any tracks. That would point to an Indian stealing the goods.

The next morning, the partners including Morrison headed to Allegan to have a word with the owners of their sawmill.

Meanwhile Ida knew she had to get the stack of letters out of Art's chest. She saddled Misty and rode to the warehouse that was locked the previous night. Jack once showed her how to get in through the back door he had made for himself, which he had concealed with lumber from the sawmill and carved on it:

"Beware. No trespassing."

Ida tore off the planks and crawled inside. As soon as she straightened up, she was facing Cameron with the mail bag in one hand and Art's letters in the other.

"Which will it be, my lady?" he laughed. "The order from Chicago or your lover's letters?"

Cameron was in her face, and Ida felt his breath on her, as he grabbed her and tried to kiss her. He pushed her into a chair, tied her with a rope, and then forced a kiss. After the forced kiss, he put a gag in her mouth, and tied a scarf around it, so she couldn't scream.

"You will get neither until you're mine," Cameron giggled out loud.

Ida tried to wiggle out in vain, as Cameron pulled the rope tighter, tying her to one of the posts. He packed the letters and the mail into a saddle bag. He locked the door behind him and walked the distance to the Indian trail in the woods where he tied his horse.

At the Big House, Cameron retired to his room on the third level with windows overlooking Broad and River streets, the busiest downtown area. He heard the stage arrive in the back and the two men arguing over the lost order from the Chicago lumberyard.

"Our neighbors upstream were lying, they stole the order," Stockbridge said.

"No, they wouldn't lie to me," Bosch said. "I do business with them. I've known them for years. You are new to this. You don't understand."

Mrs. Fisch hurried to the dining room where the two partners were fighting over the lumber order from Chicago. It was a shipment worth $20,000, and the prices of lumber were climbing up as the city was bursting at its seams.

"I am going to kill whoever has stolen that order," Bosch threatened in front of everyone.

"Calm down," said Stockbridge. "I am telling you the Richmond or Allegan people stole it to make money on our order."

Bosch slammed his fist on the table and sent cups and plates gliding across the table. Then he lifted the table on one end and sent all the dishes sliding off to the floor. He grabbed the heavy iron wrought poker by the stove and waved it around his head, hitting a glass light lamp that crashed with splinters of glass all over the floor. He ran to the sitting parlor, grabbed one of the whiskey bottles, took a big gulp and then threw it on the floor, watching it break.

"I've had enough of drinking Indians," he yelled, all fiery red.

Morrison and Stockbridge tried to calm him down as Bosch collapsed back into his chair at the table.

"Mrs. Fisch, bring out the food," he ordered as if nothing had happened, but breathing heavily.

The settlers in the Big House all have witnessed Bosch's anger before, but never this intense and violent. The evening closed in, when Bosch noticed Ida wasn't at the table or around the house.

"Where's my wife?"

Everyone stared at him and watched his anger grow on him. He ran away from the table and searched the bedroom, the offices and the entire house, as if she were hiding from him in his own building, where it all started.

"She must be at the warehouse," he said to himself and headed out to the stables.

But Cameron was standing outside waiting for him, holding the mail bag and a pile of papers. He searched the bag and found the order from the lumberyard in Chicago and handed it to Bosch.

"Where did you get this?" he raised his eyebrows. "You knew we've been searching for the order everywhere. Where did you get the mail bag, I ask again?"

He grabbed Cameron by his coat and shook him hard, but Cameron kept holding onto the rest of the mail.

"I found the mail bag tied to the raft at Fishtown," he said. "The drunken Indian missed the landing here and floated down to the lagoon and then abandoned it and ran into the woods."

"What the heck were you doing in Fishtown?" he asked.

"Well, I was looking for the mail bag just like the rest of you," Cameron said. "It occurred to me it could have floated to the lagoon."

Bosch was too happy to ride up to the warehouse to look for Ida. He grabbed another bottle of whiskey from the cabinet and poured drinks for all present at the table and in the dining room.

"Cheers, we found the order," he said taking a big gulp.

Cameron stood up from his seat at the table and corrected

Bosch in front of everybody.

"I found the mail bag and saved it from destruction at Shriver's Bend," he said. "You know how fishermen are; Charlie and Henry wouldn't have noticed that the bag was there."

Cameron, Jack and Ida had been to Fishtown and Shriver's Bend, the two fishing villages by the Oxbow Lagoon several times, fishing and hunting in the woods. They made friends with the fishermen from the villages, Charles and Henry Shriver, who sailed into the promising area with the winding river from the port of Buffalo, N.Y. The Indians helped them clear the primitive land, and Capt. John Martel built their fishing tug, the *Shriver Brothers.*

On a good day, with this tug, the brothers could bring in two-to-three thousand pounds of whitefish and hundreds of sturgeon. They were known for their hospitality, and people from Chicago arrived to venture out on the lake with the tug and watch the nets lift with loads of fish. This was the foundation for charter fishing for which Saugatuck, former Flats, has become famous for.

28

The Great Spirit

During the long Singapore winters, Jack taught Ida basic man's skills: how to use a knife that he had learned from the Indians. Back at the warehouse, Ida knocked down the chair and dragged herself to the tool box, where they kept knives and guns. She cut the rope and freed herself, pulled the gag out of her mouth, and grabbed a gun that she hid in the pocket of her skirt. Misty was still there, tied in the back, to one of the posts. Ida saddled her and rode around the hill down to the crossing with the Indian trail, where she had first seen Art on that ominous starry night. She entered the Big House while everyone was celebrating in the dining room. She changed in their bedroom into a dark green dress and then went downstairs.

"Mrs. Fisch, can you bring me a plate, please," she said. "I am starving."

Cameron, whose sight was blurry now, recognized Ida first in disbelief. The others were too drunk to notice that the lady had entered the dining room in perfect condition. Ida put on make-up, expensive perfumes and the evening dress she had bought in Chicago during one of her trips on the steamers.

"Where have you been, my love?" John Bosch stuttered the words.

"I went for a ride with Misty," she smiled. "Such a gentle horse that you gifted me."

Bosch, who loved horses, calmed down seeing Ida return and having the shipment order back in his hands.

"We're in business again, my love," he said. "We located the order."

"Where in the world was it?" Ida blushed.

"It's a long story," Bosch said. "I will tell you later."

Bosch held up the shipment order valued at $20,000 and waved it around his head. The business partners celebrated into the morning hours, and Ida heard John fall over in the bed by her side. He slept in, but Ida dressed and spent the day teaching the children from the area, which calmed her down. It was spring on the lakeshore, and even though the dunes were a barren wasteland, the banks of the Kalamazoo River blossomed with wildflowers. After school, Ida went for a walk along the banks of the river to pick lilies and wildflowers. She reached the fishing villages, as the brothers were hauling in the catch of the day. By now, Charlie and Henry knew the lonesome lady walked along the banks of the river and wandered into the Fishtown village and Shriver's Bend. The hospitable brothers greeted her, waiting to hear the news of the day coming from the big settlement of Singapore, and sometimes even from Chicago. In turn, they saved the best whitefish and salmon for her.

"What is new in Singapore?" Charlie always beat Henry with the big question. "Have they found the shipment order?"

Ida smiled at the speed of news traveling between the two settlements along the Kalamazoo River, faster than the current itself. Henry was preparing whitefish for the lady and for the visitors from Chicago. She always brought the brothers spices and herbs for the fish and taught them how to prepare whitefish, big city style--seared on a pan with white wine and herbs. She planted their herb and vegetable garden, because she couldn't have her own at the Big House that was now surrounded with stables, stages and coaches. As the main Bosch Transportation Co., Cameron was the head of the transportation company and Tobias was one of the drivers.

"We've heard that Bosch's stage is growing," Charlie said. "And so is the shipbuilding."

The smell of seared fish filled the fishermen's cottage. Instructed by Mrs. Fisch, Ida was reluctant to talk about the stage business or the shipbuilding. They were now building more ships as the payload increased with raw hides from the stockyards of Chicago and goods for the stores.

"Where was the shipment order?" Charlie persisted.

"Depends on who you talk to," Ida said. "Word has it that a drunken Indian left it here in Fishtown, and someone found it and brought it back into the Big House."

Charlie's forehead all wrinkled up with a thought of the shipment order floating to these two fishing settlements managed by the two brothers.

"Did you hear that, Henry?" he said. "They found the mail bag with the order here in our Fishtown."

"Tall tales," Henry waved off the words, shrugging his shoulders.

But the tall tales that often the wind brought in from the lake or from the dunes sometimes had grains of truth in them. Ida left for Jack's cabin in the woods, as she wanted to lay flowers on his grave. She took the Indian trail from the fishing villages to the cabin and walked inside to grab some paper and cloths for the fire.

She made the fire close to the grave behind the cabin and watched the flames. In the flames, she could see everything that had just happened; her lies and intrigues to hide her secret love for Art, Cameron's deceit and John's anger.

"The lady has done wrong," a voice behind her back startled her. "She threw her own guilt on the Indians. We did no wrong."

Ida turned around to see Indian Chief Macsaube standing behind her. Jack, who befriended them, taught her not to fear the Indians. They helped the white man settle in the area and traded with them. Macsaube often traded maple sugar, fish and venison for the "fire water." Ida, speechless, watched the Indian, wishing for old Jack to rise from the dead from his grave to help her. The chief pointed to Jack's grave and said:

"He was a good man, better than you," he said.

Ida did not move and stayed motionless as if facing a wild

animal, which Jack also taught her. Macsaube came closer to her but kept his distance. Ma used to say that one day the savage would kill her in the woods, scalp her, and nothing would be left of her except for the scalp. Ida believed her and prayed to God to forgive her for lying about the Indians.

"I will get you some tobacco, fire water and ammunition. I promise," she said. If you spare my life."

Macsaube nodded.

"I will be back for those," he assured her. "Bring as much as you can."

29

Nightmares in Chicago

Jack had told Ida about the Great Spirit residing in the woods and the forests surrounding the sand hills where he could hear the Spirit. He taught Ida to listen to the sounds of the woods, to discern a friend from enemy, human from another human. At school, the kids spoke about Indians and their innocent encounters with them. Bosch, now engaged in more lumbering and shipbuilding ventures, and sent Ida to take care of business in Chicago, once Stockbridge left for the lumber operations on the other side of Lake Michigan.

When Art and Ida finally met in the port of Chicago at the end of June that year, Ida saw the torn man suffering from loneliness. However, his longing for a vendetta for lost years of life from Bosch and Capt. Quinn hadn't subsided but outgrew him into abnormal proportions; the hate was consuming him. They went to the Sauganash Hotel on Lake and Wacker streets in Chicago for dinner.

"I have to find Quinn first," he said.

However, all his attempts at finding Quinn ended in a dead-end street with nowhere to go. He searched in libraries and in catalogues advertising steamships and trips with captains and dinners with captains. He searched in index books, and he searched endless lists of nautical navigation personnel. He searched lists of deceased people even though he knew Quinn wasn't dead, because *evil men don't die easy. They have to suffer before they die.*

"Quinn will suffer before he dies," Art said. "When I find him, he will suffer a long and painful death."

Ida feared the day when Art finds Quinn.

"Art, you're scaring me," she said. "If you don't stop, I will go back home to Singapore."

Art looked at the woman he loved to death and beyond. He would never let her leave his side again, that he had determined as he watched Ida from a distance descend the steps from the steamer and then run toward him and hug him. Art returned her hugs and lifted her in his arms. That night was filled with all the passion of all the lost nights combined; all that Art had missed because of the two evil men, Bosch and Quinn. He made love over and over to Ida making up for all the lost nights and all the lost days forever.

"They deprived me of everything," he said. "I've spent years searching for Quinn, and I haven't found him yet. I will die if I don't find him. I must find him. Will you help me find him?"

Ida watched the changed man in front of her eyes; where did the loving gentle soul go? This was a different man than she had known before. The next morning, Ida dressed well and left for the lumber offices by the harbor to talk to Stockbridge about the growing development in Singapore.

"Did you have a good trip, Mrs. Bosch?" he asked. "I've been waiting for you with a project that is just right for you, and it will keep you here in Chicago for a while."

Ida embraced the idea of a new project in Chicago but feared Art's plans. Much like Stockbridge, Art had a project for Ida as well.

"We will go to Buffalo together to find Quinn," Art said. "That's where I last saw him. That's where he is. We're going to find him."

Ida had to explain to Stockbridge that she would be gone for some time, but that she would take on the project as soon as she got back. Worried, she watched Art's face staring outside the windows of the steamer that was heading northeast from the harbor of Chicago. Two hours into sailing, the steamer hit a squall, raging the waters, and it was rocking and sliding up and down the violent waves. They both fell on the floor of the steamer, and the crew told them to stay on the floor because of the violent waves. Together, on the floor they were holding onto each other for their lives as the steamer leaned to one side, dipping the windows under the water, and only smears of gray were on the upside of the boat. Ida saw providence in that moment; they were after someone from the past with the intention to kill, yet they may not survive the storm to be able to kill. They remained on the floor.

As Art was helping Ida get up, he heard a familiar voice.

"Stay on the floor," cried the voice. "The storm is getting worse, the waves are higher, and the wind is blowing harder and faster. The ship is out of control. We're losing control."

Art saw dark circles in front of his eyelids with his eyes closed tightly. His hand reached out to find Ida, instead he grabbed cold metal rolling up and down the floor as the steamer rocked in the waves from side to side, up and down, light and dark, dark and light. He tried getting up, but each time he got up, he fell down again. Ida was nowhere to be seen as he fell again to the floor. He slid all the way to one of the cabins with passengers also on the floor. Still no signs of Ida.

He screamed, "Ida, where are you? I can't see you."

Art lay helplessly on the floor with closed eyes. He was losing feeling in his hands and arms from the constant effort to get up and falling back down on his face. His fingers were bloody now from scratching the floor and the seats as he tried to get up. He hit has face against the seat and then back against the floor, bloodying his face. When he tried touching it, blood was dripping on his jacket, and he could feel the slash on his temple from hitting the cold bar. He grabbed the long iron bar and propped himself up off the floor with it. Standing up, he could see the devastation on board, but he still couldn't find Ida standing or lying on the floor. He could hear screaming from the cabins, the floor and the seats. As the vessel leaned again to one side, he could see water flooding the deck. Art waded in the water to find Ida. He dragged himself through the passenger cabins with people soaking wet and reaching out from the water. Water was everywhere. He heard the boat sending signals for help. He fell again deep in the water choking for air and spitting out water. Someone pulled him by his collar. When he opened his eyes to see the captain, whose voice he heard earlier, he screamed into the wet darkness.

"No, Quinn. Don't kill me."

"He has a fever," the assisting doctor said. "You can go home now. He will stay overnight, and we'll see how he recovers. Come back tomorrow to see him."

Ida felt lost in the big city without Art, not knowing where to go. She was avoiding Art's apartment as long as she could. The previous morning, Art woke up sweating and screaming, so Ida took the stage to the local hospital with Art in her arms. Hate had consumed the man. She entered the quiet apartment with the covers still thrown all over the bed, as if a fight had taken place. It was a fight of a man against a man.

"That's all it was, just nightmares," Art said. "Go to work and say hi to Mr. Stockbridge. He knows me. I am one of the major investors in the new company."

Ida touched Art and kissed him as she left for the lumberyard by the harbor. Mr. Stockbridge was waiting for her with a new project for a new company. The new company bought out major interest of Bosch in the Singapore Co. Stockbridge now owned all the sawmills in Singapore, leaving Bosch with the shipbuilding, boarding and transportation.

"I will need you here in Chicago," he said. "Bosch agreed."

30

Fiery betrayals

With her newly-gained freedom, Ida walked hand-in-hand with Art through the streets of Chicago. Breaking up with Bosch will be easy now that he let Stockbridge have the major interest in the Singapore Co., making him Ida's next boss. Stockbridge in turn appreciated her experience from Singapore and named her the head of the Sales and Distribution Department, as unusual as it was for a woman to hold a position of that magnitude in the 19th century.

As such, she could travel like most salespeople. Both Art, one of the major shareholders in the new company, and Ida accepted the new assignment in Buffalo with hope for a new life, far away from both Chicago and doomed Singapore. Before leaving for Buffalo, Ida sent several letters addressed to Bosch at the Big House in Singapore, in hopes of reaching her husband, who never responded.

Bosch spewed hatred against the trio that betrayed him at the height of prosperity in Singapore, although he had sold his interest in the company of his own free will. He continued with the current operations, as was in the deal, but he wanted Ida back more than ever before.

"Go to the Indian woman," said Mrs. Fisch. "She will tell you how to get Ida back without killing."

"Where do I find her?" Bosch was saddling his horse.

"Go into the woods past the oak openings into the Indian camp. First ask for Chief Macsaube, and he will direct you to her," said Mrs. Fisch. "Oshea told me about her when she helped him."

When Oshea came to the area around the Kalamazoo River mouth in the 1830s, he got hurt several times in the unoccupied wilderness. Early on, he came across the Ottawa and Potawattomi in their camp. In order to survive in the wilderness, he was forced to make friends. After the Black Hawk War, the Indian title to lands in Western Michigan was extinguished, and Allegan County Indians received annuities from the US Government. After these ceased, the Ottawa were removed to reservations in the Grand Traverse region where the descendants of the powerful tribe enjoy the comforts of civilization. However, all great chiefs, including Muckataw, Macsaube, Ring Nose, Tecumseh, Waukazoo, Elkhart, Okemos, and Pokagon have gone to their last "Happy Hunting Ground," right in Allegan County, where they held the title to the land.

Bosch, who often hunted with Oshea, found the camp near the oak openings with ease, and the chief, having been friends with Oshea, welcomed him to his wigwam made of small saplings covered with brush and bark at the top. The chief was sitting in his abode as if he had been waiting for Bosch. Bosch entered the wigwam, and the chief pointed him to sit on a rough bench made of poles and brush and covered with matting of reed and grasses.

"Macsaube, I need your help," Bosch said.

"I met your woman not far from our camp, by Jack's cabin," the chief said.

"I want her back," Bosch said.

Macsaube offered a pipe to Bosch, and they sat in the solitude of the woods listening only to the sounds of the singing sands, the wind and the leaves shivering in the wind. The forest was speaking its own language of eternal love woven into its trails and creeks. It was high summer, the golden rays covered the grass with a yellow shimmering coat, as the stems bent in the wind.

"The curse of the white man has been passed onto us," said Macsaube. "Your squaw lied about us."

Bosch puffed on the pipe listening to the chief speak about the curse of the white man. The curse of the white man was the "fire water" and love. Bosch himself sold and traded whiskey to both tribes, the Ottawa and the Potawattomi, even though other pioneers and settlers despised that after seeing the devastation it had caused among both the Indians and the white settlers. Whiskey made the Indian warriors, and white men alike, weak, childish and angry.

"Do you have some fire water on you?" asked Macsaube.

"I do," Bosch offered Macsaube a bottle brought on one of the ships.

Macsaube took a deep gulp from the bottle and swallowed, enjoying the fire that it set inside him. He felt bold in front of this white man like never before. He drank more, as Bosch watched him get drunk, and throw the bottle away.

"You want to get back the squaw I met by the cabin?" Macsaube asked in a drunken daze in the heat of the day. "That's why you came here to see me."

"Yes, chief, that's why I am here," Bosch said. "I hear you have a squaw of your own who heals broken love."

"So does your fire water," said the chief. "At first before it's gone. Do you have more fire water on you?"

Bosch pulled out of his saddle bag another bottle of whiskey but didn't give it to the chief yet. The chief stumbled outside and brought back in a leather and fur pouch from another wigwam. He searched it and then shoved it aside with disappointment and searched again, fetching a buffalo's tooth on a leather string with a small sachet.

"It's empty," the chief said exhausted. "Shaman Aiyana gave me this when I was suffering from broken love and broken bones when I fell."

Bosch took the sachet from the chief's hands and smelled it.

It still smelled of soothing herbs of valerian, ephedra, and sweet leaf.

"Where can I find Aiyana?" said Bosch as he handed another bottle of whiskey to Macsaube.

Macsaube collapsed, snoring on his rug. Bosch walked to the other wigwam where the chief got the empty sachet from the Indian women.

"Where can I find shaman Aiyana?" he asked the women, who didn't understand him.

Exasperated Bosch rode back to the Big House and ran to the basement where Mrs. Bosch stored herbs, spices and dried wildflowers. None of them smelled like the chief's sachet. On his way out, he ran into Cameron by the stables. He remembered that Cameron wanted to show or give him something on that wild night.

"You wanted to show me something," said Bosch.

Cameron was readying his horse for a trip around the sand hill to the warehouses. He had the bag with Art's letters on him, since he didn't want Bosch to find the letters on his own.

"Yes, I do," said Cameron holding onto the bag tightly. "But I want some money first, before I show you these letters."

Bosch pulled out of his wallet several banknotes and handed them to Cameron, who checked if they were not the infamous Singapore bank notes. Bosch watched him inspect the money.

"You know we burnt them at the bank back then in a stove," he said. "These are good."

Cameron handed Bosch the stack of letters all addressing Ida and sealed with eternal love from Art. Cameron jumped on his horse and left Bosch standing there by the back porch and reading the secret letters of love. He felt anger growing inside him, the letters confirming in writing what he had suspected all along. Beautiful Ida was never his to have; she was a butterfly with broken wings and heart. She didn't want him or the town of Singapore.

The chief was up and drinking water to wash down the taste of the fire water. He had been dancing outside to get the bad spirit of the fire water out of him.

"Where can I find shaman Aiyana, chief Macsaube?" Bosch demanded. "I don't have time to waste. You've spent the entire morning drinking."

"Well, you've wasted a lifetime on yourself and business, so there was no time left for your squaw," said the chief who sat down in front of the wigwam. Sit down, or I won't speak."

Bosch obeyed the chief, knowing he was telling the truth.

"You have to go to the Ottawas, and ask for shaman Aiyana," he said.

The Ottawa Indians camped and traded at Peach Orchard Point north of the village of Douglas. The post was called that because Indians had planted peach pits and had trees growing there before the white settlers came into the Kalamazoo River area. Bosch saddled his horse and took the trails to Peach Orchard Point, a large trading post and an Indian camp. It was a high summer day, with the sun directly above his head between the dunes; this setting calmed him down enough to sit and read the letters of forbidden eternal love.

"Dear Ida,

I love you more than ever before, since I can't touch or see you. You've carved yourself in my heart forever……I need you.

Each word he read hurt more and more, as Bosch realized the power of love between the two, who were thrown apart by the lake, with only the waves and the wind carrying those words of love across the distance and whispering them into his ears.

"She never loved you," whispered the voice. "She used you for your money and had all these men at her feet."

He got up and rode the trail until he reached the Peach Orchard Point camp and trading post established by the American Fur Company, with John Jacob Astor at the head of the company. The trading posts of the 1800s with mostly French or French half-breed traders were small, but they did big business, trading fishhooks, ammunition, steel traps, hats, caps, boots, and beads, jewelry, calicoes and colorful cloths. The traders cheated the Indians, trading brooches of poor quality, made of a cheap white metal that cost less than 25 cents for fine fur pelts.

Whiskey was a big trading article; even though it was forbidden by law, the profits on whiskey were enormous. The stock for French traders came by water or land; it was brought from Detroit on pack horses or transported by the lakes in large open boats from Detroit, Mackinaw or Montreal. Large traders brought their goods from Mackinaw in barges down the lake, and then up various rivers like the Kalamazoo River, where the posts were located. These traders kept runners in the Indian camps all winter. The runners carried their goods in packs on their back and returned with furs for which they have traded.

The Indian camp at Peach Orchard Point counted more than 30 wigwams. An Indian showed him to shaman Aiyana's wigwam by the creek emptying into the lake. The elderly medicine woman was dividing herbs into sachets when he entered. The wigwam smelled of herbs, spices and dried wildflowers. He took off his hat and greeted the woman by her name. It was hot in the wigwam, and Bosch was sweating from the ride in the dunes. He could smell his own sweat, which Indians considered healing in their "sweat dances."

"Hau, Aiyana," he said nodding his head.

At first, Aiyana didn't even look up, busy with the dried herbs. Thinking she was deaf, Bosch addressed her again louder.

"I can hear you," she said. "Who sent you here?'

"Chief Macsaube," he said handing her the empty sachet from the chief.

Aiyana took the sachet and breathed in the long-gone fragrances of the past: musky with sweet undertones. She looked up at Bosch with a slight smile, crinkling up her entire face into a grimace.

"White man wants love," she held up the empty sachet in front of his face. "He needs hehaka tapejuta. He will get me elk oil from the post."

The old medicine woman showed him out of the wigwam to the post.

"Aiyana will make hehaka tapejuta," she said. "White man will go to the post."

She turned away from Bosch and walked back into the healing medicine wigwam. The trading post wasn't far away from the camp, so Bosch walked to it in the summer heat. The post was bustling with horses, wagons and runners coming in and unloading the wagons with goods. He walked inside the main log cabin with furs, hats and raunchy elk oils. He had nothing to trade with, so he paid with the few remaining ornate Singapore banknotes without flinching. The robust trader took his money and gave him a small bottle of elk oil, winking at him.

Aiyana mixed the elk oil with sweet leaf into hehaka tapejuta; but she also made a sweet-smelling ointment, mixing sweet leaf with buffalo fat. Both Mrs. Fisch and Chief Macsaube warned

Bosch that Shaman Aiyana will want something in return. Bosch packed all sorts of cheap trinkets in his saddle bag, not knowing what the shaman will want.

"White man will give me the cameo brooch that the lady has in her possession," Aiyana said. "It has magic powers, because it was given to her from the heart by her Scottish lover."

Bosch, startled that the shaman woman knew about the cameo brooch, stepped back from her. He remembered on a few occasions that Ida wore the brooch that she had bought in Chicago while visiting her mother, according to her story.

"I don't have the brooch," he said. "I don't know where to find it. She bought it in Chicago."

"Then you're not going to get hehaka tapejuta," Aiyana turned away from Bosch and hid the sachets and the ointment in her pocket. "White man, leave my wigwam now. Bring the brooch when you want love. Hehaka tapejuta will bring you love, if you bring the brooch that your squaw wears."

31

Art's vendetta

Art and Ida boarded a steamer in the port of Chicago and headed for Buffalo on a beautiful summer day. They stood on the upper deck watching the silhouettes of buildings against the setting sun. They looked ahead to the new assignment in Buffalo where Stockbridge established land sales offices. He purchased land surrounding Singapore and speculated as to the soaring prices of land, due to the increase in trade and the tannery business south of Singapore on the Lake Michigan shore. The tannery used the tanbark, abundant in the hemlock forest of Western Michigan, to produce leather. Untanned hides came in from Chicago on northbound boats and provided for additional cargo as tanned leather on the return trip.

In Buffalo, Ida insisted on taking separate rooms in the hotel that served as a boarding house. Once they established the land sales office in town, Art searched in business and ship directories for Capt. Quinn, since he remembered Quinn mentioning that Buffalo was his home port. He went to the port authorities to inquire about Capt. Quinn. His patience paid off when one of the officers said he was on the same steamer with Quinn on their way to Chicago and back to Buffalo.

"I believe that Capt. Quinn lives farther southeast of town; he talked about building a house in the country," the officer said, pulling out a big logbook. "He's scheduled to leave tomorrow for Milwaukee, if you want to talk to him. Are you his friend or relative?"

"Yes, I am a distant cousin," Art lied.

"I can give you his address," the officer said.

"That would be great," Art smirked as he jotted down the captain's address.

That evening he never went back to the boarding house and took a stage into the countryside. Ever since they arrived in Buffalo, Art carried a gun on him. He hid in the shrubs at the front of the house and waited until the morning, until the captain boarded the stage to the port. He jumped on the back of the stage, and when they were at full speed, opened the door and bounced inside to Quinn's brief shock. Art shot him in the head--a clean shot--that left Quinn dead on the spot with blood on his face. The stage continued on the bumpy road as Art jumped off and walked back to town.

Ida was heading out to the land sales office for the day; her main task was to find a person and a partner to manage the operations after the initial set-up of the land office. She worked all day long and late into the afternoon. As she reached for her hat, someone grabbed her by the arm and turned her toward him. Shocked, she saw Bosch right in front of her eyes holding a gun.

"You didn't expect me, did you, my love?" Bosch quipped.

She backed away shocked and screaming.

"No one can hear you here," he said. "You know that. We picked this location for a reason, Stockbridge and I. This time you're not getting away. You're coming back with me once and forever. Your escapades must end. I will put an end to them right now."

It wasn't until now that Ida realized that Bosch was in cahoots with Stockbridge all along to trick her into going back to Singapore. He hooked his arm into her arm and led her into a stage waiting for them. There he tied her to one of the handlebars on the stage for a long trip back to Singapore. They only stopped for the horses to feed and get water. In three days, they arrived back in Singapore. Bosch led her up the stairs and tied her in the former room she had before they got married. He locked her in, sticking the key into his pocket.

"Do not let her out, no matter what," he said. "Keep her locked in there."

Mrs. Fisch was too scared and disturbed to answer and walked away into her own rooms in the basement. The next day, Bosch entered Ida's room with breakfast and tea, setting it on the stand by her bed. He rummaged through her bags, still unpacked from the unwanted trip, until he found the cameo brooch, kissed it and stuck it in his pocket.

"Give it back to me, it's mine," she cried. "Art gave it to me. It was his mother's."

Bosch slammed the door and locked it, returning the key to his pocket.

"You can't keep me locked in here forever," Ida yelled banging on the door. "Open the door. Let me out of here, you bastard."

The screaming followed Bosch all the way to his office, where Stockbridge was waiting for him. The two looked at each other relieved. The operation was almost complete.

"Now you have her, and all we have to do is get rid of that miserable Scott in Buffalo," said Stockbridge. "But that has been taken care of too."

"He will fall into his own trap," smirked Bosch, smoothing his beard.

In the meantime, Art walked inside his own room in the boarding house to change and then he knocked on Ida's door and opened it. From behind the door, the kind officer from the port hit him on the head with the back of a gun. However, Art kicked the gun out of the officer's hands and sent it sliding underneath the bed. As the officer fell on the floor and reached for the gun, Art stepped on his upper back and shot him in the back of his head, a clean shot in the head. In his own room, he packed up his bags and left for the next stage out of town.

32

Snuff & Pirate Cappy Jack

Stockbridge and Bosch took on a new partner, Otis R. Johnson, a shoemaker and leather worker from Maine, who built the tannery. The firm, O. R. Johnson & Co., now owned both sawmills and the general store in Singapore. Johnson brought to the firm the lumber mill, a lumberyard and a general store in Saugatuck, originally Flats. The company owned many acres of land in western Allegan County that were sold through the sales offices in Chicago and Buffalo, now manned by Cameron, after Ida's abduction. The firm ran other mills and stores in Allegan County near Pearl. Many investors in O. R. Johnson & Co. branched out into other lumbering operations, including the Menominee Lumbering Co. in Wisconsin and the Mackinac Lumber Co. in the Upper Peninsula of Michigan.

"Ida, Art is dead," he said to his crying wife. "Stop thinking about him."

Bosch and Ida were seated in the sitting room for breakfast before they headed out to their jobs; Ida started another school year, and Bosch was embedded in O.R. Johnson & Co., forever as the major investor of the sprawling company.

"How do you know he is dead?" she wept. "Did you kill him?"

"They found him dead in our own offices in Buffalo, he killed himself," said Bosch. "He slit his wrists and bled out. You know he was mentally instable. There was a reason why he was in an asylum."

"Who found him?" Ida persisted.

"I sent Cameron to Buffalo to help out in the vacant sales office, and he found your friend dead," said Bosch.

In the sprawling town of Singapore, Ida felt like she was living in the land of the dead, as she looked at the barren sand hills with cut down pine trees, on her way to the school at the end of Dugout Road. With the growing area, more kids were attending the one-room schoolhouse, chattering about the Indians living in a camp by Oxbow. She still rode her horse Misty to school along the Kalamazoo River and tended to her garden by the schoolhouse. Since Ida couldn't have children or a garden of her own, she made the schoolhouse her second home. When the kids came hungry, she fed them with produce from the garden and from the goods taken from the Big House. Mrs. Fisch once noticed goods disappearing from the pantry and the basement. So did the other residents in the Big House. But everyone used the common storage space in the basement.

Mrs. Fisch counted over and over again, but the numbers were not adding up. She still had fewer bags of flour than what the inventory showed on paper, as well as potatoes and salted pork. Someone must have been stealing groceries from the basement. One evening, she decided to wait in the far dark corner of the basement. Soon she heard the rustle of a skirt, but she couldn't see from the corner in the basement. The sounds lasted only a few minutes, and it was dead silent again. It could have been the Hollanders' 'de vrows' running low on supplies, much like everyone else in town.

Ida cooked for the kids at the schoolhouse in a kitchen that she made out of the small room in the back of the school and put some tables in there. She cooked on the big stove that was used for heating of the schoolhouse. But she also bought goods at one of the general stores; to avoid the first company store in town, she went to Johnson's or Morrison's stores in Saugatuck. O. R. Johnson & Co. owned dry goods and groceries in the nearby town.

She always enjoyed the ride to the village that had close ties to Singapore. At that time, Saugatuck located upstream from Singapore, was a small but growing community with a post office, a general store, and Coates Drug Store, located in the Plummer House. Early on, Ida became a member of the Women's Club of Saugatuck. She was friends with Morrison. Despite the shady past of the misplaced mail, they continued to do business together.

In the early pioneer days, the need to survive overshadowed old gripes, and grit prevailed, as in the case of Morrison and Ida's snafu over the mail. The drug store in Saugatuck carried much more than medicine; it was a gathering place where small talk, exaggerated into gossip, was exchanged between the village residents and nosy visitors like Ida. Ida always bought candy for herself and for the kids in school. The candy counter displayed licorice, mint candy, peanut butter and caramel candy, and chocolates. She packed her saddle bags full of candy for the kids.

A funny incident once happened at the Union School in Saugatuck. Druggist Bird often talked about it, and he gave Ida the poem "Snuff" that his wife Hattie Wright had written.

Snuff

We had a funny time one day,
We pupils of the Union School.
Ote Johnson brought some snuff up there
And each one took some, like a fool.

To make the matter worse and worse,
Unto Steve Newnham, Emma spoke,
"My dear," said she, "If we could make
R. Brainard sneeze, 'twould be a joke."

"All right," said he. So, Emma put
Into Steve Newnham's hand some snuff.
We never thought the end of that
That would be so bad, the horrid stuff.

For a while we all a-sneezing were,
And scarce could breathe, for so much snuff
Professor Brainard came and said,
"Who brought to school this horrid stuff?"

And while we trembling there for fear,
"Who brought this here?" again he cried.
At last poor Otis raised his hand
And said, "Twas I," and then he sighed.

And then, but stop, we will not tell
For what ensued we all well know.
The worst we'll tell, one schoolmate's gone.
And Lizzie Wallin's lost a beau!

The major protagonist in the poem was Otis W. Johnson, whose father Ida knew well from Singapore's new company Johnson & Co. They laughed together with druggist Charlie at the story about bringing snuff to school.

"So, Charlie, can I buy some snuff here?" Ida charmed laughing.

Charlie handed her a lovely box of scented powdered tobacco and showed her ornate snuff bottles with different flavors: vanilla, coffee, chocolate, Bordeaux, honey, cherry, orange, apricot, plum, cinnamon, rose, menthol, spearmint and camphor.

"I can mix you your very own special snuff, Mrs. Bosch," Charlie offered. "The next time you stop by in town, I will have it ready for you.

Ida smiled, adding to her weekly shopping list the pungent and sharp snuff and more candy for the kids. She stopped at one of the grocery stores to buy flour to replace Mrs. Bosch's supplies in the basement. She replenished the flour supplies, saving some for the school.

It was one of those community Saturday evenings at the Big House, again where everyone pitched in. The Hollanders brought in a lot of original dishes from the old country of Holland, along with Henry Post who was spending his honeymoon with Anna Coatsworth in Singapore before moving onto the new settlement north of town.

"What's the occasion, may I ask?" Mrs. Fisch said.

She was surprised at the variety of dishes at the common table from Holland in Europe; even Cameron traveled in for the community Saturday dinner from the Buffalo offices. He changed in his old room and came all dressed up for dinner, glancing briefly at Ida whose cheeks were glowing again in the candlelight, from their flickering flames casting shadows on the walls. He watched her from his place at the table directly across from Ida. Partners Stockbridge and Johnson chimed in ten minutes late.

Hollander dishes included: new herring, fried cod, krokets, cheeses, pea soup, and oliebollen that Anna made together with Mrs. Fisch in the kitchen using an enormous amount of oil. Stockbridge and Johnson brought in with them fine wines and whiskey. Bosch stood up with a speech ready:

"Cheers to our Holland friends, who have been here with us in Singapore, through the bad and the good," he toasted to the Hollanders.

John Loukes explained that the Hollanders were joining a new settlement north of town, Holland, founded by Albertus Van Raalte. They were leaving Singapore, where they landed by chance, because of the slush ice blocking the mouth of the Black River by Holland.

"We would like to thank you for your hospitality, for your free spirit and for pioneering us through our first days in the new world," said Loukes.

Ida felt her chest tighten; the Hollanders and 'de vrows' were one of the first people she met in Singapore when she overheard their singing and worshipping in the unknown language. Mrs. Loukes handed her in front of everyone a knitted shawl and mitts.

"I made these for you, Mrs. Bosch," she said.

The Hollanders had been waiting for good weather and putting off their trip for days until late that evening when they embarked on an Indian mackinaw boat and sailed north to the settlement of Holland. Even without the Hollanders, the loud evening extended into the night. Cameron looked at Ida with deep inquisitive eyes, and for the first time she dared to look at him as well.

"You are the messenger of bad news," she said. "Did you see Art dead?"

"I discovered his bloody body, he cut his wrists and bled out," he said. "I found him dead at the Buffalo offices. I wanted to let you know, but you know how it is with mail. You can't rely on it these days."

Ida felt her last hope vanishing from her body; a big part of her died with Art. She was only half alive. It was late at night when she retired into their bedroom suite next to the company office. She couldn't sleep, put on her coat and walked to the beach to wave goodbye to the Hollanders. She stopped at the light house manned by Nichols who was still up and let her in.

"Did they make it out on the lake alright?" she asked hoping they didn't sail out at all.

"With difficulties, but yes, they're gone," he said. The old Frenchman, Joseph Victor, took them out on the lake."

"They were my only friends here in Singapore," Ida cried. "Now I am by myself. I am surrounded by the cold breath of death. Everyone has died; my dear Jack and Art."

Nichols offered her hot tea and words of hope as the waves of Lake Michigan met the current in the Kalamazoo River and mixed together into a swelling vicious concoction whipped up by the wind.

"You're never alone in Singapore, you're only alone in your heart that misses the Scottish man," he said. "But your heart will heal with time. I am your friend too. And I am here for you. You can come and see me anytime."

The lighthouse keeper reminded her of old Jack when she first met him that stormy night in the harbor house and took his maps and charts. Nichols too had nautical charts, maps and logs, and treasures from old Jack's harbor house. She looked at the various pictures of the ships built in Singapore; they were mostly pencil or ink sketches and drawings of the first schooner, *Octavia,* built in Singapore and enrolled in the port of record for all of Lake Michigan, which was Chicago.

"Why do you have only *Octavia* on your walls?" Ida said. "There must have been other schooners nearby."

But the three-masted schooner built at Singapore was the closest to Nichols' heart, as he danced with his wife on her deck before and after she was launched.

"We were aboard when she went in," he sighed looking at the drawings.

On May 9th, 1874, schooner *Octavia* loaded 100 cords of wood at the north pier of Kewaunee in Wisconsin and left the pier that evening. However, the wind died away and "she was carried by the groundswell northward toward the stony shoal off the village limit." Her master was unfamiliar with the area, dropped the anchor too late, and *Octavia* went hard aground about 800 feet from shore. The schooner ended up with her stern toward shore and listed to the south.

"Most of the cargo was saved, including us, but the schooner was a total wreck," said Nichols. "A local person painted her."

Ida pulled her coat tighter and wrapped it around her as she headed back to the Big House. It was a dark night with the only light coming from the lamps in the lighthouse, but she had her oil lamp to guide her back into Singapore. She entered through the back entrance by the porch and sneaked in her bed, with John snoring by her side.

She kept busy at the schoolhouse with the **children, giving** them licorice from the drugstore; then they baked biscuits. It was story time in the afternoon.

"Mrs. Bosch, tell us a story from Chicago," they asked. "And the boats, the pirates and the captains. Tell us about Cappy Jack."

The kids always wanted to know stories from Chicago or aboard the steamships, or the pirates, since Ida often talked about her travels, using Jack's navigation maps of the Great Lakes. Ida kept those as a souvenir when she found them in the deserted cabin by the Oxbow camp. The maps were all yellowed and stained. And Cappy Jack was the main character of all her pirate stories from the Great **Lakes that** she made up when the kids wouldn't give up. The story about Cappy Jack grew each school day until it became the main story of the Singapore school.

"Cappy Jack Blackbeard was a saltwater dog in the Atlantic Ocean before a squall took him to the Great Lakes. Cappy and his pirates ruled the high fresh-water seas of the Great Lakes and searched for treasures not known to Jack **Sparrow--lumber**, *fire water and wild-game meat. Cappy Jack had a long beard and set fires on the shore to trick boats mistaking the fires for port* **lights,** *and they would crash on the rocks. Cappy and his pirates stole the cargo, beaver pelts, timber and sometimes entire ships. One night, the Cappy's pirates stole the little schooner, Nellie."*

"Did they also steal *Octavia?* " asked a little girl.

The little girl was one of her Indian students from the camp by Oxbow. She made friends with the kids from Singapore and wanted to go to school with them. Chief Macsaube, who was a good friend with Oshea and Bosch, allowed the girl to attend, if Oshea guaranteed that the girl would be safe. Her name was Dakota.

Ida looked at the girl with long black braided hair seated in the third desk by the window.

"Dakota, how do you know about *Octavia?*" Ida asked surprised.

"My white aunt and uncle danced on it," the girl smiled. "I wish I could dance on *Octavia* with my boyfriend. Why did Cappy let her crash? He was a good sailor."

Ida continued with the story about Cappy who turned pirate

on the Great Lakes, mainly on Lake Eerie, and made a good living by stealing treasures from schooners and sloops.

"Cappy Jack lived in Singapore for a while, and he still directed ships into the harbor, bringing in goods like candy, until one night a squall took him away from us into the night and out on the sea. It just swept him with his harbor house off the docks. He left maps behind, so you can enjoy exploring the lakes with him. That way he lives with us forever. That's the story of Cappy Jack."

"Wow, did you know Cappy Jack?" asked the girl. "What was he like? What did his pirate boat look like?"

Ida cried and couldn't answer the little innocent girl, who reminded her of her own innocence, two decades ago, before her ominous trip to Singapore. She rang the bell and let the kids outside and shut the door. She cried hot tears that were rolling down her cold cheeks, and then she cried more until she lost track of time and fell asleep on the bench made of grasses, reed and bark. She woke up with the sun rising above the last pine trees still standing that the lumberjacks hadn't managed to cut. The new morning was fresh, and she could smell the herb garden in the school backyard. She had planted new spearmint, mint, lavender, basil, bee balm and parsley.

33

An Omen

At the crack of dawn, the sleeping town of Singapore woke up to a fire raging on the north industrial side of town where the sawmills were located. A very hot summer left the dune grasses and brush yellow and rustling in the strong wind, blowing steadily across from the lake and creating eddies on the Kalamazoo River and the lake. The wind had persisted all summer long, lifting the grains of sand and sending them inside the wooden frame houses.

All the pioneer communities along the lakeshore were suffering from the unrelenting heat. In the summer heat, Ida visited the Indian camp by Oxbow to talk to chief Macsaube about Dakota going to her school in Singapore. Ida lovingly called the first school in Allegan County her school, because it was. The school replaced the empty spaces left by the death of the old seadog Jack and her lover Art.

Ida went to the schoolhouse, even in the summertime when there was no school, to tend to her garden, to read and write. Devastated by the deaths, she enclosed herself inside a protective pearl shell like a mussel, determined never to come back out again. She got up with the sunrise above the few lone pine trees left standing, saddled Misty and rode to the schoolhouse. Mrs. Fisch packed her food for the entire day.

"It's summer, my dear," she said. "Why do you go there every day? You need a break too."

Ida looked at aging Mrs. Fisch, who still parted her hair in the middle and tied it back in a bun. Only now it was gray. She must have had that same faded black dress that she was wearing when she opened the door for Ida many years ago. In recent years, with the passing of her close friends, Ida felt closer to the woman, who saw it all happen. Mrs. Fisch was the first to know about Art, but never said anything.

"It's going to be hot out there," she said. "Stay home for once. We'll have some lemonade."

Ida took the food and jumped on Misty who was still swift, in spite of her cantor getting slower. The short ride to the school refreshed her with new energy. She went through the old workbooks that were her constant companions along with other books. When she talked to the chief, he was agreeable to having Dakota go to the little school in the fall. They sat across from each other in the sun outside his wigwam.

"I forgive you for placing the blame on the red man, who was innocent," he said.

"Oh, chief I was desperate," she said. "I didn't want John to find the letters."

"I know," he nodded. "You are still desperate searching for something you have lost. Stop searching, let it go; it will come back to you. Dakota can go to your school in the fall. Take good care of her."

On that ominous day in 1866, the fire kept raging for hours, burning down the first sawmill started by pioneer Oshea Wilder, whose dream was to build out Singapore to the glory of big port cities along the east coast. In its heyday, the sawmill cut 14,000 board feet of lumber each working day with the wood harvested from white pines crowning the sand hills.

Gossip had it that someone started the fire seeking insurance profits. However, the fire spread from a tug and burned down five houses along with the sawmill. At that time, Singapore had the three-masted schooner, *O. R. Johnson,* built by master Aurelius C. McMillan at Saugatuck and tugboats *W. B. Minter*, *L.B. Coates* and the *Spray*. But it became clear that the future transportation on the Great Lakes would be by steamboats

Schooner *O.R. Johnson* was built for speed and cargo. The Saugatuck paper, *Saugatuck Commercial,* wrote that the schooner was the fastest sailing vessel on Lake Michigan, and that it made the round-trip from Singapore to Chicago and back to Singapore in 38 hours, including loading and unloading.

When Ida arrived at the scene of the fire, it was burning strong and the wind carried it further to the houses on River Street, but it ran out of fuel and didn't spread to the hills that had no standing trees on them due to lumbering. The brave men of Singapore extinguished the fire, preventing it from spreading to the other sawmill.

A new sawmill was constructed to replace the burnt one at the end of Dugout Road. It was the most productive of all the Singapore mills, cranking out timber to replace buildings for the fires to come. Ida smelled of smoke when she came back to the Big House, where the main talk was the devastating fire of the first sawmill in town and gossip how it happened. Built by New York and Michigan Co, in the western wilderness of Allegan County, the first sawmill was considered sacred, giving life to the entire area of Singapore.

The partners of the new company got together to rebuild the sawmill with the lumbering industry still being the lifeline of Singapore. However, it was now competing for the emerging tourist business from the big cities of Chicago and Milwaukee. Beyond lumber, the vessels on the Great Lakes were now bringing in tourists to the lakeshore communities like Saugatuck.

Ida saddled up and headed to Saugatuck to pick up her order of snuff, candy and flour for the pantry and for the school. She could still smell the smoke billowing to the sky behind her, as she took the lakeshore path instead of the one along the Kalamazoo River. Unlike

Singapore, the town was protected by a large sand dune known as Mt. Baldhead, covered with standing forests. As she approached the town, Mt. Baldhead was towering in front of her in all its 794 feet of sand glory with trails to its top and the beach at its foothill on the northside of the natural harbor. That day she tied old Misty at the bottom of the hill and climbed to the summit of the *"Monarch of Sand Dunes."*

She sat down to take in the beauty laying at her feet covered with sand. The vast lake was shimmering in the afternoon sun in all the hues of blue and green undercurrents. The sun rays painted streaks of gold, orange and yellow on the blue surface. It was a true Indian summer that fall, when the summer heat never subsided and caused the ominous fire at Singapore. A beach stretched far to the north. The sand running through her fingers was still hot as she laid in it watching the untouched blue sky. She threw off her riding boots and dipped her feet in the hot sand. The soothing hot sand became her healing spa, along with the lake and the sky. The breeze from the lake brushed her face and took away with it the wet sweat on her forehead that the hat could not absorb. She untied her bun and let her blonde hair lay loose on her shoulders, making it a pillow. She opened one of her students' workbooks to read in the soft afternoon, far away from the billowing smoke of Singapore and the ambitions of the Singapore men, whose lost dreams were replaced by new dreams forged in the fire of the first sawmill.

Ida wrote in her own notebook about her fiery trip to Singapore that would last a lifetime; her tarnished dreams of love that never came to fruition, her lost friends and a lost lover to ambition, greed and vendetta. The wind lifted, so Ida packed up and walked down the path adorned with wildflowers and hemlock woods. Misty nickered when she saw Ida coming down the sandy path from the hill, thirsting for company and fresh water from the lake.

Rather than going the distance around the river, Ida took the old chain ferry, piloted by "Grandpa Jay" also known as the "Sky Pilot," across the Kalamazoo River to the Butler Dock in downtown Saugatuck.

"How is the lady doing on this beautiful day?" Grandpa Jay asked. "I've heard that a fire raged in Singapore and burnt down all the buildings."

Jay had been waiting for hours for a passenger, so when he saw the lady with the horse, he welcomed her aboard the chain ferry, blew the airhorn and cranked the three pullies that moved the ferry along the line. The slow ride took them to the docks in town, as Jay admired both the lady and the horse.

"How did you know I was coming from Singapore?" she asked surprised. "I never take this route. I usually take Dugout Road, but the sun brought me out to the lakeshore."

"I saw the smoke on my way to the ferry this morning," he said. "No doubt, it was coming from Singapore."

"Yes, we had a fire, but the men put it out," she said.

"Ah, the brave men of Singapore, I've heard a lot about them," he said. "I even met some of them during my lumbering days."

Jay, an expert lumberman, had been farming north of Saugatuck before he sold the farm to become the famous ferryman on the chain ferry across the Kalamazoo River.

"I could tell you stories," he said with eyes shining in the sun. "Do you want to listen?"

"I do," Ida said. "When I get back from town. You will be here, waiting for me?"

Jay smiled as he landed the ferry at Butler's Docks in town.

"I will be waiting for you with my stories," he nodded.

She rode Misty along the old Butler docks with tugboats to the drug store on main street in downtown Saugatuck. Druggist Charlie wearing a white coat, was mixing up something behind the counter. When he saw Ida, he lightened up and extended his hand to the lady from Singapore, who had become a regular at the drug store.

Charlie was an apprentice at the C. A. Ensign drugstore and bought out the business with the help of O.R. Johnson. His drugstore was well-stocked, but he kept the best medicine stored away in a cabinet close to the counter. This is where Charlie displayed bottles with pain-killing laudanum that made people feel better, as well as snake oils and his famous snuff. Suffering from a headache, Ida sat in a chair in the nook of the drugstore, its windows overlooking Main Street. At the time, there was also a general store on Main Street. But the pain brought her back into the nook of the drugstore, and she wiped her forehead.

A woman in a floral dress wearing a hat walked into the

store, handing Charlie a small box, and then she left without a word. Charlie set the box aside and devoted all his attention to the lovely lady from Singapore.

"I heard there was a fire in Singapore early this morning," he said. "What happened?"

"The sawmill caught on fire from a tugboat," she said holding her head in her hands. "It burnt down the sawmill and some houses but didn't spread to the hills, because it didn't have anything to feed on. The sand hills are barren. It's a wasteland. I have this terrible headache from the stench and all the smoke.

Charlie sat across from Ida in the nook of the drugstore and offered her strong herbal tea, when he noticed the cameo brooch on her blouse. He stared at it intensely, until Ida started touching herself all over trying to find out what was wrong with her riding outfit.

"It's the brooch, beautiful," Charlie sighed. "Where did you get it?"

Ida blushed and touched the brooch and covered it with her hand, still blushing.

"I would like to buy that from you," he said.

"It's not for sale," she said.

"I will trade it with you, then," he said.

"For what?" Ida showed remote interest.

Charlie walked to the counter and picked up the small box the lady in the hat had left on the counter by the medicine cabinet, and he sat back down again. He then opened the box and pulled out a small bottle with a pharmaceutical label that read in big blue letters, TINCTURE. He shook it and eased the cork out, smelling the contents. He walked back to the counter to pick up a spoon and a bottle of rhubarb tincture, along with a glass vial. He mixed the rhubarb tincture with a few drachms from the bottle with the blue lettering and shook the vial well. He added a few drops to Ida's tea.

"Drink that, it will help you get rid of your headache," he said.

Ida took a sip of the tea with the drops and sat back in her chair holding her head.

"Charlie, I am going for a walk to get rid of this pain," she said. "Can you watch Misty and give her some water. I will be back soon."

Charlie watched the beautiful woman leave the drug store

and quickly took all the bottles with tinctures and the vial and stored them away in the back room. Dizzy and nauseated, Ida walked down Main Street toward the old docks and sat down on a bench by the ferry. Jay had just docked the old chain ferry on the other side and waved to her, gesticulating that he would soon be back on the town side. She watched Jay crank the pullies and move on the line closer to her. In the afternoon sun, Jay danced on the deck and turned into a fire flame. Ida touched her forehead that was hot in spite of the light breeze coming from the lake. She waved off the heat like a fly and got up to greet the man who turned into a flame that was licking her skin. The flame was flickering in front of her eyes, and then out of the flame stepped weather-worn Jay, who operated the chain ferry year- round, in the cold, rain and in the heat of the day. The sun too was dancing on the water, and Ida felt the pain leaving her head, that cooled down a bit. Jay walked to her looking closely into her eyes, but she couldn't see his. They both sat down on the bench.

"Are you ok?" he said. "You look different than when you rode my ferry. What happened to you?"

"Nothing, I just have this horrible headache from the smoke and the fire," she said. "I've been trying to shake it all day long."

"Ask Charlie at the drugstore for his drops," Jay said. "I can't remember what he calls them. He keeps them hidden. Where's your horse?"

"I am not going back yet," she said. "I left Misty in town. I just needed the walk, that's all."

Jay was concerned, but Ida insisted that she must return to town for Misty.

"I can come back with you," he offered.

"No, I am fine," she said. "I feel much better now. I got rid of the headache from all the smoke. I will be back with Misty; we have to ride home."

Back at the store, Ida offered to pay for the tincture, but Charlie didn't want any money for the magic drops that drove away Ida's pounding headache. He handed her a new bottle of the tincture and put it in a nice small box.

"Here, take it," he said. "You will pay me next time when you're in town."

Ida put everything in her saddle bags: candy for the kids, a box of peach snuff and the tincture in a box. She left light like the breeze from the lake.

34

Strange Encounters at Oxbow

The ride along the lakeshore on Fishtown Trail that connected Saugatuck with Singapore to Shriver's Inn in the setting sun comforted her, even though she was still upset that Charlie wanted to trade the magic pain drops for her brooch. She was free to wear the brooch with Art's death, and she did. Ida only took it off for the night, and even then, she put it under her pillow, so she could feel it and touch it. The cold soft feel of the brooch reminded her of Art's touch and his stories from Scotland and about his arrival in the New World on the steamboat.

Misty was slowing down and had to stop often on the short ride to Shriver's Inn at the bend near the Oxbow Lagoon. Halfway, with her headache gone, she got off Misty and waded in the lake to cool off, and she sat down on a small dune. Henry came to greet her and took the tired horse to the stable to rest. Autumns in Michigan by the big lake were made of gold, with leaves turning yellow, orange and red.

Ida walked inside the nice inn that greeted tourists from all over including Chicago. The chatter was loud, and she sat by the window with the view of the lake and the lagoon. She feared the worst, but her headache was gone, and she was happy to see the messenger boy delivering mail from Saugatuck. He recognized her and smiled. He was a grown handsome man now and mail delivery was his job, and he had a big route between the towns of Saugatuck, Singapore and Allegan. He walked to her table.

"I am Joe," he said. "We met many years ago somewhere in this area, I believe. You were looking for some letters."

But Ida still saw the small, scared boy in this tall man with blonde, red hair and a mustache. He was wearing the blue clothes and a hat of a mailman that he set aside.

"I am Ida, have a seat," she nodded toward the chair at her table.

Joe sat down after a long trip from the Abronia post office in Allegan County where he picked up the mail from the main post office. Sometimes he missed floating on a raft down Kalamazoo River with bags of mail; the postal service gave him a horse and a uniform. When Joe smiled, he had dimples in his cheeks. He was all tanned from his routes in the countryside. Joe was happy to see Mrs. Bosch here at the inn, as he had a letter for her. It had been several years since she had received a letter. She was surprised.

"I always come here to Fishtown first, and then go to Singapore," he said handing her the letter. "I am glad I found you here."

She felt the painful memory of the past hurting the messenger boy. Ida took the letter and put it in her bag, fearing more bad news, as if there was anything left to hurt her. By now everyone whom she loved was dead. Owner Henry sat down with them and brought them drinks. In later years, Ida switched to drinking wine, while both men drank beers.

"My guests from Chicago drink wine, so I go on these trips in search of fine wines, but I still get it from the steamers," Henry said.

The chatter was louder and louder. As the messenger boy had to continue on his route to Singapore, Ida walked with him and stayed outside for the rest of the evening.

"Please let them know at the Big House that I am not coming for the night," she said teary-eyed. "I have to take care of Misty, she can't continue. She's too old."

Ida spent the night in the stables with her beloved Misty.

"Mrs. Bosch, come inside, you need some rest," said Henry.

She finally retired to a room on the second floor overlooking the lake and slept in, exhausted from the trip. She woke up to a bad headache. Ida walked to the stables, but Misty's stall was empty. Henry was standing behind her and touched her shoulder.

"She passed, I took care of her," he said. "Stay here for another night. I will send word to the Big House. Come and have breakfast with us."

They ate, yet Ida couldn't see through the tears that kept filling her eyes with a steady flow.

Ida, weeping out loud, ran into the woods past the Oxbow Camp and to Jack's old cabin in the hemlock forest. She was surprised to find ashes from a fire that burnt not long ago. She walked first around the cabin, and then inside; there was Art as though he had been expecting her on that autumn morning in the hemlock forest. His handsome face brightened as he walked to her and hugged her with a passion until she couldn't breathe. Ida stepped back, touching her forehead. Little orange flames and circles were dancing in front of her eyes, and she fainted on the plank floor with rugs. Art took her in his arms and laid her on a bed he made from grass reed and covered her with blankets. He kissed her on her head in her golden blonde hair and sat by her side.

Art tried to wake her up, but Ida was breathing heavily and shaking. He gave her some cold water; she came alive to see his face above hers and closed her eyes again. It must be the magic drops from the druggist in Saugatuck. With her eyes still closed, Ida touched his face to feel flesh. She felt Art's warm skin from the sunshine and the fire.

"Dead men are cold," she whispered to herself. "You're not dead."

As she touched Art's warm face again, Ida dared to open her eyes, and she saw the loving face again leaning above her, Art's soothing eyes and his lips, as he kissed her on the cheek. During her nightmares, Ida envisioned them meeting again on a boat or in Chicago, or in the land of the dead, when she visited the cemetery in Chicago. He helped her get up, and she looked around the cabin.

"Where am I?" she asked.

"You're in Jack's cabin with me," Art said.

"I have to go outside," she cried.

Art helped her, and they walked outside where Art had made a fire to warm her up and put a kettle of water on it. Ida touched him again on the arm and his warm cheeks, looking into his eyes. They were the same warm eyes that had always stayed with her. Art hugged Ida and kissed her to wake her up. Being fully awake, she searched her bag and showed him the letter.

"I haven't had time to open it," she said. "The messenger boy Joe gave it to me last night at Shriver's Inn."

She held the unopened letter, reluctant to open it.

"You're dead, Bosch and Cameron said so," she shook her head and held it again. "You're not alive. This is a bad dream. I am going to wake up and you will be dead just like Jack and Misty.

Nothing can bring you back from the land of the dead."

Art sat close to her and took her hand, then he poured her hot tea. He had gray hair on his temples and a little bit of gray in his mustache; some wrinkles around his eyes adorned his high cheeks. His hands were strong and would not let go of her.

"You're mine forever," he kissed her. "I will never leave you again."

But in her head, Art died so many times, over and over again. She returned the kiss and the hug that sealed their eternal love.

"You're all that I have left," she cried. "Memories of you kept me alive and the letters. Your letters that I would kill for and die for."

They walked to the lakeshore and waded in the warm water of the lake.

"Bosch won't be looking for you?" Art asked.

"John thinks you're dead," she said smiling for the first time. "They all think you're dead. You should stay that way. It's safer if they think you're dead. You're better off pretending that you're dead."

They sat on the small beach clearing with waves washing their feet. The rhythm of the waves was like their heartbeats and the blood pulsing in their veins, that no one had slashed. Ida touched his wrists to see if Art had bled to death. There were no marks of wounds on his wrists.

"I will bring us some food from the inn," she said.

Ida felt alive again, and they fell into the dune grasses kissing and making love in the setting sun with the waves and the sand singing the eternal song of love. Love filled their hearts and heads and bodies. Art watched Ida walk on the beach toward Fishtown; she was swinging in the evening breeze, her blonde hair flowing on her shoulders. He laid back in the dune grasses.

"We were worried about you," Henry said.

"I needed a walk on the beach and in the woods," Ida said. Then she asked, "Where did you put my Misty? I would like to be with her this evening."

Henry looked at the beautiful woman glowing with love, all the previous sorrow had disappeared from her peaceful face. The inn was a hideout for many city guests, and Henry was used to not asking questions and keeping secrets. They walked together by the

Oxbow Lagoon and the oak opening in the nearby woods. She immediately saw the large mound of dirt to the right under a big oak tree. She kneeled by the mound and prayed for all the souls she had lost recently.

Ida ate at the inn and retired to her room early. She packed leftover food from dinner, got dressed and headed into the hemlock woods, where she could see the fire. Under the starry sky, Art and Ida made love by the fire, redeeming all that had been taken away from them in the years gone by. The infinity of the warm autumn night stretched beyond the boundaries set forth by man. Only the unbounded nature existed now and their pure love, unspoiled by tomorrow's worries. The crackling fire and the night forest were the only sounds of the night, with the waves washing the shore in the distance. There was no need to talk about the gap, because they had just filled it with love.

"What if you're a ghost," she said. "And you're not real."

"Then I wouldn't be hugging and kissing you," Art kissed her again. "Am I a ghost?"

She returned the kiss, making sure Art wasn't a ghost and was pure flesh. She felt for his pulse and touched his chest to feel the rhythm of his beating heart. Then she touched her own chest between the breasts that Art was kissing and holding in his hands. His warm body was gliding on her body in the rhythm of the night, and Ida felt him moving inside her. The movement stirred a flow of love from her body in unison with his flow, warming her inside and out.

"I know you're human," she kissed him from above. "We both are humans united into one being."

Ida kissed Art's entire body from his forehead, his lips, his hairy chest, his stomach, and in between his warm thighs. They fell asleep in each other's arms as the sky lightened up with pink streaks of dawn on the horizon, signaling a new day.

35

Booming Railroads & Hotels

Ida walked barefoot along the beach from Fishtown to the mouth of the Kalamazoo River at Singapore, holding her riding boots and saddle bags in her hands, as the sun rose higher in the sky. Mrs. Fisch came rushing to the entrance as Ida stepped inside the Big House, barefooted, throwing her boots in the cloak room.

"Where's your horse?" she said taking Ida's hat.

Ida was glowing from the walk on the beach in the fresh morning air, and from the night spent with a man she found and loved.

"Misty entered eternity," Ida said with a tear rolling down her warm cheek. "That's why I stayed overnight in Fishtown."

"Oh, my dear, come to me," Mrs. Fisch hugged her and took her to the sitting room. "The messenger boy said you wouldn't be coming for the night. I will make you some tea."

In the parlor, they sat together face to face, woman to woman, bound by years spent together amidst the wilderness of western Allegan County, at the confluence of the river and the lake, where the swells of the lake meet the current of the river.

The two women accompanied the brave pioneer men who had founded Singapore on a foundation made of evaporating dreams, timber, and shifting sands; and somewhere along the way, they crossed paths. Their joint path was paved with determination and the basic instinct to survive, when others didn't. Fires and flames blazed the path and forged dreams to come true. Some dreams were forgotten while others changed. The forged product was eternal love that rose from the ashes of the fires. The smoke from the fire at the first sawmill dispersed into the sky, and its ashes were carried by the wind and the waves out onto the big lake.

They sipped herbal tea and Ida showed Mrs. Fisch the little box from the druggist. But Mrs. Fisch, overjoyed with Ida's arrival, didn't open the box and left it on the stand.

"I was wondering if you would come back," Mrs. Fisch said to Ida's surprise. "I thought we would never see you again."

"But Mrs. Fisch where would I go?" Ida said. "This is my home; this is where my children are. It's my school, just like this house is your house. Without you, the house would be nothing."

The big frame three-story boarding house, at the corner of River and Broad streets, built on a pricey lot, was one of the first houses in Singapore, kept alive with its housekeeper and maid for all, Mrs. Fisch from New England. The robust young woman, like many others, came with her own dreams of sandcastles on the shore of Lake Michigan. She worked hard to keep the dream of sandcastles from being washed away by the unrelenting waves of the lake. She mended and nurtured her sandcastles, braving the life of a pioneer woman without the luxuries of the east coast. She never flinched, never wavered, she was always there by Ida's side without Ida knowing about it.

"Oh, just drink your tea. All I ever did was to accompany my husband to this wilderness," she waved.

"Would you do it again, Mrs. Fisch?" Ida asked.

"In a heartbeat," she said laughing. "I wouldn't have met you, If I didn't."

It was time for one of the famous Saturday community dinners at the Big House that still welcomed immigrants, much like Ellis Island, from all over the world and pioneer settlers from the east coast. Cameron arrived via the early Central Michigan Railroad from Detroit to St. Joseph, in which the O.R. Johnson Co. had invested. Rail was getting more common as it transformed from horse-drawn railcars to railroad wagons transporting lumber, troops and passengers. Cameron managed the company's interest from various offices in New York, Detroit and Chicago. Cameron arrived well-dressed for the occasion, too busy with his career to get married.

"Beautiful as ever," he nodded to Mrs. Bosch, handing her a shining red box tied with a white bow and flowers."

"Thank you, Cameron," she said, and laid the box aside. "Are you bringing us good news?"

Cameron often wondered if Ida knew the truth about Art, that in fact when he entered the apartment room in Buffalo, there was no one there, and the company offices were vacated as well. Art left no traces behind him, as Cameron was determined to find the Scott. He searched through both the apartment and the office, but all he found was Ida's diary.

"The good news is that I took the rail," he said.

"Tell us all about rail travel," Ida said breathless.

They sat at the big table across from each other. Ida and Mrs. Fisch decorated the dining room for the gathering that included the company business partners, all the guests in the boarding room and friends from town. They called on Stimson from the Astor to help out Mrs. Bosch. Michigan autumn, with its red, orange and yellow hues on the blue backdrop of the lake, provided the perfect setting in a wilderness that had been tamed down by the early pioneers. Tamed but not conquered, nature showed its dominance, as it thundered over the lake with striking lightning bolts. Mrs. Fisch, with Ida's help, stocked up for the upcoming winter. They dried berries, apples and fruit from the peach orchards during the "Peach Boom" of the 1800s started by the early French fur traders in what was known as the "Peach Growing Era" in Allegan County, and mainly in Ganges Township, when all Ganges was one vast peach orchard.

They decorated the dining room in the fall colors, fresh and dried peaches and apples graced the table to honor a trade that was rivaling the lumbering industry, with fruit being transported to Chicago on vessels from Singapore, now carrying a full two-way payload. The prosperity was reflected in the increased trade between the villages along the Kalamazoo River.

Ida picked up on the conversation after bringing in more dishes.

"You must have encountered some interesting people on the rail," she said. "Was it dangerous, Cameron?"

Ida had never called Cameron by his first name. Stunned, he looked up from the table at the glowing woman he never could have. The rail was dangerous, since the cars were made of wood, and any collision resulted in the death of the passengers.

"Do tell us about your ride, Cameron," she stressed his name. "I've heard about all these railroad accidents where the occupants got killed in collisions. Right, Mr. Fisch?"

"Yes, the rail is very dangerous," seconded Mr. Fisch who recently traveled on rail to St. Joe.

"You're no stranger to danger, right Cameron?" Ida persisted piercing Cameron with her eyes.

Cameron took a sip of red wine and paused before he answered. He accepted money from Bosch for a crime he never committed and kept the oath of silence known as "omerta" to keep it a secret. Cameron, like a wild bobcat, trapped himself in an intricate web of lies.

"Dangers are always in front of us, but we face them, Mrs.

Bosch," he said. "I've never been the one to run away from a scare. We create our own dangers. We nurture them into monsters."

Ida took a deep breath and stabbed Cameron with her eyes that had flames flickering in them like a cat's eyes. At that moment, she looked like a cat ready to attack and pounce on him. Bosch interrupted the fiery conversation in his half- jovial, half-sarcastic manner.

"How is our traveling salesman doing?" he said laughing. "You are brave to venture out on the rails, so I've overheard."

Everyone at the table wanted to know about railroad travel that now ran close to the pioneer settlements in Michigan--mainly St. Joe--and complimented stage and steamboat travel.

"We've placed great faith in railroads," said Bosch. "We see the future in them."

"Our investments have largely shifted to railroads," said partner Stockbridge, joined by O.R. Johnson. "And hotels."

The railroads were the foreshadowing of an era of grandeur of grand hotels to accommodate the traveling tourists and business people alike. The partners had a vision that had always preceded them, as in the case of Singapore.

"Let Cameron tell us about his rail travels, John," Ida said. "And his other scares."

The trains were powered by steam engines, much like everything else including the sawmill engines and the steamboats. The first trains chugging through St. Joe were pulled by steam locomotives. The story of early railroading is fraught with starts and stops, lines that didn't quite make it to their intended destination, mudslides and wrecks.

Cameron sat back in his chair and watching his audience, mainly Ida, the words started pouring from his mouth. He talked about train collisions and crossing the river valleys on high trusses on the East Coast, and railroad cars falling off these with passengers screaming. Often, foul play was involved.

"If you want to get rid of someone, you just plan it over a truss and push the person out of the railcar who's waiting by the door for the next stop," he said.

"Is it that easy, my dear Cameron?" Ida smirked, "to get rid of a person?"

Bosch interrupted again with anger rising in him, wondering

if Cameron had told Ida about the murder in Buffalo. He touched Cameron on his shoulder and showed him to the parlor, excusing them.

"What are you doing? Are you crazy?" Bosch hissed at Cameron. "Do you want her to find out about what you did?"

"I think she knows," said Cameron.

"That is ludicrous," Bosch said. "I went to great extent to cover up for your murder. She thinks he's dead."

"Excuse me," Cameron said. "You ordered me to kill that Scott and threatened me. I can report you."

"You have no proof," said Bosch, "just your own foolishness. If anything leaks out today, I will kill you, and the wildcats in the woods will feast on your flesh."

The two angry men, all red, returned to the dining room trying to cover up their argument with pretense. The women were bringing in more dishes; desserts, wine and whiskey were flowing in abundance. Ida drank red wine, and together with Mrs. Fisch, they made fruit wines from peach orchards by the trading post. The tension in the room dissipated in the wine. Someone knocked Ida's wine glass down, and it spilled on her pretty pink and white dress. Upset, she ran into their bedroom to clean the stain and found the present from Cameron on her dresser. She thought she had left it in the dining room, but the box was here. Ida opened the box with letters, Art's diary and a small Indian knife. The short knife with feathers must have been from the Ottawa camp by the Oxbow Lagoon or from the trading post by the peach orchards. Either way, Cameron wouldn't have the time to stop and buy the knife. She hid the knife, the diary and the letters under her clothes in the bottom drawer of the dresser.

All cleaned up, she entered the dining room only to find Cameron and Bosch at each other's necks. Others were trying to tear them apart, but they were glued to each other. She pulled angry Bosch away who was swearing at Cameron.

"What are you two doing?" she yelled. "Stop it."

Cameron stumbled out of the dining room, into the hallway and out on the main street, while Bosch ran after him. Cameron disappeared into the dark night with the wind howling from the lake. Bosch came back and downed a shot of whiskey and sank back into his chair, breathing heavily. The oil in the lamps was running low, and it was getting dark in the dining room, to Bosch's dismay, since he couldn't see his own glass, plus Cameron had ripped his evening jacket.

"Why can't we even have light?" he stuttered.

"We don't have any more oil left," said Mrs. Fisch. "Ida and I will have to restock."

Bosch's anger was growing as he smashed his fist on the table, and the wine glasses clinked, spilling more wine on the table. But partner Stockbridge brought some oil with him and poured it in a lamp, lighting up the room.

"You shouldn't have let Cameron leave," Stockbridge said. "The company needs him to conduct our business. You can't get rid of people you need."

36

Shaman Aiyanna

On a sunny autumn morning, the two women took the stage to get supplies at the Peach Orchard Trading Post. Ida pinned her beloved cameo brooch to the lapel of her jacket. She still wore her riding boots, even though she didn't have a horse. They stopped on their way at the Pine Plains Tavern, five miles east of Fennville. At the trading post, they encountered traders from Mackinaw City and Mackinac Island. Mrs. Fisch had come to know many of these men over the years of getting supplies for the Big House. These traders were rough men, often of French origin or from the American Fur Company, started by America's first millionaire, Jacob Astor.

Ida wandered around the post, while Mrs. Fisch bought kerosene and paraffin oils for all the lamps at the big house. While Mrs. Fisch chatted with the traders from Mackinaw, Ida walked over to the Indian camp. She had heard about the medicine woman Aiyanna who welcomed her into her healing wigwam. The wigwam was decorated with dried herbs, plants, sandalwood, and containers with teas and opium.

"I've been waiting for you," Aiyanna said. "Have a seat."

Ida sat on a blanket, inhaling the sweet floral scents and

smells in the wigwam.

Medicine Woman Aiyanna donned a heavy blouse and skirt, and her wrinkly face adorned a colorful headdress of feathers. Aiyanna was also a spiritual healer for the tribe, sought out by people from far and near. She was burning incenses in a caldron. She was known to foretell future and heal physical and spiritual wounds.

"Your heart brings you to me," she said. "You're not bringing it with you today; you left it a long time ago in a foreign land behind the seas. You're looking to find your heart."

"Yes, I am hurting for love," Ida said, now lightheaded from the scents. "I've been hurting for love for a very long time."

Aiyanna handed her tea that smelled of roses and lavender, and she never looked up from her caldron.

"I see flames in your heart that you left with a man from foreign lands," Aiyanna said.

"Does he love me?" Ida asked.

"He loves you," she said.

"What do I have to do to be with him?" Ida asked.

Then Aiyanna stretched out her hand. Ida wanted to give her money, but the Indian shaman shook her head, as she pointed to her brooch. Ida touched it, and in disbelief looked at the shaman woman. This was the second person who wanted her brooch from Art, that he had received from his deceased mother. A Scottish legend has it that whoever receives a charm from their lover is spellbound by that love forever and cannot escape the bond forged in the fire of the ancestors. However, its owner can also bring love to others, even if it's forbidden love. The magical powers of the ancient charm can only be released by eternal love.

"I cannot give it to you," Ida held onto the brooch. "It's a gift."

"Then you're cursed, and you will never be with your lover," Aiyanna said looking into the smoke.

Ida ran out of the wigwam, crying and holding her head. She stumbled several times on her way to the trading post that bustled with activity. Mrs. Fisch handed her cans with oil, and they loaded the supplies for the winter into the horsecar.

"You forgot what time it is," Mrs. Fisch smiled looking at the sun that had traveled westward on the horizon and painted the maples deep orange and red. Ida, breathing heavily, was covering up her brooch on the jacket, as if Mrs. Fisch or someone else was to steal it from her. They took the old trail through the woods, but had to stop in Fennville, where the corduroy roads crossed, as the night settled in on the late autumn day. However, since there was no place to stay, they had to head back out into the night.

"You're cursed, you will never be with your lover," the shaman's words kept ringing through Ida's head.

"Mrs. Fisch, do you believe in magical powers?" she asked. "And in charms? Do you believe in spells and curses?"

But Mrs. Fisch was counting the money spent on winter supplies, and paid little or no attention to Ida, who took off the brooch to kiss it. This was the first time she looked closely at the mysterious gift from her Scottish lover.

"What are you holding onto?" Mrs. Fisch looked up from counting her money.

Ida blushed and tried to hide the brooch into her pocket, but Mrs. Fisch's eyes had spotted the brooch a long time ago. She never said anything in fear of Mr. Bosch.

"Did Aiyanna want the brooch?" Mrs. Fisch asked. "I thought she might have."

Ida shook her head in fear that Mrs. Fisch might want the magic charm too. They continued on the bumpy road in the dark woods with only a lantern hanging onto the stage that was swinging with the stage from side to side, its flame flickering. All of a sudden, the stage came to a stop and leaned into the ditch to one side, with one small wheel rolling away. They both could hear the driver swearing, as they slid to one side of the coach. They had to get out and help the driver put the coach back on the road. The driver was fuming with anger, as the large wheels were heavy. They found the smaller front wheel in the woods. Ida stumbled in the dark several times with branches scratching her face. Back on the road, both Ida and Mrs. Fisch, exhausted from the road, fell asleep until the sudden jerk of the horses woke them up.

They arrived on Main Street in Singapore in the middle of the night. The driver was still swearing from the incident in the woods, as Mrs. Fisch paid him to leave. They hauled into the basement of the Big House all the heavy supplies, including potatoes and flour. When Ida finally crawled into bed in the wee hours of the morning, she couldn't sleep.

"You're cursed, you will never be with your lover," the words of the Indian shaman woman took on deeper tones and raged her head with pain.

Ida walked to the cabinet with medicine and took the bottle from the druggist in Saugatuck. The purple label clearly stated that just a few drachms of laudanum will bring on sleep. She didn't waste time mixing it up with milk or vinegar and closed her eyes as she fell on the bed. The pressure behind her eyelids loosened and evaporated into the air. In front of her eyes, a golden warm meadow unrolled and a clearing in the oak woods opened. She was walking barefoot on a trail on a hot summer day with a light breeze coming from the lake and her long blonde hair loose on her shoulders. She came to a smaller lake and walked into it to cool off her feet. The water caressed her feet lightly. A hand touched her shoulder, and she turned around.

Art took her in his arms and kissed her from her lips and neck to her chest and breasts. He laid her on the warm grass and made love to her in the warm sun rays that entered her body along with him. The sun flooded their bodies with warmth and loving touch. The unison movement of the bodies synced with the movement of the grasses. She wouldn't let go as he raised his body above her, and Ida pulled Art back into her body. He stayed laying on her body that he loved and idealized that of a goddess. He entered this goddess again with the love of an angel. Ida saw the angel above Art and tried reaching out to him, but before she could touch the angel, Art disappeared underneath his wings.

"Don't take him, Angel," she cried reaching out. "Don't take him. He's mine. Leave him with me."

"You had a bad dream," said John. "You need some rest. Maybe we should leave Singapore for a while."

Ida got dressed and shook off the suggestion to leave Singapore for her wellbeing.

"I have to go to school to my kids," she said.

37

The Old Chain Ferry

On a misty morning, Art walked to the old docks by the chain ferry in downtown Saugatuck. The ferry was docked on the Mount Baldhead side, and old sailor Jay waved to him, before he cranked the pullies and the ferry moved along the line across the Kalamazoo River. Jay pulled to the shore landing and greeted the strange man. The old ferryman knew everyone in the area from as far north as Holland and south to St. Joe, east to Allegan, but the lake to the west with its moods remained a mystery to the old timer.

"I don't know you, sir," said Jay. "Are you from far?"

"I have moved here recently from Chicago," Art said tipping his hat.

"What brings the gentleman here to our small resort?" Jay asked. "Just vacationing?"

Art searched for an answer in the morning mist in vain.

"I am in love," Art said to Jay's surprise. "I am looking for my love. The only woman that I have ever loved."

True, people who came to Saugatuck on boats from big cities often searched for love as if it could be found in the streets or in the hemlock forests, or on sandy Mount Baldhead known as the Monarch of Sand Dunes. Jay smiled his wrinkly smile at the strange man from Chicago who was looking for love.

"I think you've come to the right place," Jay squinted his eyes in the sun breaking through the morning clouds. "We make love here by the pound."

The old chain ferry inched along the way, and Art could see the widening of the Kalamazoo River upstream into the Kalamazoo Lake. In front of him rose the majestic Mt. Baldhead covered with trees.

"Will you be coming back this way?" Jay asked. "I might have some stories about love ready for you before you get back."

Art nodded and shook Jay's hand and headed out to Mt. Baldhead, walking on a trail up the sand hill. Halfway up the hill, overlooking the lake, was an opening in the woods where Art paused to look if he could see Chicago in the distance. In the mist, he could see the silhouette of Ida wearing her blue iconic dress. He climbed to the top of the mountain, and there she was in her radiant silk beauty of a goddess. Art touched her to make sure he wasn't dreaming, and he touched real flesh. He touched her face and hair and reached for her hand, locking his fingers inside hers. They sat down on the grass, where they made love. The waves and the wind were celebrating their love in unison with the sun. Time stopped to search for its own meaning and measure that which no longer could be measured between a man and a woman.

Together, hand in hand, they walked to the beach to wade in the lake with the endless waves washing their feet. The sand was deep yellow with scattered driftwood on the shore, and no one was there to witness their love except for the lake and the wind.

"What will become of us?" Ida asked.

"We will become one," Art said. "I gave you a token of my love a long time ago in that warehouse on top of the hill above Singapore."

Now, many years later, they were standing at the foot of a hill they had just descended.

Together, they walked to the old chain ferry on the river. Old Jay recognized them from a distance and nodded his head toward them. As they boarded, Jay reached his hand to Art and smiled that wrinkly smile. He tipped his sailor's hat to Ida.

"I told you that you will find love here in our little town," Jay said. "I said the same thing to the lady just a few weeks ago. And now you found each other."

Jay cranked the pullies, and the ferry moved along the line across the river, with the two aboard holding hands. Jay watched them kiss in the setting sun above the lake, as he recalled the long walks on the beach with his own love from the lumbering days, now gone and buried in the cold dirt at the cemetery in Singapore.

"I wanted to tell you one of my stories, but you showed me your own love; that makes the best story of all," he shed a tear. "Let me tie this around your hands."

He tied a sisal rope around their hands and murmured words that were not meant to be heard. Feeling dazed and speechless, they left the ferry and walked away on the old docks behind the boarding house. Jay stared at them with tears in his eyes that he wiped off with his sleeve. He pulled out his log from a trunk by the pullies and the hand crank of the ferry. He sat down and wrote:

"For years, and since the beginning of time, I have been searching for love that has been hiding from me. It was a forbidden love, as it was another man's love that I wanted to make my own. I couldn't find her, until she found me in the woods, in a cabin, that belonged to another man, a sailor, a friend. Since she wasn't mine to have, I kept losing her over and over again. She disappeared from me like the sun in the evening, and she would reappear in the morning, rise high, and shine on me, only to disappear with the next sunset. I set out to find her in the singing sands of Singapore, this time for good. I prayed in the woods and on the sandy beaches, I prayed on the trails until I found her on the beach, at the foot of a mountain washed by the lake. An old ferryman sealed our love forever aboard an old chain ferry, that never stops, like love."

Jay placed the log back into the trunk as some townsfolk arrived and needed to cross the river from the old docks to the Mt. Baldhead side, where the big lake meets the sand, and together they play in the wind. They were too eager to arrive on the other side, on the beach, asking how long does it take to cross the river. As Jay cranked the pullies to start the trip, he looked into the distance, but the two had already disappeared.

"How long does it take to cross the river, old man?" another man asked.

"It takes eternity," Jay smiled his wrinkly smile. "To find love."

Art and Ida walked to the boarding house where Jay had a room. The boarding house was on the dock side of the Kalamazoo Lake with scows and barges. The boarding house was a legacy of one of the first settlers, John Butler, who had previously tried his luck north of town, in Singapore, but the wilderness drove him away from the sand hills to the shores of the Kalamazoo Lake where he had started the settlement of Saugatuck.

"You can stay here with me," Art said. "I can ride over to Singapore and tell John that we got married by the old chain ferryman aboard a ferry."

"He will kill you, but first he will not believe you," Ida said. "He will not believe you and then he will kill you."

"I have proof that we got married," Art said.

"Where is your proof?" Ida asked.

"Give me your brooch, and I will show it to John," Art said.

157

"Then he will believe me."

"That won't convince him, but do you want it back?" Ida said touching her lapel where the brooch used to be pinned.

Ida gasped for breath in disbelief, then she searched her pockets and her bag.

"What's wrong, Ida?" Art pulled her closer to kiss her.

But Ida pulled away to avoid his kiss and searched more. It was then that Art realized she wasn't wearing the brooch all along. She never had it on when they were at the mountain or rode the ferry. Ida was afraid to face Art and stepped back toward the door.

"I don't have it," she cried. "John must have taken it from me; the old shaman woman wanted it too, so did the druggist."

Art turned Ida toward him.

"Look at me," he said. "I love you no matter what. I am going to Singapore to tell him that we got married by the old ferryman."

Art stormed out of the door that shut with a loud bang. He walked along the docks to the stables and the stage service by the sawmills.

"I need a horse now," he said gasping for air.

"What's the hurry?" the horse boy asked. "We have stage service. Where do you need to go?"

The boy invited Art into the stables. He saw all the horses feeding in their stalls.

"Where do you need to go?" the horse boy asked again.

"I need to go to Singapore now," Art said.

The horse boy paused and shook his head.

"You will have to wait until Friday," the boy said.

The stage line ran tri-weekly to Allegan, South Haven and Holland. The coach to Allegan stopped in Singapore by the Dugout Road and the schoolhouse.

"Don't you have a horse?" Art demanded. "You have horses in the stables. I need a horse now. I can't wait for the coach until Friday."

The horse boy struggled to understand Art's hurry to get a horse to Singapore that same day.

"I will have to talk to my father and ask if you can ride one of our horses," the boy said. "I can't just give you one of our horses."

"I don't want one of your horses," Art said. "I need a ride to

Singapore on anything that moves."

The horse boy looked up at Art, back at the horses and at the harbor. He pointed to the nearby harbor with the scows and the barges.

"You can probably ride one of those," he said. "They'll take you out to sea."

38

Lumber Baron's Plight

Art walked to the harbor by the old docks on the Kalamazoo River when Ida caught up with him breathless. He pushed her away from him.

"You can't come with me," Art said. "You stay here, and I will be back."

Ida, all disheveled, remained standing at the old docks watching Art as the sun moved down the horizon, coloring the shimmering waters with orange and gold. A light breeze was picking up from the lake, lifting her skirt and loose hair. Captain Joseph Victor was an old Frenchman, a descendent of the French traders from the Louis Campau Trading Co., which established trading posts in Saginaw, Grand Rapids and St. Joe.

There were several steamboats, schooners and tugs docked in the harbor, as the shipbuilding industry in Saugatuck was growing in the mid1800s through the 1900s.

Victor was an old trader turned sailor. Art requested to be taken out to sea on any available vessel. If you wait a few hours, we will be heading out with "Dawn" to Singapore, Holland and Grand Haven.

"What time are you leaving?" Art asked.

"After we load her up," he said.

Art returned to Ida who was relieved that he wasn't leaving while his head was still hot. Hand in hand, they browsed the streets of Saugatuck until they reached the drug store with Charlie behind the counter. The druggist looked through his glasses at the Singapore lady with the stranger.

"Oh, the lady from Singapore is back," he smiled at her. "And this time with a friend."

They both chatted, while Art stared into the cabinet with the exotic tinctures and herbs.

"I would like more of the tincture from the poppies," Ida said looking directly into Charlie's eyes. "The one that kills any pain in the world."

The drug store smelled of fresh coffee, and Charlie offered coffee to both of them as they sat in the nook overlooking Main Street. The street bustled with coaches and walkers in the evening hours. A newspaper was laying on the coffee table that caught Ida's interest as she held it to the light to read the headlines.

Charlie talked about the news of the day which was big. Dr. A. H. Pattee (a fakir) established the first newspaper in the area, The Saugatuck Commercial, which published tidbits of news from all over the country. It was considered a duty to submit news of interest. Ida was delighted that the little town of Saugatuck had a newspaper, like her hometown of Chicago. She read the news about the new schooner *Dawn* with its master Morrison.

She showed the article to Art who read it along with the entire newspaper, while the two engaged in small talk and town gossip.

"We will be moving into town soon," Ida couldn't hide her secret anymore.

Charlie raised his eyebrows, knowing that Ida was married.

"Do you mean with Mr. Bosch?" Charlie looked at her through his eyeglasses.

"No, with Art," she said. "Let me introduce you."

Art shook hands with Charlie, nodding his head.

"Mrs. Bosch has been a good customer of mine for years," he said. "We've struck a few good deals over the years. I hear you're taking the new schooner out to sea for her maiden voyage."

"I have to go to Singapore," Art said. "I am one of the partners in the company, but I won't be talking company business."

"So, I hear from Mrs. Bosch," said Charlie nodding. "I'd be careful; Mr. Bosch is known to be a hot head."

The door opened wide, sweeping in leaves from the street and bringing in the autumn chill. In the doorway, a robust tall man in a hat was looking around the shop, as if searching for someone.

Then his eyes stopped in the nook and rested on Art. He bolted toward Art and grabbed him by his jacket trying to pull out a gun from his pocket, but Charlie jumped forward and knocked him to the floor and knelt on his chest. Art got up and hit the man in his face, as his nose started to bleed on Art's fist. It was bloodied John Bosch fuming with anger, knocked down on the floor of the drugstore. They tied him up and loaded him on a stage to the old harbor, as the schooner's loud horn blasted through the air, announcing that *Dawn* was heading out to sea soon.

Art spoke with Frenchman Captain Victor, giving him directions about Bosch as they loaded him inside a cabin.

"He will stay tied until you reach shore," Art said. "There you will unload him along with the flour and everything else. Further instructions are in the letter. Give him the papers."

Art handed Victor a big wrapper with sheets of paper, inside the old sailor found money, more money that he had ever made in his entire life trading, lumbering and sailing.

"I will take good care of him, sir," he said. "You have my sailor's word of a Frenchman from the Louis Campau company. We keep our word."

Standing on the docks, Art could hear the struggle of the robust man locked up in the cabin of the schooner *Dawn,* soon to head to unknown shores. With a smirk, Art walked away and joined Ida at the boarding house. She was all dressed up in her evening red and black dress with a conic skirt, her hair parted and combed into a chignon curling behind her ears, Art put on his best evening jacket. They invited Charlie along to stand witness to their love. Art sought out the old ferryman Jay who had docked his chain ferry for the night.

They walked to the T. Dole's Union Hotel, dubbed as a quiet house with peace and plenty, to celebrate the union of Ida and Art. The hotel was repaired and had a bar after a dry run by the former owner; the new owner, Mr. Rode, fitted his building up in good shape and opened his saloon for business. The foursome, relieved by the day's events were joined by the mysterious lady in a floral dress that had previously brought in the box to the drug store. Charlie introduced the elegant woman as one of his longtime suppliers of herbs and tinctures from the country.

"I should send a messenger to Singapore to bring Mrs. Fisch

and her husband," Ida said. "Without them I wouldn't have survived my stay in the Big House."

The couple all dressed up arrived by a stage owned by the Johnson Co., of Singapore.

"Will you live here in Saugatuck?" Mrs. Fisch asked Ida. "What about your school and the children in Singapore?"

"I will ride my horse there," glowing Ida smiled.

"I am so happy to hear that," Mrs. Fisch said. "The children love you and miss you."

"I will be back as soon as Art and I get our affairs straightened out," she said. "I cannot leave the school and my children."

Mrs. Fisch leaned to Ida and whispered in her ear. They both got up and walked to the parlor for ladies at the Union Hotel. It was all decorated with paintings of white scows and schooners on the blue lake, and the lighthouse at the end of the channel. The walls of the parlor were covered with green and yellow wallpaper, and a painting of a woman hung above the mantel of the fireplace. There was an etagere displaying books and mysterious containers. Mrs. Fisch handed Ida a small box, but Ida set it aside; she was too anxious to hear out Mrs. Fisch.

"When he couldn't find you around town, he left for the Peach Orchard camp," Mrs. Fisch continued to whisper, "to seek out the Indian healer Aiyanna."

Back in Singapore, angry Bosch rode his horse to the Peach Orchard Indian camp to look for Ida, who never came home or let the house know about her whereabouts. He tore into Shaman Aiyanna's wigwam, scaring the medicine woman into her corner. He yelled at the wrinkly old woman.

"Where is my wife?" he demanded. "I heard she was here. She gave you the brooch for your shaman tricks."

Aiyanna looked up from her herbs and sachets and shrugged her shoulders, as she burnt some herbs in the caldron. Her long skirt rustled on the reed mattresses, as she moved to her shelves with containers and opened one.

"Give me back her brooch," Bosch persisted.

"You were not the one who gave it to her," she said. "It does not belong to you, just like the lady does not belong to you."

Bosch turned red and grabbed the medicine woman by her blouse and pulled her closer into his face.

"You, old witch," he barked. "You stole the brooch and cast a spell on her."

Aiyanna freed herself from Bosch's tight grip and pushed him away from her large chest adorned with a necklace from tusks and bones that rattled loud with her every movement. She called on young Alo.

"Alo, come here," she said. "Show the white man out."

"I won't leave until you tell me where Ida is, or I will cut your throat," Bosch stepped closer to the medicine woman who was hiding behind the young Indian.

Then, Bosch pulled out his gun at both of them, scaring them into the corner."

"She's with a man you know from the past," Aiyanna said. "They are at the Mouth of the River."

Bosch gasped for breath and felt his blood rushing into his head.

"You old lying, witch," he grabbed Aiyanna again by her blouse. "You tell me where the woman is, or I will kill you and him too."

Alo freed the old woman and pulled her away from the robust man fuming with anger.

"Go to the mouth of the river," Alo said. "You will find her at the medicine store."

Alo turned to Aiyanna who shook her head as she stepped out of the wigwam and pointed southwest toward the setting sun. Bosch followed her arm and squinted his eyes into the sun at the white pine forests that covered the hills and dunes until they touched the blue water.

"You will find her where one lake flows into the big lake," she said.

"Give me the brooch," he demanded.

"I don't have her brooch," Aiyanna said. "She never gave me the brooch. She loves the man who gave it to her, not you. She never loved you. You will never have her love. Leave now. And never come back again. You are not welcome here."

Both Aiyanna and Alo disappeared inside the wigwam, as

Bosch kept staring into the setting sun. He squeezed his gun as he jumped on his horse and headed to the "Mouth of the River." The vista unraveling at his feet marveled his fuming brain. Like all the pioneer settlers from the east coast, Bosch loved the rolling hills, the bountiful orchards, the sandy beaches, the hemlock forests and the majestic big blue lake. He could see the winding Kalamazoo River and would follow it all the way to its mouth, where he would carry out the revenge that had been eating him up like a wasteful disease against the Scottish man who had destroyed his life by stealing his wife's heart.

The resort town of Saugatuck greeted him like every other stranger, with love and open arms. Bosch planned to fight Art like a man, a man against another man, carrying out the duel with guns in the streets. However, when he saw him seated in that nook, a wave of anger rose up in him and flooded his brain, and he attacked in the store like a coward.

And now like a coward, he laid tied up inside a cabin on a schooner that had lifted its sails and flew on the water. In vain did Bosch try getting up, he kicked the boards until the Frenchman appeared in the door peeking in. Victor walked inside and sat on the bench nodding at Bosch laying on the floor, while he opened the wrapper and the letter with instructions of what to do with this angry man who lost his valor like the great brave pioneers helpless in the face of love.

"Did you know that you never attack a Scottish man indoors?" Victor asked him. "Or any man from the old country?"

Victor took the gag out of Bosch's mouth but left him tied up and wrestling to free himself.

"Cowards shouldn't be sailing aboard beautiful scows schooners like this gal," said Victor lovingly. "I will decide what to do with you."

"I will give you anything you want," Bosch begged. "Just leave me in Singapore."

The setting sun cast its last orange and yellow rays and dipped below the horizon. Victor poured some oil in the lamp and brought food for Bosch.

"Now, don't move, here is some food for you," he said.

Victor tied one hand to a post in the cabin and freed the man's other hand, but before that, he handed the cabin key to the second mate.

"Keep us locked in until I call you," Victor said handing over the key. "Just making sure this bird doesn't fly away before we land. Can you hand me the chart?"

Victor studied *Dawn's* course.

"How much will you give me if I leave you at Singapore?" he said.

"Anything," Bosch said.

"My instructions from the Scottish gentleman are different," Victor said. "Finish your food."

Bosch freed his other hand and jumped the Frenchman and knocked him to the floor. He hit the gun against the Frenchman's head and knocked him out. He changed into Victor's sailor's clothes and tipped the sailor's hat into his face, while dressing Victor into his own clothes and sliding him to the corner. He rang the bell for the second mate.

"We're docking briefly at Singapore," said Bosch. "The man stays in here until further instructions. Give me the key to the cabin."

Bosch threw a blanket over Victor's body and locked the cabin. They passed the lighthouse and entered the sleeping harbor at Singapore.

"Here are the charts," he said. "Your next stop is in Grand Haven. Let him out there."

The second mate took the charts from Bosch, but he kept the key.

"I will stay here for a few days," said Bosch. "I have business to conduct here, and then we will meet back in Saugatuck."

Bosch ordered to unload a few barrels of flour and leave them at the harbor. He watched the schooner sail away north, as he hurried to the Big House to find it empty, with the Fischs gone. He found a note from Mrs. Fisch on the dining table.

"We've been invited to a party at the Union Hotel in Saugatuck," she wrote. "We will stay for a few days to vacate."

Bosch jumped on his horse and flew through the night woods into Saugatuck. All the lights at the hotel were out, and the lamplighter had dimmed the street lamps a few hours ago. Standing in front of the dark hotel, Bosch realized he had lost track of time aboard *Dawn*.

Darkness surrounded him as he squeezed his gun tight. There

was nothing left for him but to return through the night woods back to Singapore.

39

The Mouth of the River

They woke up to a beautiful autumn day, relieved of their burden of the past forever. Upon Art's insistence, Ida planned their official wedding at the Congregational Church in town, but they had to go and see the pastor to arrange for the ceremony. Pastor J. F. Taylor held the pulpit of the first church in the town of Saugatuck, that became known for holding the first war meeting upon the outbreak of the Civil War in 1861 before the new building was finished. The members first met in the schoolhouse in Pine Grove, in January, 1860.

Pastor Taylor looked at their birth records; Ida was born in Chicago and Artemas was born in Edinburg, Scotland.

"My dear children, what brings you to the Mouth of the River?" Taylor asked. "You picked this wilderness over your big cities on the other sides of the lake and ocean."

Ida feared the meeting with the pastor. Even though Ma and Pa back in Chicago were religious, she wasn't, because there was no church in Singapore, only a town hall, and she didn't seek it out. However, Artemas was a stout catholic, but he had no place to practice his religion except when he lived in New York and Chicago. At one point, Ida suggested to bypass a church ceremony and leave their matrimony to the old ferryman Jay.

"Do we have to marry at a church?" she said.

"Well of course, my love," Art said. "My parents would turn in their graves if we didn't."

Art would have preferred to marry in a catholic church, but there were no catholic churches in the surrounding area. He insisted on having an official ceremony to forever cut the ties of the past with Bosch and the Johnson Co., as well.

"Will you stay here with us in this wilderness?" Taylor asked. "As you may have found out, it's not for everyone."

They both agreed to everything that Taylor wanted to hear.

"I see you both were baptized at catholic churches," he said.

Artemas was baptized at the High Kirk of Edinburg, an old famous cathedral where John Knox, the leader of the protestant reformist movement, served as a minister. The wedding of Art and Ida was set for next Saturday at noon, before the onset of winter.

"If there is anyone in attendance who has cause to believe that this couple should not be joined in marriage, you may speak now or forever hold your peace," said Taylor.

"I do, she is my lawfully wedded wife," John Bosch bolted to the altar.

Shocked, Taylor dropped the book with the matrimony script and backed away behind the pulpit. Bosch picked it up and faced the couple in front of the small shocked congregation reading the passage:

The joy you'll find as you pursue your shared lives will fuel you to face head-on the challenges you'll encounter on this Earth. On your journeys together, keep your spouse in the space of highest priority in your heart. The love you share must be guarded and cherished, it is your most valuable treasure.

"The challenge on this Earth from the start was this man from Scotland who snaked his way into my house, took my hospitality and my wife," Bosch said. "For that he will suffer in eternal hell. May they both burn in hell.

"And to you Art, I will come and get you once and for all."

Bosch slammed the book against the table and punched Art in the face, who however showed the other cheek, according to the Bible. John walked away down the aisle without turning his head. Scared Taylor reappeared from behind the pulpit as the small gathering murmured and whispered.

"Continue, please," Art said.

"Under the eyes of God, I solemnly consecrate these matrimonial proceedings and the sacred covenant you shall both enter into on this day. Marriage is an ancient rite. As you enter into this union, you are choosing to take part in a historical human establishment and are pledging your commitment, before the witnesses present here today, to enter into that tradition with honor.

As Jesus said: *"Have you not read that He who made them at the beginning* **made them male and female?"** He also taught that, *"For this reason a man shall leave his father and mother and be joined to his wife, and the two shall become one flesh'? So then, they are no longer two but one flesh. Therefore, what God has joined together, let not man separate."*

Taylor shut the book and looked at the couple with anger.

"You two have separated what God has joined," he said. "You will not have my blessings."

The two never exchanged vows or rings at the botched ceremony. So, their impromptu matrimony on the chain ferry presided by the ferryman Jay remained official. Taylor made it clear that the two were not welcomed in the church, and the word spread around the small town, raising the waves of gossip.

"I told you we shouldn't have gotten married," Ida said. "Not officially. The ferry was enough."

"We didn't," Art said. "The Revered refused to marry us."

"You really can't blame him," said Ida. "We should have gotten an official divorce."

"Like where?" snapped Art.

Divorces were a taboo at the time. Unhappy couples separated instead.

Later, in the afternoon, they went to the old docks where ferryman Jay had been busy cranking the pullies along the line moving the ferry across the river. They boarded the ferry and sat on an old trunk by the pullies. Jay nodded at them.

"I've heard from the townsfolk," Jay said. "Pastor Taylor backed out scared of John Bosch. No wonder. Everyone is scared of him. He lost his mind a long time ago because of Ida."

Ida was sobbing in despair.

"He ruined us forever," said Art.

"How come he escaped from the schooner?" Jay shook his head. "You should have had him killed."

"That would make me a murderer in the new land," Art sighed. "My ancestors had already paid for their own sins in the old country. I didn't want to introduce new customs here."

Yes, Art was a descendent of a Scottish nobleman whom love had turned into a ruthless killer in the wilderness of the hemlock woods and white pines gracing the hills and the dunes.

They climbed up Mt. Baldhead and watched the misty lake at their feet as afternoon turned into evening and darkness enveloped them. Art hugged Ida and kissed her.

"He will come after you," she said. "There's no escape."

Art looked at the woman whom he cherished and loved and kissed her again to seal their destiny. They took the chain ferry back into town and went to the Union Hotel and asked Jay to join them later. Jay brought in a gift for them from the sea being an avid fisherman and a down-to-earth man.

"What are you going to do?" Jay said.

"We should leave town," Ida said.

"No, I will not run away from destiny," said Art. "This is where I found my destiny many years ago on that night when we met at the Indian trail crossing by Singapore."

"It was a curse that we've met at an Indian crossing," Ida said. "Mrs. Fisch mentioned that, and so did old man Jack."

"Old Indian tales," Art waved off the bothersome thought.

But they left for nearby Fennville to escape the town's gossip and Bosch's stalking.

40

Indian Curses

The curse was put on the Indian trail crossing in the woods by the Pottawatomi Indians by "Ring Nose" on the white men for taking their lands and driving them out of the Kalamazoo River valley after the Black Hawk War in 1832. Furthermore, the Singapore area was cursed by the surviving sailors of the steamer *Milwaukie,* who almost froze aboard the doomed steamer carrying flour from St. Joe. One of the sailors who staggered inside the lifesaving lighthouse cursed Singapore and its inhabitants.

"May Singapore never see the fruits of its labor, know love or happiness," said a sailor who had lost his mind from the endured hardships. "It will suffer from great destruction and suffocate from a slow death."

Bosch called Mrs. Fisch into his office, showing her the note she had left for him when Ida and Art were celebrating their matrimony at the Union Hotel in Saugatuck.

"You have known all along and took part in this unlawful, sinful union of my wife with that scoundrel from Scotland?" he demanded an answer. "I've been feeding you all these years, and you have betrayed me."

"No, it's the curse of "Ring Nose" and the freezing sailors," she cried. "Please do not let us go."

Bosch himself had heard about the curses, and everyone at that time in Singapore was superstitious. The sailor whom he had pushed into the river with Jack, has never been found.

"Do you know anything about that drunken sailor?" he asked.

"You pushed him in the river, and Jack saved him, but he froze aboard *Milwaukie*," Mrs. Fisch said. "He had time to put a curse on Singapore, and you were in it. He cursed you as well."

Bosch saddled his horse and headed to the nearby Indian camp by Oxbow to see Chief Macsaube. The ride in the autumn woods was like from the legend of Nenabooshoo, a trickster, who was a spirit of great power, able to perform any miracle. It was Nenabooshoo who painted the emerald forests with the dew from the goldenrod, pink from the eastern sky, crimson from the maples and fire flames, purple and blue from the waters of the big lake.

He entered the chief's wigwam, who pointed to the reed grass bench for him to sit right across from the chief.

"You come here to seek love again," the chief said.

"Yes, and I want you to break that old Indian curse on the lands surrounding Singapore," Bosch said.

"I cannot break a curse I did not create," said Chief Macsaube.

"Is it true, there is a curse on Singapore?" asked Bosch, "And on me?"

Chief Macsaube stood up and walked outside the wigwam and came back with a string of beads known as wampum.

"There is a curse by Ring Nose on the trail crossing," the chief said.

"And Singapore?" Bosch asked.

"If there is a curse on Singapore, the white man cursed it," the chief said. "It wasn't the Red Man."

"How do I break the curse on Singapore?" Bosch persisted.

The chief extended his hand and shook his head to the rustle of his colorful headdress, as Bosch pulled out money from his pocket.

"No, you know what we want," Chief Macsaube said. "We want the brooch and your fire water, and then we can break our curses. I don't know about the ones on Singapore by the White Man."

Bosch handed him two bottles of whiskey, which Macsaube gladly accepted, and immediately took a gulp from the bottle.

"Oh, it's better than fire," he said offering the bottle to Bosch.

Bosch took a gulp from the **bottle and** kneeled in front of the chief.

"You are the big chief of everything, please take away the curses from Singapore," he begged. "I will give you more fire water and the brooch. Come to our monthly Saturday dinner."

They both walked outside of the wigwam into the emerald forests to a sand hill overlooking the big lake in all its majesty. Chief Macsaube lifted his right arm and swiped the clouds to the **ground and** evening dew appeared on the beach grasses. He reached for the setting sun with his eyes shining and brought down to the ground golden rays.

"The curse has been broken," said Macsaube. "Leave and bring me the brooch as a token of trust between the white and the red man."

"Will Singapore be saved from destruction?" Bosch whispered.

But the chief was gone as the sun set over the big lake.

Back at the Big House, Mrs. Fisch was readying the Saturday community dinner for house guests and townsfolk. She decorated the table with autumn bounty, and Mr. Fisch brought venison and salmon. Sometimes, Bosch and Fisch went hunting together to provide food for the **house and** the company store.

"We're expecting an honorary guest tonight," Bosch announced.

All present stared at the master of the **house, their** imagination stirred by the vision of having an honorary guest in the wilderness of Singapore, trapped between the lake and the sand hills.

"It's a surprise, most of you don't know our honorary guest," Bosch said.

And there he was, standing in his full dress and a headdress, entering like the Great Spirit of the Woods, Chief Macsaube from the Oxbow Lagoon. He brought jewelry and a red and black blanket, "Rhythm of the Land," remembering those lost and the future. Macsaube handed the blanket to Bosch.

"This is to our future, as we honor those who died so we can live," Macsaubee said.

As the feast was in its full swing with luscious dishes of venison and salmon being passed among the guests, the mailman tore in breathless, disturbing the balance among the guests.

"Fire, fire," he yelled. "Holland is on fire. Fennville is on fire. There's fire everywhere."

Everyone ran outside in fear that the fire was also raging in Singapore. However, the surrounding woods were cut down and there was little danger of fire moving its way. Nearby Saugatuck escaped the flames, although fire threatened the bridge between Saugatuck and Douglas which had been built in 1868. Much credit was given to the newly-formed fire department. However, the outlying township and inland portions of the county were not as fortunate, and acres of uncut timber succumbed to the fire.

Mr. Wallin, who owned the old Wells tannery on the creek between Goshorn Lake and Moore's sawmill on the Kalamazoo River, had all men on guard, night and day, at the tannery. They remained on the roofs and the bark piles, armed with pails of water and wet blankets, watching for the sparks that were carried by high winds from the burning woods. The whole county between Dingleville and Holland was burned.

The entire territory north and east of Singapore was burned.

41

The Great Fire of 1871

The disastrous series of fires struck the Midwest on Sunday, October 8, after a hot and dry summer, and they burned communities north and east of Singapore, Chicago and Milwaukee across Lake Michigan. The flames consumed wooden structures and woods and scorched them to the ground. More than half of Chicago was destroyed, Holland was devastated, and nearby Fennville was left with a little more than a church and a half-finished hotel.

The fire leveled a broad swath of Michigan and Wisconsin, including the cities of Peshtigo, Holland, Manistee, and Port Huron. That same night, the Great Chicago Fire erupted in nearby Illinois. Holland resident, G. Van Schelven, witnessed the fire's advance on Holland in the following account, *"The Burning of Holland, Oct. 9, 1871" from the "Collections of the Pioneer Society of the State of Michigan Together with Reports of County Pioneer.*

At 2 o'clock in the afternoon the wind turned southwesterly and began gradually to increase. The fire alarm was rung, and from this time on the fighting of the fire all along the timbered tracts south and southwest of the city, was kept up uninterruptedly.

As night advanced the wind increased in force, until at midnight it blew a hurricane, spreading the fire and the flames with an alarming velocity toward the doomed city. The huge bark piles at the Cappen & Bertch tannery in the western and the Third Reformed Church in the southern part of the city, were among the first points attacked; from thence on, the devastating fire fiend had a full and unmolested sway.

Back at the Big House, the party guests were staring at the consuming flames and billowing smoke in nearby Fennville and Holland north of Singapore. Bosch jumped on his horse and galloped toward Saugatuck in fear for Ida. The bridge connecting Saugatuck and Douglas was in flames, and the fire department worked to contain it and to prevent the fire from spreading. He stopped at the Congregational Church to ask pastor Taylor where he could find Ida. But Taylor refused to give Bosch the address of the couple, which he didn't know himself.

Saugatuck was on alert and frenzy ensued. As chaos prevailed, in vain he searched for Ida. Helpless, Bosch ran into the office of the newspaper of the Commercial Record. But he couldn't find anyone, since they were all outside. Bosch tried to catch the druggist entering his store, where he had previously fought with Art. He caught druggist Charlie packing his things and on the run for his life. Bosch grabbed him by the jacket and turned him to see his red face and fear in his eyes. Charlie stopped for a while from throwing his belongings in a large flour sack. He was stuffing the sack with bottles of laudanum, herbs, and medicine.

"Stop, tell me where my wife is?" Bosch shook the man in front of his face. "Where do those two live?"

Charlie shook his head and dragged the bag after him out the door into the street and left Bosch in the unlocked store. They could hear the Saugatuck Fire Department alarm and horns announcing the spreading devastating fire. He ran to the post office where postmaster Morrison was hurrying to escape and dropped his mail bag with letters.

"Morrison, where does my wife live?" he barked at the postmaster. "I fear for her life. Give me her address. We're still friends and company partners."

"I can't do that, my friend," said Morrison, "that would compromise my integrity. I am the servant of the government."

"You have no integrity," Bosch barked into his face.

Bosch, suppressing his anger, stared in disbelief at his old-time friend, Morrison.

"I fear for her life, do you understand?" he shook Morrison.

"I do, but I am not giving you her address," Morrison said as he escaped Bosch's grip on his jacket. "Are you crazy? They didn't hand out their address to everybody in town."

Bosch was sweating in the October heat, enhanced by the sweltering nearby conflagrations. The inferno grew by the minute, inside and outside of him. He grabbed the mailbag and ran to the old docks with the chain ferry where he could see the flames licking the bridge connecting Saugatuck with Douglas. The long bridge was built by piling edgings and slabs from the mills, covering them with sawdust. Old sailor Jay ferried panicked people and their cattle across the Kalamazoo River. Bosch had to wait to fit on the overcrowded ferry that moved slowly across the river; he made his way through the crowd to Jay by the pullies. The wind from the lake carried the wailing of the scared animals and the smoke from burning Chicago across the lake.

"Have you seen my wife?" Bosch yelled over the crowd's panic. "Where is my wife, Ida? You know her."

Jay shook his head as he cranked the pullies to get the ferry moving across the river.

"You married them right here on this ferry," he yelled over the heads of the crowd, "Against the will of God or my own."

Jay completely immersed in his task ignored angry Bosch screaming at the top of his lungs. The cattle snorted, grunted, and bellowed as the crowd pressed against the cattle, until the equipment broke, and the chain ferry stopped and swayed in the middle of the river. The crowd pushed Bosch to the equipment, where his arm got stuck in the pullies. Somebody from the shore called the firefighters to help the stranded ferry with the passengers and the cattle. The firefighters pulled the chain ferry back to the old docks, increasing the chaos.

"No one goes on the ferry," they yelled. "The town is safe. We contained the fire by the bridge."

The crowd and the herd hit the ground bellowing and ran loose through the streets of Saugatuck. The deafening sounds of the sirens finally stopped at night. Fuming with anger, Bosch found himself at the unlocked drug store opening the bag with mail. He went through the letters and then through hand-written receipts in the drawer by the register. He found Ida's address on a satin box tied with a bow. He shoved the box in his pocket and ran to the address on the box. When Bosch reached the boarding house, he was breathless, and the house was dipped in darkness. Bosch pulled out of his pocket a can of oil with a wick, that he had stolen at the drug store. He lit the lamp so he could see the stairs. He stumbled through the dark hallway upstairs and knocked open room 202. The oil lamp shed light on the room, and he searched for the dresser on the right side of the bed, opened it and under the clothes, he found the little box that kept appearing and disappearing at different events and times. It was tied with a bow. He grabbed it and put it in his pocket. No one was in the room. Ida left behind her all her combs and brushes, expensive perfumes and most dresses, that she had purchased in Chicago.

He was back out on the darkened streets of Saugatuck. Bosch stared helplessly into the dark with flames shooting into the night sky northeast of town. The night was lit by the conflagrations in the northern territory; he could hear bellowing of the cattle and screaming into the night, as people were still looking for shelter. Bosch's scared horse ran away from the post by the drug store.

Charlie was back at the store, and this time let him in and locked it back up.

"Is it safe now?" asked scared Bosch.

"The firefighters put out the fire by the bridge, and nothing spread beyond the abutments," Charlie said breathless. "You can stay here until the morning. You have no horse."

"I need to find my wife," Bosch begged. "She is in danger with that Scottish scoundrel Artemas."

"Well, you're not going to find them in the middle of the night," Charlie said. "Get some rest. Lay there in the nook on the blankets."

The morning found the two exhausted men sleeping on the floor in the nook with dim light coming in. Charlie made some good coffee brought in from the steamships. He kept a fair stock of Brazilian coffee beans that Charlie grinded at the drug store, and he made a full pot that daunting morning. Charlie ran out to get the paper from the Commercial Record. The headlines were screaming in bold letters:

"Fire in the Midwest"

On Sunday, October 8, 1871, fire leveled a broad swath of Michigan and Wisconsin, including the cities of Peshtigo, Holland, Manistee, and Port Huron. At least 1,200 people died (possibly twice as many) as a result of the fire. Approximately 800 fatalities occurred in Peshtigo, Wisconsin. That same night, the Great Chicago Fire erupted in nearby Illinois.

Conditions were ripe for major conflagrations that year. Rainfall during the preceding months totaled just one-fourth of normal precipitation; early October was unseasonably warm; and winds were strong. Vast tracts of forest burned for a week in parts of Michigan and Wisconsin, and Chicago firefighters battled blazes daily. Contributing to Chicago's Great Conflagration were the facts that the bustling midwestern city was built primarily of wood, and several woodworking industries operated within the city limits.

Bosch found in the letters exchanged between Ida and Art a mention of nearby Fennville.

"If everything else fails, meet me in Fennville," Art wrote. "I will be waiting for you there, always until the end of time. Love Art."

"Where can I get a horse in town?" Bosch demanded.

"By the sawmill," Charlie said. "I doubt they will have any. You should stay put until it's over."

Bosch slammed the door behind him and headed to the sawmill, but found a horse tied to a post by the Saugatuck House owned by K.S. Smith of Battle Creek. Without hesitation, he untied the horse and turned on the road out of town toward the devastation southeast of town, where he could see the smoke billowing to the sky darkened with ashes. About four miles up the river, he traveled through the marshes of Willow Bar, Squaw Cut and Devil's Neck, where in the early days, Indians camped until Bosch could see the flames consuming the village of Fennville. The fire was licking the half-built hotel, the boarding house and several dwellings. At the railroad depot of the Chicago and Michigan Lake Shore Railroad (C&MLS), he found a train conductor; a train had arrived from St. Joe on its way to Holland and Muskegon but had to stop because of the raging fires.

Desperate, Bosch shouted at the train conductor.

"Anyone aboard the train?" he cried. "I am looking for a couple."

"No, they all had to get off here, and no one is boarding until the fires are done," said the scared train conductor. "We're staying here in Fennville. You can't board."

The C& MLS train escaped the Great Fire of Chicago by minutes, as it headed out the previous day before the onset of the devastating fires that leveled four square miles including the business district, leaving 300 Chicagoans dead, and 90,000 of 500,000 residents were left homeless.

The exhausted train conductor saw the flames behind him and in St. Joe from across the lake consuming the wooden structures of Chicago.

Bosch turned back to the burnt downtown of Fennville to search the remnants of the boarding house, but a firefighter sent him away swearing.

"Damn you, go back to where you came from," he said.

"I need to find a woman that stayed here last night," he hurled the words. "Alive or dead. Please help me."

The firefighter looked at the desperate man whose clothes were covered in ashes and had burnt holes in his hat. Bosch's gray face was smeared with ashes and dirt, and he could barely breathe. Bosch collapsed into the firefighter's arms, losing consciousness. Covered in ashes and fire debris, the firefighter eased the heavy body on the ground still hot from the previous fire. The lifeless body lay on the ground in front of the burnt down boarding house, that served as a hotel. He got some water from the water cans and poured it on Bosch's face to wake him up, but Bosch remained still. The firefighter lifted Bosch's head and gave him cold water from the can. Bosch's white and blue lips were shaking as he took the first sip and swallowed it, breathing heavily. The firefighter wiped Bosch's gray face and lifted him off the ground until he could stand on his own. He helped him into the saddle.

"The boarding house burnt to ashes," said the firefighter. "If she was here, she would have burnt alive. Was she alone or with someone? What did she look like?"

He could barely talk because of his dry mouth and throat, and Bosch felt the pain of the questions about his dead wife.

"She was with a man," he said. "Maybe it's good that they burnt alive."

Bosch bent to shake the firefighter's hand, shook his head and turned away out of town. Bosch was standing at the crossroads of hell burning behind him in Fennville and to the north in Holland, and beyond the big lake in Chicago and Peshtigo in Wisconsin. He headed west to the lakeshore stopping at Hutchins Lake, where he used to go with Ida on Sundays for a picnic. Once, they borrowed a canoe from the Indians and boated on the lake until sunset, when everybody left, and they made love in the nearby woods by the campfire. In vain, Bosch tried to find the clearing where they used to make love. Everything was overgrown with shrubs and new seedlings. Then he found a young hemlock tree in a beautiful grouping of hemlocks.

He hadn't been to Hutchins Lake in years, and so he sat down and opened the box he grabbed from the dresser in the boarding room on the night of the fire. Inside was the beautiful cameo brooch that Ida used to wear on her jackets and dresses. He held it up against the sun and saw the Scottish coat-of-arms engraved in the silver backing. It finally dawned on him where Ida got the brooch.

42

Chicago must be rebuilt

With Holland and Chicago crying for lumber to rebuild their cities after the devastating fires of 1871, Singapore mills and other sawmills in Allegan County were working around the clock and throughout the winter. The harbor at Singapore was busy with a two-way payload. Schooner *O.R. Johnson* made 63 trips across Lake Michigan that year. According to a commercial report, printed in the Commercial Record newspaper for the month of October, 69 vessels were carrying lumber, board, shingles, lath, cords of wood, railroad ties, staves, leather, apples, fish and butter.

The company, which also held interest in the Saugatuck Lumber Co., was back at the helm of all lumbering operations, and the fleet was growing to accommodate Chicago's need for lumber. John Bosch had to travel to Saugatuck for business, both company and personal.

Saugatuck mills were equally busy fulfilling demands of the big cities scorched by the fire. He visited with druggist Charlie, who couldn't help him.

"I have no clue where Ida is," Charlie said. "Go to the boarding house."

The boarding house was back in operation, and the clerk opened his books and searched for the names of the occupants until he finally found Artemas Wallace.

"Can you give me his permanent address?" asked Bosch.

The clerk looked up from the books and through his thick eyeglasses and then back into the books.

"He wouldn't give his permanent address," said the clerk. "This is the only address I have, and he's not here. The last time I saw him here was right before the fire. But he left a note here."

The clerk gave Bosch the note with Art's handwriting.

"Dear John,

By the time you get this note you will be searching for us.

You cannot change the bond between Ida and myself, just like you cannot change the Indian curse that was put on all of us by crossing the trail that ominous night. If you don't give up now, you will spend the rest of your life searching like Odysseus. Ida is mine into eternity. I took her with me. God bless you, Art."

Fuming, Bosch tore the letter apart and stomped the pieces into the ground with his boot as he jumped on his horse heading to Fennville, where the couple was seen for the last time before the great fire. But on his way, he stopped at the medicine woman's wigwam and showed her the brooch with the Scottish engraving in silver.

"I have the brooch now," he barked at the old woman. "Can anyone of you lift all of the curses, if I give it to you? Chief Macsaubee didn't lift them all."

Aiyanna looked at the desperate man standing in front of her inside her wigwam and offering her the brooch that she coveted so much all these years.

"Take it as a token of trust between us," he said.

The old woman took the brooch and ran her fingers over the engraving of the coat-of-arms, kissed it and put it in her pocket. She murmured a few words.

"Go and find peace and love," she said. "Like I told you before, don't come back here again."

Back in Fennville, Bosch searched for the owner of the burnt down boarding house, where Ida and Art stayed that fatal night of the great fire. The owner vaguely remembered the couple.

"Yes, they stopped here, and they were going to stay, but then changed their minds," said the owner. "I haven't seen them since."

"Did they mention where they were going?" Bosch persisted.

"No, they left in a hurry," he said. "That's all I know. Then the fire broke out, and we had to evacuate all the guests, and all hell broke loose in Fennville. I don't know anything else about the couple."

Bosch went to the depot, but the delayed train had left a long time ago. He stood by the tracks as if he was waiting for a train to come, to take him away to Ida.

The Big House in Singapore now seemed empty, even

though it had new guests and mill hands flocking in due to the increase again in lumbering, and shipbuilding. A disaster on one side of the lake brought prosperity to Singapore that was bursting at the seams. The curse must have been lifted, so Bosch thought. He rode to the schoolhouse at the end of Dugout Road, as the new teacher had taken Ida's place. He walked inside and found Ida's notebooks, ink pens, pencils and stories.

"Can I take these?" he asked the new teacher.

"Yes, please. What happened to Mrs. Ida?" she said.

"Mrs. Ida may not be alive," he said with tears in his eyes. "She may have burnt in the great fire. I don't know. I would like to believe she didn't and that she is alive and will come back to Singapore. She has before."

"But she left behind everything, her beloved books, notebooks, and stories," the new teacher said. "Surely, she will be back to pick up her belongings. Hasn't she stopped by at the house?"

The talk about Art and Ida hadn't engulfed the area yet. The townsfolk were convinced that Mrs. Ida had left for Chicago for a vacation just like many times before. Bosch packed up Ida's books and left the schoolhouse for good without looking back. He rode the horse along the river to Fishtown to chat with the Shriver brothers. He hadn't seen them since their last fight over the lost mail and the shipment order; Bosch was convinced they were part of the stolen order conspiracy with Ida and later, the conspiracy to cover up her illicit relationship with Art. He had never forgiven them. The brothers rarely visited Singapore, only to peddle their fish.

Both brothers were outside on the fishing docks engaged in a live discussion, that suddenly stopped, when they saw Bosch on the horse. He never got down from the horse.

"Have you seen my wife lately?" he asked.

"She hasn't been here in a while," Henry said. "Is she ok? We are worried about her."

"I don't know," Bosch said. "I am trying to find out."

Bosch got off the horse, tied him to the post and asked for a glass of wine. All three of them walked inside the inn to talk about the fire and the rebuilding of the major cities, and how Singapore was contributing. Many tourists escaped Chicago before the devastating fire and stayed at the inn, others came later to seek reprieve from the conflagration. One Chicagoan described his experience on the night of the fire:

"I jumped out of bed and pulled on my pants. Everybody in the house was trying to save as much as possible. I tied my clothes in a sheet. With my clothes under my arm and my pack on my back, I left the house with the rest of the family. Everybody was running north. People were carrying all kinds of crazy things. A woman was carrying a pot of soup, which was spilling all over her dress. People were carrying cats, dogs and goats. In the great excitement, people saved worthless things and left behind good things. I saw a woman carrying a big frame in which was framed her wedding veil and wreath. She said it would have been bad luck to leave it behind."

Bosch stood up in front of the guests at Shriver's Inn and spoke about the greatness of Singapore and how it was helping the major cities in their rebuilding efforts. The Singapore mills had been working around the clock, spitting out lumber and boards by thousands of feet, and they didn't stop in the winter.

"Chicago must be rebuilt," he said. "It will rise out of the ashes and soar high on the west shore of the great lake. We are proud to help our sister city in need."

Everyone toasted to Singapore for the rebuilding efforts of Chicago and to the spirit of survival. Bosch breathed in new energy from the waves in the lake, from the remaining white pines, and from the sun over the sand hills and beaches. He no longer felt self-pity over the past, smeared with ambition, greed and lost love, but the survival instinct prevailed in this robust man, who was one of the founding pillars of Singapore.

"We will increase the capacity of the mills ten-fold and build new vessels to carry the lumber over the great lake," he said.

Henry made salmon and whitefish in the outdoors pit, paired it with white wine from the steamboats and the gifts the brothers had received over the years from their Chicago guests.

The saws at the mills in Singapore ran at full speed cutting timber while new vessels were under construction, and the Johnson Co. held interest in small tugboats, including the *W.B. Minter* built in Saugatuck, *L.B. Coates*, the *Spray* and *Saugatuck*.

The company held several meetings with Cameron present at Bosch's office at the Big House. Bosch named Cameron the head of the rebuilding efforts of Chicago.

"Cameron, I will need you here now as we rebuild Chicago,"

said Bosch.

Cameron moved into the Big House that was now full of workers, but the tradition of Saturday community dinners remained. The head table was occupied by the company partners including Johnson and Stockbridge.

"We're missing Art," said oblivious Stockbridge. "He is one of our major stockholders."

Cameron hurried to respond.

"I sent him an invite," Cameron said. "He will be here on Monday for the company meeting."

"I doubt that," said Bosch. "We can buy his stock. I don't want to see that man ever again in my life."

"But now, it would be at its highest," argued Cameron.

"I said we are buying him out," Bosch persisted. "I don't want him involved in the company affairs. I doubt he is alive; he and my wife burnt together."

The conversation turned back to the aftermath of the great conflagration that brought prosperity back to Singapore. This time, the company's grandiose plans and vision spun as far as the Mackinac Island, due to the proposed expansion of the Michigan Central Railroad, the Grand Rapids and Indiana Railroad, the Detroit and Cleveland Steamship Navigation Co., which formed a new company, the Mackinac Island Hotel Company in 1886.

Although Bosch found new life and hope in the company's growing transactions, Cameron was running the show, with his sprawling contacts and connections between the east and the west.

"I will arrange for the buyout with Art," said Cameron.

"I am telling you he's not alive," said Bosch. "We don't have to worry about him. His share is our share."

"How do you know he's dead?" Cameron argued.

Cameron had a new office in Singapore but was gone most of the time conducting business on behalf of the sprawling company, with interests in the Chicago and Michigan Lake Shore Railroad (C&MLS) and its ventures to build railroad hotels. Art didn't show up for the company meeting on Monday at Bosch's office at the Big House, as was expected.

"I am telling you all, he is dead. They both died in the fire in Fennville," Bosch said. "Several people confirmed that. Cameron, go to Chicago to oversee our operations."

Cameron was on the next train to Chicago, boarding in Fennville, which was the closest station to Singapore. Fennville rebuilt fast, much like the other communities with no time to mourn. Out of the ashes rose the "Queen of the West."

43

Queen of the West, 1873

"The capitalists, the mercantile and business interests of this country and of Europe cannot afford to withhold the means to rebuild Chicago.... What she has been in the past she must become in the future, and a hundred-fold more."

Upon his arrival in the newly rebuilt Chicago, Cameron stayed at the third Potter Palmer Hotel, known as Palmer's Grand Hotel, located at State and Monroe streets. Before commencing his work for the Johnson company based in Singapore, Cameron was set to find Art in the heart of the newly-rebuilt Chicago.

The lumberyards and mills along the Chicago River survived, and the railroad tracks were not damaged. These allowed shipments of aid to come pouring in from across the country and around the world. Book donations collected in England became part of Chicago's first free public library, which opened its doors in 1873 along with other buildings, as most of Chicago had been rebuilt by 1873.

Chicago reigned again as the Queen of the West on the east shore of Lake Michigan, a major gateway city to the west in the 19th century.

Cameron rode to the lumberyards on the river and found the company office untouched by the fire. At times he worked out of the Chicago office, where he made a few contacts. He arranged for a meeting with Johnson and Francis Stockbridge, who was elected to the Michigan Senate and later to the United States Senate, at the Palmer Hotel to sign lumbering and railroad contracts. Cameron also invited one of the leading men of Chicago, Long John Wentworth, to the clandestine meeting that would determine the fate of Singapore across the lake. The meeting was set for next Monday afternoon at the Palmer.

Inside his room on the sixth floor, he pulled out the old letters that Cameron had taken many years ago from the Singapore warehouse. They had Art's old address in Chicago at a boarding house near the wharf. The wharf, the mills and the meat-packing plants didn't succumb to the fire. The clerk at the boarding house pulled out the old guest books, and found Art registered in them.

"Sir, he had no other permanent address registered here in Chicago," said the confused clerk. "I can ask around about the gentleman. What is his profession?"

"He is a businessman in the lumber trade from New York," said Cameron. "But he was born in Edinburgh, Scotland and has ties to Europe."

The clerk pulled out a thick, leather-bound book with the title, "Biographical Sketches of the Leading Men of Chicago."

"If your gentleman or his friends are not in this book, you won't find him in this city," said the clerk with a smirk. "If he is in the book, your door to this city is open. No need to look any further."

The clerk handed the thick book to speechless Cameron who turned red.

"You may borrow the book until your meeting at the Palmer," he said. "They ran out of copies early on. A gentleman from the Palmer left it here for me to keep. The book holds a lot of secrets on these fine gentlemen."

The illustrated book was first published by Wilson & St. Claire Publishers, with photographs of the leading men by Chicago artist, J. Carbutt, in 1868, who had mastered the new art of photography, then described as the process which draws down the rays of the sun and makes them paint with unfailing accuracy varied scenes of nature and life, so that one can sit in his own room, and by means of the stereoscope, visit all nations and climes.

Cameron opened the book to look at the photographs of the leading men of Chicago since its incorporation in 1833 as a town, and in 1837 as a city. Determined to penetrate the intricate Chicago businessmen network, Cameron was going to read up on Wentworth before their meeting at the Palmer Hotel on Monday.

Chicago now had a population of 500,000, and to find the Scott, Artemas Wallace, was like looking for a needle in a haystack in the human beehive. Bosch never convinced Cameron about the death of Artemas in one of the great fires raging in West Michigan in 1871. That night Cameron went to one of the pubs that popped up in the neighborhood by the meat packing plants, where Ida used to live with her parents. The old pub was filled with workers from the factories. The noise was deafening, but Cameron ordered a beer and went through Ida's letters where he found both her address and a mention of other siblings. The next morning, he headed to Ida's old home and knocked on the door. A young woman answered the door.

"I am looking for your sister, Ida," he said showing the shocked woman a letter from Ida's mom.

The young woman invited him inside the house.

"I wish I could help you sir, but we haven't seen our sister since the funeral," she said.

"Did she have any friends, or where did she like to go," Cameron asked.

"She had a passion for newspapers and was involved in women's clubs," the young woman said. "Please let me know if you find her."

Cameron promised to find Ida in the big city.

"When I find her, I will let you know," he said.

Cameron invited Long John to the Palmer for a late afternoon drink once he identified him as one of the "Leading Men of Chicago," thanks to Ida's correspondence that mentioned publisher Long John Wentworth as a kind man, who had helped her on several occasions.

Wentworth gladly accepted the invitation when he saw that the gentleman wanted to talk about Ida. He remembered Ida and the lumber lord from Singapore quite well and still kept the Singapore fake bank note as a souvenir from his heydays as the publisher of the Chicago Democrat.

The two men greeted each other with inquisitive looks.

"How did you know about me and Ida?" Wentworth asked. "Do we know each other?"

Cameron explained his business connections with the lumber lord of Singapore, John Bosch.

"I am here to conduct our lumber operations, but I would also like to know where I could find Ida?" Cameron said.

Wentworth raised his eyebrows in a surprise.

"Well, I am neither a lumber baron or a matchmaker," Long

John Wentworth laughed. "I thought Ida had been happily living with John Bosch in Singapore across the lake. She was in my newspaper offices a long time ago. I don't know if I can help you now. Everything has changed. I haven't heard from either one of them."

Cameron pulled out the book with photographs of the leading men of Chicago.

"Do you know any of these fine gentlemen of Chicago?" he asked.

Wentworth took the big book in his hands and reached for his belly. Laughing without opening the book, he ran his hand on the cover, tracing the fine engraving with his finger. He looked up at Cameron with a wide smile.

"I know all of them. They're my friends," he said. "And they know me. How may I help you?"

Cameron leaned back in his chair and watched the big man closely.

"Which one of them has any ties to Scotland in the old country?" he asked.

It was Wentworth's turn to hide his surprise in front of this fella from Singapore. He was steadily growing suspicious of the man's intentions, in regards to Ida.

"May I ask what is your relation to Mrs. Bosch?" Wentworth said.

"I am her friend, and I need to find her," he said. "She left Singapore in haste during the Great Conflagration. We are worried if she is alive. Mr. Bosch sent me to find her while working on lumber contracts for our company. He's been wasting away without his beloved wife."

Experienced Wentworth took a sip of his coffee and ordered another glass of wine. He looked around the fancy fitted Palmer Hotel restaurant. The hotel owner, Potter Palmer, was Wentworth's good friend who funded and supported Long John in his election campaigns that resulted in Wentworth being twice the mayor of Chicago and elected to the Congress.

"Do you have a proof that Bosch is looking for his wife Ida before I tell you anything about my friends that this book doesn't reveal," Long John remarked, growing impatient and tapping his fingers on the engraving on the cover of the book.

"I do not," Cameron said. "Other than a man's word."

"That's not good enough for me. How should I trust your intentions with Bosch's lovely wife?" Long John searched Cameron's face for any signs of betrayal.

Cameron's face muscles were of steel with equal color of cold gray coloring his eyes that stared straight into Long John's. Frozen to his chair, Cameron didn't twitch a muscle in his entire body.

"Everything you need to know is in this book," Long John tapped his fingers again on the cover of the big book. "The rest I won't tell you unless I have a proof beyond your word, a physical proof that you know those two so well beyond any doubt. Mrs. Bosch used to wear a brooch. I remember that brooch."

Long John ordered another glass of wine to stand up to his reputation of being a drinker, but Cameron halted him and called on the waiter.

"Bring us a bottle of your finest French wine," Cameron ordered. "Bring me your wine list first."

Cameron was stalling trying to think of a proof that Bosch wanted to find his wife.

"Where is that darn brooch?" Cameron whispered to himself.

All of a sudden, he remembered the clerk's words at the boarding house about the sixth floor of the hotel being sealed off to regular guests and reserved for the "leading men of Chicago" and a reference to their secrets. He turned red as he made the connection between the fine men of Chicago and the sealed off sixth floor of the Palmer Hotel, as well as the reason why the clerk had the important book that was nowhere to be found at the hotel.

In the meantime, the waiter brought the wine list. Cameron studied the wines extensively for a clue of how to turn his assumption about the crooked men of Chicago into a fact, and mainly to gain time.

"Do you have a favorite wine, Mr. Wentworth?" he asked the big man.

In vain, did Cameron try to remember the list of fine wines that the company drank at the Big House in Singapore, because he wasn't present at most of the community dinners. One time when he got back from Buffalo, he asked Ida what wine she was drinking, just before he offended her with the stolen letters. She smiled a sly smile and winked at him.

"I only drink wine from Chassagne-Montrachet," she said. "That's where my great grandparents owned a vineyard."

"Do you have Chassagne-Montrachet red?" Cameron asked.

"I will bring it right out," the waiter said.

"You have good taste my dear friend," said Long John, "and deep pockets."

They enjoyed their Chassagne-Montrachet as the night settled in on Chicago, and Cameron still didn't have any leads. The only thing Long John admitted to was having a friend of Scottish origin, but that he couldn't give out his name. Cameron was fuming, because the company meeting was coming up with Johnson and Stockbridge, and he would have no time left to search for Art. He walked Long John to the stagecoach that would take him home. Before retiring to his quarters on the fifth floor, he stopped at the reception desk inquiring about a room on the sixth floor.

"I would like to have a room on the sixth floor," he said offering additional $100 to the clerk.

"You can't have a room on the sixth floor," the clerk said. "They are all reserved for meetings of the leading men of Chicago at any given time. Mr. Palmer arranged it that way."

Cameron felt a little woozy from the taste of Chassagne-Montrachet and had to lay down, promising himself he would study the book about the leading men of Chicago to find leads. It was on his nightstand, and he managed to open it before he fell on the bed asleep.

44

Wallace Scottish estate

Ida was writing in the boudoir, when Art, all dressed up, appeared that morning. She had a fine view of the large estate with rolling hills from her bay window. The housemaid served breakfast in the parlor. She was her usual chitty chatty herself, which Ida despised; she was nothing like discreet Mrs. Fisch back in

Singapore.

"Is the gentleman heading out to the big city this morning?" she asked.

"Yes, Art is heading out to Chicago," Ida snapped. "We will eat alone this morning."

Ida stood up and poured the coffee and tea for them, ignoring the housemaid who turned away and scurried to the kitchen with a sigh. The housemaid never liked this blonde educated woman who came from Singapore, which equaled to coming from nowhere in her head. The blonde intruder into the household only wrote, read, and sent her out on different errands into the big city to the library.

"Why can't the lady go herself to the big city?" she dared to argue once.

"I can't ride in the stage," Ida lied. "I have a motion sickness."

The housemaid didn't believe a word Ida said. She was suspicious from the very beginning since Ida and Art arrived one evening soon after the great conflagration of 1871, telling her stories about their home being burnt to the ground. Mr. Wallace took the two in without any explanation.

"He's my great nephew from the old country," Wallace said. "That's all, and yes, their home burnt down on the other side of the lake."

"But Sir, I don't know anything about these two people," the housemaid argued.

"They're my family," Wallace said. "We're going to leave it at that. Go and take care of business, and my nephew."

No further words were spoken since that exchange between Sir Wallace and the housemaid. But housemaid Anna didn't like to be shoved aside from the happenings at the large estate. She couldn't snoop around the couple's rooms, because Ida never left the estate, except for Sundays to go to church and once a month for a clandestine meeting. Ida turned to religion after the Great Conflagration.

Housemaid Anna was listening behind the door to the parlor trying to catch a word from the conversation.

"I have to go to Chicago today," Art stated.

"But what if he finds you," said Ida. "Don't go."

"You are paranoid, Ida," Art snapped. "How in the world do

you know that they are looking for us? They all think we're dead, that we burned alive in Fennville during the great fire."

Anna pressed her ear to the door to catch more words from the heated conversation until the door opened and she was in the parlor facing the two.

"What are you doing?" screamed Ida at the housemaid.

Anna grabbed the sugar bowl and offered some sugar to Ida who stepped back in front of the maid.

"I didn't ask for sugar," Ida snapped. "Leave us alone. Please leave."

Ida turned to Art breathing heavily.

"Go if you have to, that woman is driving me nuts," Ida said. "I don't know how long I will be able to take it."

Art kissed her and put on his hat and left for the courtyard with the stage waiting for him. Wallace was already seated in the stage headed for Chicago. Ida returned back to her writing, when she was disturbed again by housemaid Anna, who brought her more tea.

"I apologize for intruding," Anna said all red. "The messenger left a letter for you yesterday. I didn't get a chance to give it to you."

Anna handed the letter on a small tray to Ida, who took it with the utmost care.

"How do you know it's for me?" Ida said.

Anna shrugged her shoulders and watched Ida, waiting for her to open the letter.

"Thank you, Anna," Ida said. "You may leave now. I need you to go to the public library in Chicago and do some research for me. You have shopping to do."

For once, Anna jumped at the opportunity to get out of the estate that was suffocating her along with the educated blonde woman.

"What is the lady looking for this time?" Anna asked. "Aren't you going to open your letter?"

Ida turned her back to Anna and stared outside the window into the sunny morning on the rolling hills of the estate. She wore her pretty morning dress and decided that she would write outside, as she often did when the unpredictable seasons allowed for that.

"Not right now," Ida said. "Can you get the porch ready for

me before you leave for the library, Anna?"

"Well, of course," Anna hurried to set the porch so she could leave for the big city.

The Victorian mansion had an enclosed porch facing the west with the setting sun, which Ida had always favored. It nestled on 200 acres of rich farmland in Galena Country northwest of Chicago.

"Come back before it gets dark," Ida ordered. "Not like the last time. Where were you anyway?"

Anna left the question unanswered in a hurry to leave the estate.

Ida felt relieved that everyone had left the estate for the day. Ida was savoring the moment before she would open the mysterious letter with strange handwriting. Anna made food for all of them for the entire day; she packed lunches for the gentlemen and separate dishes for the ladies. The sun moved on the horizon over the vineyards, coloring them in gold and bronze. It reminded Ida of her trips along the lakeshore to Mt. Baldhead in Saugatuck. Deep nostalgia for the lake and the sand hills settled in her heart. She missed her friends in Singapore and in Fishtown. She set the letter aside on the coffee table and rode her horse to the vineyards, absorbing the sun and the scents of the afternoon outside.

Whenever she spoke with Art's great uncle Thomas aka Sir Wallace, he mentioned the vineyards of Chassagne-Montrachet in Burgundy, where his mother came from before marrying into the Scottish family in Edinburg. Uncle Thomas grafted some of the vines to bring back from the old country to his estate in Galena. She sat down amidst the vineyards and by the chapel dedicated to Mother Mary. Ida couldn't get rid of the sad feeling that filled her heart now that she was alone, and the letter with the strange handwriting was still waiting for her on the porch. The grapes were ripening, and they would soon harvest them. She tried to remember how many harvests she had spent on Uncle Thomas' estate. It must have been three harvests at least since the great conflagration. She rode back to the house and picked up the letter from the coffee table and rode back to the chapel in the vineyards built according to an old European tradition. The chapel reminded her, much like the housemaid, that she never officially got married to Art, other than on the chain ferry across the Kalamazoo River by the chain ferryman Jay.

"Are they living in sin?" Anna gasped for breath. "How can you let sin enter under our roof?"

Ida overheard one of the first conversations at the mansion between Uncle Thomas and the housemaid in the early days.

"He's my nephew and needs my help," Thomas said. "I am not going to punish him for his love life."

Housemaid Anna acted offended by the loose manners of the landlord.

"But they can't live here unless they get married," the housemaid protested.

"I make the decisions around this house," Thomas stressed. "He is my nephew and my blood. You can never change that with your beliefs."

"You were a catholic too, and so is Art," the housemaid argued. "I will not support any reforms here."

Anna's angry words kept resonating in Ida's head, a hundred times magnified and hurting her. They fought with Art over their illegitimate union made by a chain ferryman in Saugatuck.

"What do you want me to do?" Art said. "I tried once, and you know what happened at that church where Bosch broke up our wedding."

"We can try again," Ida said, "here at the chapel."

Ida even found a priest willing to marry them at the chapel in the vineyards, but fate had it otherwise. The priest had found out through the parish grapevine, that Ida was still married to a Singapore lumber baron.

"My dear, you cannot have a catholic wedding," he said. "You're still married, and even if you divorced you wouldn't be able to have a catholic wedding. You have to find a different religion if you want to get married."

Ida still cried over the botched wedding in Saugatuck, and now at the chapel, until she couldn't cry any more. She went into the rows of vines and picked the ripe purple grapes of the Pinot Noir varietals. She stalled in the vineyards to put off opening of the letter, but she finally sat down by the chapel and opened the letter with the strange handwriting.

"Dear Ida,

I am the little Indian girl you used to teach at the schoolhouse in Singapore. Shaman Aiyanna is my aunt, and she told me about you and the curse the Indians had put on you and the white man. That is why you cannot find love. Aunt now has the brooch, and she wants to return it to you. You are the owner, and it will bring back love to you. She can't write, so she asked me to write this letter to you. If you could come back to Peach Orchards, she will have it for you. We will be waiting for you. Don't go to Singapore, they all think you died in the great conflagration; that your big love was consecrated by the fire......"

Ida was shocked as the past was peeking at her from the letter written by the little Indian girl that she loved as her own child. Without finishing the letter, she folded it carefully but held onto it in the palm of her hand. She rode her horse back to the house, ran into her bedroom and started making preparations for the big trip across Lake Michigan. She had previously discarded all the suitcases determined never to travel again beyond Galena. Ida stood in the middle of the bedroom helpless. But then she remembered the attic of the house and climbed the stairs into the attic in search of a luggage, a trunk, anything that she could pack her few belongings into. In frenzy, she threw blankets around that were covering up the old furniture. Uncle Thomas accumulated a lot of things over the years. It reminded her of the warehouse in Singapore on the sand hill with other people's belongings. She was afraid to open old trunks in fear of finding more clues to Art's past.

"What are you looking for?" Uncle Thomas was standing in the trap door to the attic.

He was a tall, gentle man respected by all. Ida lost track of time in the vineyards and even forgot the basket with grapes by the chapel. She stood up and looked the man directly into his eyes.

"I was just looking for luggage," she admitted.

What do you need it for?" uncle asked surprised. "Let's go downstairs and have some dinner. You look hungry and exhausted. You didn't get any rest while we were gone?"

Uncle Thomas shut the trap door, and together they walked into the dining room where Art had already been seated and Anna was running around getting the dinner ready.

"I am sorry, I lost track of time in the vineyards," Ida apologized for her disheveled looks.

Ida realized she was still holding onto the letter in one hand and tried sticking it into the pocket of her dress. But it was too late, as both Art and Uncle Thomas noticed the folded paper in her left hand.

"It's nothing, just my writing from this morning," Ida turned all red as she lied. "How was your trip to Chicago?"

Anna served salmon with herbed mashed potatoes, beans, and asparagus, as Uncle Thomas brought out the best Pinot Noir from his wine cellars.

"What are we celebrating?" Ida asked.

"It's my birthday, my dear," Uncle Thomas' laugh roared through the house. "I invited a few dear guests from Chicago. They will be here in an hour, just in time for dessert and drinks."

Ida was embarrassed that she didn't remember this important date for all.

"Art, why didn't you tell me?" she asked. "I wish I had known about this."

"You're always so busy, my dear, distracted by your writing," he said. "You never pay attention to your surroundings. Forgive her, please Uncle Thomas."

They toasted to Uncle Thomas' robust health, who was well into his late 80s. He was a widower and often talked about his deceased wife, whose ashes he transported back to the old country into her family vineyards in Burgundy.

"That's when I got some of the Pinot Noir vines that you're drinking today," he sighed. "That was a long time ago."

Ida excused herself and ran into the vineyards for the basket of grapes. She was glowing when she came back.

"These are for you," Ida handed Uncle Thomas the basket, "Happy Birthday."

They all ate the grapes from the basket and drank the fine wine to celebrate their discoveries. Startled, Ida recognized the deep voice outside hollering:

"Happy Birthday, Tom."

It was Long John Wentworth, the publisher of the Chicago Democrat, who helped her so many years ago. The big man entered the dining room with all his grandeur.

"This lady needs no introductions," he laughed. "We're old friends. Give me a hug."

Ida stood up as Long John gave her a big hug, squeezing the breath out of her. When she could breathe again, Ida shook his hand.

"What brings you here to friend Thomas' house, dear Ida?" he asked. "What a surprise."

Ida smiled and sat down across from Long John as Anna brought out a sterling silver tray with desserts. The French assortment included cheeses and more cheeses in honor of Thomas' wife's French heritage.

"You're just in time for cheese and drinks," Thomas welcomed his old friend.

"I wouldn't miss it for anything in this world," said Long John looking at Art. "Who is this fine gentleman?"

"That is my nephew from Scotland," Thomas said. "He's staying for a while with your friend Ida."

Long John chuckled into his beard trying to hide his surprise at the Scottish nephew Artemas.

"Well, we need to drink to that," Long John giggled. "Scotts seem to be in high demand nowadays."

They all laughed not knowing what that statement about Scotts being in demand meant. The tall wine glasses clinked, and Uncle Thomas drank first to prove the honest quality of the wine. Art leaned closer to Ida and whispered into her ear:

"I love you," he said. "I got something for you. You look lovely tonight."

Ida was glowing with love and the heat coming from the wine and the afternoon spent in the vineyards. She changed into her favorite evening light blue bustle dress that Art had bought for her in Chicago. Wentworth turned to Ida.

"How is Mr. Bosch?" he said. "I've heard that he is looking for you. Are you hiding here with my dear friend Thomas?"

Ida and Art froze in shock, staring at Long John's red face heated by the Pinot Noir wine from the estate of his Scottish friend Thomas. But Thomas jumped in.

"We're family," Thomas said. "We met at the memorial for Art's parents in Chicago. Ida is just visiting with us for a while to teach here at our Galena schools. I recommended her with her expertise and considering the dire shortage of teachers."

Long John looked at the trio pondering whether to pursue his quest for truth.

"I choose to believe you," he laughed. "Galena is lucky to have you, Mrs. Ida. I've always had second thoughts about

Singapore. It wasn't the right place for you to begin with, considering all the lumberjacks."

The tension fell to the floor like a heavy flower whose stem couldn't hold its blossom any longer. The evening continued to glide into the night filled with sweet promises of everlasting love and the sweet grapes of Pinot Noir. After the last glass of wine and dessert, Art carried Ida into their bed and they made love. When they woke up, Art gave her a beautiful ring.

"To our love," he said sliding the ring on her finger. "This seals our love forever before you go to Singapore, if you say you must go."

The estate's stagecoach with two black horses was awaiting Long John and Ida for a trip to Chicago. Anna let Ida borrow her luggage and helped her pack in the bedroom and straighten out the sheets and the covers.

"Don't forget your pretty dress," Anna reminded Ida, holding the blue dress in the light coming from the window.

Ida packed the blue bustle dress without wavering and kissed the new ring from Art.

"Don't forget anything," Anna looked concerned. "How long will you be gone?"

"Not too long," Ida said. "I have new classes coming up soon."

"The kids in Galena School will be waiting for you," Anna said.

Neither Art nor Thomas understood Ida's quick departure for Singapore. Art worried about her trip alone and offered to travel with her to the forbidden spot.

"No, she must go alone," Uncle Thomas insisted. "If anyone is looking for you, they can't find both of you together. But do you have to go, Ida? You're safe here."

Ida couldn't explain the longing to go back to where she found love, peace, and friends far across the lake and by the shifting sand hills. Her heart was half filled with Art's love, but half empty longing for the dunes, the beaches and the hemlock forests. She felt split and torn apart. She leaned out of the stage window and waved to the threesome standing in front of the Victorian mansion overlooking the vineyards. She never said a proper goodbye.

She felt with her fingers for the letter from Dakota in the

pocket of her coat. She never showed the letter to anyone despite Art's and Uncle's inquisitive looks. Ida pulled out the letter from her pocket to read the rest of it that she didn't have time to finish in the vineyards:

..........*"if you do go to Singapore, don't go beyond the Indian trail crossing. There could be great danger awaiting you."*

With love,

Dakota

For the longest time, she stared behind her as the Victorian mansion got smaller and smaller until it disappeared from her view. Ida watched the beautiful Galena countryside go by as she chatted with Wentworth.

"I didn't want to talk about it back at the mansion, but a businessman by the name of Cameron has been looking for both of you," Long John said. "I just wanted to warn you that you could be in danger. I didn't tell him anything."

Worried, Ida reached for the letter in her purse and showed it to her long-time friend, Long John. Wentworth, being a master of letters, studied the handwriting.

"Do you think it's the girl's handwriting?" he asked concerned.

"She wasn't writing yet when I taught her at the Singapore school," Ida said.

"If there are any doubts in your mind you shouldn't go," Long John said. "Do you have to have the brooch back? What do you need it for?"

"It's more about the curse that Singapore has been plagued by," she sighed. "I want to live a normal life with Art. We can't hide forever. I don't want to stay at the mansion any longer. I want to come out of my hiding."

They arrived by stage at the Galena depot of the Galena & Chicago Union Railroad from Chicago. The railroad travel took off well, to the great joy of investors, such as Bosch and his company on the other side of Lake Michigan.

Wentworth accompanied Ida to the harbor in Chicago with steamers awaiting the passengers. The steamboat travel in the 1870s took on new speed as the railroads connected more and more resorts, and companies like Johnson and Stockbridge invested in building hotels. Ida boarded the steamer to St. Joseph and took the railroad to Allegan and the stage to Saugatuck.

45

Passages

Ida first visited with druggist Charlie, who was delighted to see her.

"Oh, Ida, you're alive," he said. "I almost believed the lies that you two had burnt in the great conflagration."

They chatted in the nook of the drug store like nothing had happened since their last chat when Art was present, and the hopes were high for their marriage.

"I see you're doing well, my friend," Ida said smiling.

"Let me show you around town," Charlie offered.

Post fire Saugatuck was firmly established as a resort for Chicagoans with charming hotels such as Hotel Saugatuck overlooking the Kalamazoo Lake. They entered the hotel, former Twin Gables Inn, which used to be an icehouse for the Clipson Brewery at the bottom of the hill and a barrel stave mill owned by Francis B. Stockbridge. They ordered wine so they could catch up on old times.

"I see that a lot has changed in Saugatuck," Ida sighed with a hint of nostalgia.

But the old charm never disappeared from her heart, mind or from the town and its people that had been so kind to both her and Art with its mainstay druggist Charlie. They went for a walk to the old docks and to the chain ferry and boarded it. The old ferryman turned around surprised by the visitors at the late hour and late season for the resort. His old face under the sailor's hat wrinkled up and he tipped his hat to Ida. Jay hugged her until she couldn't breathe.

"You've become a stranger," Jay said. "And I kept telling Charlie that you were alive; he wouldn't believe me, old bastard. They almost had a funeral for you in Singapore to convince everyone that you were dead."

Ida leaned on the rail of the ferry and listened to the cranking of the pullies and the chain, trying to imagine her own funeral with flowers, music and criers. She shivered at the thought that Bosch was trying to bury her alive.

"Jay, I think they did have it," Charlie said squinting his eyes into the setting sun over the big lake. "Bosch had a eulogy printed in the paper for Ida. I read it."

Druggist Charlie pulled out the clip from the newspaper with Ida's obit and eulogy to Ida's disbelief. The words sounded familiar to her resonating in her nightmares at the Victorian mansion in Galena. She had always wondered about a particular dream that kept coming back. In the dream, Ida was lost in a big unknown city to her, wandering the streets and searching for something that she couldn't find.

Charlie remembered that afternoon in winter after the great conflagration, when Mrs. Fisch came into his drug store all bundled up, freezing and red in the face. She tore into the store all upset and breathless, holding the Commercial Record paper in her hands.

"Calm down," Charlie said. "I will make you some tea with laudanum. You need it. What happened? What's that?"

Charlie made raspberry leaf tea and put 15 drops of laudanum in it. Shaking, Mrs. Fisch reached out for the porcelain cup and downed the entire cup in one long gulp. Charlie sat across from her in the nook of the store where he kept drops and herbal liquors on display for all to see. Too excited to speak, Mrs. Fisch stretched out her hand with the empty cup.

"Can you give me more tea, please," she begged, all shaking.

Charlie made a fresh pot of tea for both of them, adding laudanum drops without counting them. The housemaid from Singapore stopped shaking and shook her head in disbelief.

"He arranged for a funeral for Ida," she sobbed. "A real funeral."

Charlie gasped at the words coming out of the mouth of this well-behaved Christian woman.

"That can't be," Charlie reasoned. "Mr. Bosch doesn't know if Ida's dead. It's all small talk without any proof. No one has ever found their bodies. Neither one of them."

But the word had it that the bodies were scorched so bad that only ashes were found at the burnt-down boarding house in Fennville.

"Mr. Bosch had the ashes brought in from Fennville for the

funeral," Mrs. Fisch added.

Charlie shook his head in astonishment.

"How the heck did he know those were Ida's and Art's ashes?" Charlie exclaimed in disbelief.

"They found the brooch in the ashes of the boarding house," Mrs. Fisch was sobbing. "He put it on her coffin."

"That damn brooch again," said Charlie, "I don't believe it. Where did he get the brooch? How do we know it's the same one?"

Charlie couldn't quiet the Singapore housemaid who was now crying out loud in desperation.

"Where did he get the damn brooch?" Charlie demanded.

"From the ashes," the housemaid whispered. "I saw it. He made me go to the funeral."

John Bosch arranged for the funeral for Ida soon after the fire. The news circulated around Singapore, and many came to the funeral at the town cemetery. Bosch bought a plot and had a tombstone made for Ida. It read:

Ida Bosch, burnt in the great conflagration of 1871.

Bosch held a funeral dinner after the ceremony at the Big House for his beloved wife lost to the great conflagration. The dinner was well attended, and Bosch read the eulogy for Ida:

A Chicagoan by birth, a Michiganian by heart and marriage, an entrepreneur and a teacher,

My beloved Ida touched everyone like the breeze coming from the lake,

> *Like the ferocious waves, she swept the shores of Singapore,*
> *Turning lumbering souls into unforgotten heroes,*
> *The wild savage into a gentle friend,*
> *Diving into the blue waters of Lake Michigan,*
> *She found treasures lying at the bottom,*
> *Forbidden love, painful love, encompassing love,*
> *Emerging anew, a white dove,*
> *Buried at the foot of the sand hill,*
> *Ida conquered the hearts of Singapore forever.*

The funeral dinner was just as loud as all the parties at the Big House, and it happened to fall on one of the community Saturdays attended by all. Mrs. Fisch added extra tables for out-of-town guests, and Bosch ordered more bottles of wine and whiskey. As a rule, business was always discussed at the gatherings.

"To her soul, may Ida live forever," teary Bosch raised his glass but quickly had to sit down, his head spinning.

Discussion at the table turned to railroad hotels as the newest trend of the 19th century. The Mackinac Straits area has always been of interest to Johnson and Stockbridge for its strategic position; the trading post at the Straits connected to the posts in the Lower Peninsula of Michigan. Bosch longed to get his company's name on a historic marker on Mackinac Island to commemorate his love for Ida. The company bought land on the southwest end of the island later to be acquired by the Mackinac Island Hotel Company that built the Grand Hotel in 1887.

Once, Bosch took Ida along on a business trip to the Straits, and they traveled by ferry to Mackinac Island. They walked around the island, hand in hand, falling in love all over again. The island was their haven and reprieve from the intricacies of the growing railroad, steamer and hotel business.

"I want to stay here forever," Ida said.

46

Singing Sands

Ida shook herself back to reality on the chain ferry with ferryman Jay and the Saugatuck druggist, heeding their words of warning. The sun was setting over Lake Michigan and she decided to stay overnight at Hotel Saugatuck before heading out later in the week to get her brooch from Indian healer Aiyanna. The hotel overlooking the Kalamazoo Lake was fitted to her likes as she longed to write on the enclosed porch. Ida always carried her leather-bound journal from Art with her. The inscription in gold read: *"To my eternal love, Ida."* That night after dinner she explored all the nooks and crannies of the lovely hotel with twin gables.

She couldn't sleep after the long trip, hearing the words of her own eulogy composed by her husband. Ida woke up sweating in the middle of the night. She put on her jacket and walked to the old docks underneath the stars. It was a clear night, and the full moon was shining bright on the shimmering river and the lake. She could hear the waves washing ashore. Ida walked along the river to its mouth where the waters mixed together in a staccato of words:

"Forbidden love, painful love, encompassing love."

"Like the ferocious waves, she swept the shores of Singapore."

Ida sat down in the cold sand clutching her cold, leather-bound journal. She opened it to the first page.

"For getting to know you was the biggest pleasure of my life. Art."

She couldn't remember if she said a proper goodbye to Art back in Galena, but she could feel the new cold ring on her finger. She felt for the stone. It was a fiery garnet originating in the royal lands of Bohemia in the old country. She kissed it and walked back to the hotel. In the morning, the hotel owners readied her horse, and she headed out into the hemlock woods clad in their autumn beauty.

When she arrived at Peach Orchards, the Indian healer Aiyanna was waiting for her in her medicine tent.

"You wanted to see me," curious Ida said sitting down on the grass reed bench.

The Indian healer woman was making tea and mixing herbs from different sachets.

"You know that the white man buried you," she said.

Ida sighed that another person was confirming her own death.

"Where?" Ida asked wondering if she had been buried next to her favorite, the old sailor Jack.

"In Singapore at the little cemetery," Aiyanna said offering her tea. "It's official. You're dead."

The little cemetery of Singapore had only a few tombstones with names of the early settlers that were later transferred to the cemetery in Saugatuck.

"I don't have the brooch, one day it disappeared," Aiyanna said nodding her head.

Ida sighed and gasped for breath.

"Can you still lift the curse?" she asked.

"You have to get back the brooch," Aiyanna said nodding her head. "But don't cross the Indian trail."

But the only way to get to Singapore was to cross the Indian trail which was forbidden.

"How am I going to get there without crossing the trail?" Ida said. "Who has the brooch?"

Aiyanna flashed her eyes on the new garnet ring, but Ida quickly covered it. The horse neighed outside, and Ida left the old medicine woman with haste longing for fresh air. To avoid crossing the Indian trail, Ida retreated west toward the setting sun, down the rolling hills with orchards and vineyards to the lakeshore. The warm breeze brushed her face. She touched it to feel if she was alive. She reached the sand dunes where Jack's shack used to be not far from Oxbow, but the sand had been shifting and covered his dwelling; Ida could only tell by the three tall pine trees where Jack used to make the fire.

The evening was setting in by the lakeshore as she continued to Fishtown on the beach. She could see the fire from afar. Charlie and Henry cooked the daily catch over the fire for the Chicago guests at the Shriver Inn. With the onset of fall, the fishing colony grew quiet with only the waves washing the few docks with the fishing barges. As she came closer, Ida could smell the grilled fish that she loved. Only the Shriver brothers knew how to make it the right way, blackened with herbs and lemon. They were outside by the fire and jumped to their feet when they saw her, and they stepped back in fear as if they had seen a ghost.

"Hello, Charlie, hello Henry," she greeted them seated in the saddle. "Hello, my friends."

Only the waves were washing ashore grains of sand and taking them back into the green depths of the lake and the wind whispered the day's stories. The brothers stared at the dark silhouette in fear and Charlie shrieked:

"You're dead," he cried. "I was at your funeral in Singapore. John Bosch praised your soul. I heard the eulogy. I heard the music. I cried at the funeral. You are dead."

The Shriver brothers attended Ida's funeral put on by Bosch and laid red carnations on the fresh dirt mound in the first row at the cemetery in Singapore. The violinist from the Astor House played for Ida the song to the rhythm of the waves:

"Nearer, My God, to Thee."

Charlie and Henry remembered weeping to the sad sounds of the violin that brought back memories of Ida when she stopped at their Inn and enjoyed their herbed salmon. Now, they saw her in flesh and in all her blonde beauty in front of them.

"I came to taste some of your salmon, before I head out to Singapore tomorrow morning," Ida said.

She jumped off the horse, took off her hat and approached the shocked brothers backing away toward the fire. Henry almost fell into the fire. She walked closer to them until she stood right in front of their faces, breathing her warm breath on them. Then she touched Charlie.

"Charlie, I am here and alive," she said. "Henry it's me, your friend from Singapore and Chicago.

Charlie felt the warm touch of the woman whom he had admired all these years for her courage to brave the wilderness of the sand dunes, and to live with lumber baron John Bosch. He noticed a strand of white hair in the blonde waves, as he reached out for her hand.

"It's you Ida," he said. "We missed you. We thought you were dead."

"Most people do," Ida smiled. "Don't let that fool you."

They walked to the outside seating by the fire warming up the autumn night. The night was full of promises and forgotten lies, betrayal and deceit. The Shriver brothers grilled the fresh catch of the day which was king salmon.

"He made it look like you were dead," said Henry in disbelief.

"That's what he wanted all along to see me dead rather than in another man's arms," Ida wiped off tears from her face. "This pretense funeral worked out fine for him as always."

They ate blackened salmon with herbs and drank white wine from the steamers by the fire.

"I fear for you if you go to Singapore tomorrow," Henry said. "What do you need the brooch for anyway? Go back to Art. Go back to Galena. Forget about the brooch."

The night moved in with a chill coming from the lake, and Ida went into her room on the second floor overlooking the lake. It was the night of the waxing gibbous moon shedding light across the water. Ida pulled out her leather-bound diary from Art to write before going to bed. Henry's warning resonated in her head and so did the words of her own eulogy, written by John. She decided to continue the words in the eulogy:

A bleeding heart between two men,
Lost in a sea of waves,
Picking grains of sand,
That through her fingers fell,
Trapped in a heart-shaped box,
With feathers and wings that only laudanum gives,
Rising like the moon in the afternoon.

Exhausted, she fell asleep in the chair by the window as the super moon set at 2: 30 a.m. and bathed her room in cold white. Rising up with the sun, she said goodbye to the Shriver brothers before they headed out on the lake for the first victorious catch of the day. She rode on the beach to avoid the cursed Indian crossing further northeast of the Kalamazoo River above the Oxbow lagoon.

She passed the lighthouse and turned the horse around to stop at the beacon of light to say hi to light keeper Nichols only to find that he had left to take up farming, and Timothy Coates had replaced him. But the drawings of the doomed ghastly steamer *Milwaukie* remained.

"I remember when that happened," she pointed to the drawing on the wall. "It was a horrible winter. Most sailors froze, trapped in the sunken steamer. Those who made it out, covered in flour, were never normal again."

Coates smiled at the pretty stranger with long blonde hair who came in like the wind blowing from the lake picking up the sand grains.

"I heard about it," he said. "What brings you here to the lighthouse?"

Ida sat down in the main room as Coates rushed to the kitchen to make some coffee and tea. She never noticed the family pictures hanging on the wall. Coates' dad had a general store in Singapore that competed with Bosch's company store during the good times.

"I used to live in Singapore," Ida said slowly, weighing every word.

"My father owned a store in town," Coates said.

"What happened to the store?" Ida asked.

"You know John Bosch & Co. drove him out of there," he said. "They hated any competition and wanted everyone to buy at their own store. Bastards. They made life miserable for him, until he left. They pulled all sorts of tricks on dad."

Ida got up and walked to the drawing of the doomed steamer, searching for an answer.

"What else is new in Singapore?" she asked.

Coates waved his hand to brush off unpleasant thoughts of Singapore.

"Nothing a stranger like you would care to know," Coates said. "The sand is shifting toward the town."

She was startled and taken aback by the simple statement.

"What do you mean that the sand is covering the town?" she asked.

"It's burying it alive," Coates said.

Ida shivered at something being buried alive.

On her way to Fishtown and Singapore, Ida couldn't find the large dune where the warehouse used to stand and the pine forests were gone, all lumbered out. A barren wasteland dominated the landscape instead of the majestic golden dunes rising from the earth to heavens bathing in the sun and singing glory to God. The few remaining trees were buried in the sand with only a few treetops peeking out of the sand.

"People are moving out before the sand buries them alive," Coates said.

Startled, Ida walked outside to look toward the town beyond the river.

"It's not safe for you to go there," Coates said. "There's been looting and nothing but trouble in the last few months."

Ida stopped to think about all the warnings.

"But people are still living there?" she gasped.

"Yes, they will be there for a while," Coates said shrugging his shoulders. "What do you need from there?"

Hesitating for a minute, Ida remembered the old medicine woman saying that she-- and no one else--would have to be the one to get the brooch, to retrieve the power of love and break the curse.

"I need to get my things from my old house," she said. "I have to go there by myself."

Coates walked to the cabinet and pulled out a handgun and offered it to Ida.

"Here, take this," he said. "Do you know how to use it?"

Ida nodded, took the gun and put it in her bag. In her mind, she thanked good old Jack for teaching her all the man's tricks. She turned around to wave goodbye to lightkeeper Coates who remained standing in front of the lighthouse. The town wasn't too far from the lighthouse. She walked the path at least a hundred times, but this time it seemed like eternity before she reached the docks all covered with sand. Ida stopped at one of the sawmills. Deafness and silence engulfed the machine room where the steam-powered machines used to hum to cut endless timber into boards and planks.

She remembered Oshea running around the sawmills like crazy bossing the mill hands around. But he always had a kind word for her. Piling sand shut the machines down. Ida gazed in disbelief at the sand's devastation. As she was standing in the middle of the sawmill, sand was blowing in over her boots, and she had to run out so as not to suffocate.

A crew was working at the large sawmill taking apart the machinery, also covered with sand. The men had scarves tied around their faces to protect themselves from the sand. Everything was crunching against the grain of sand. A man with a scarf on his face grabbed her by the arm and escorted her outside the sawmill.

"You shouldn't be here," he said. "It's too dangerous. Leave town if you can. If you can't, you can stay with me."

Ida looked surprised. She didn't recognize Cameron in the red scarf amidst the rubble and the sand.

"Meet me tonight at the Astor," he said. "We have unfinished business to conduct."

"I will give you the money tonight," Ida said, looking Cameron directly into his eyes. "I can't leave town without the brooch."

Ida has always felt that she had a lot in common with this slick businessman; they shared the same business ecumene and hatred for Bosch. At times, they even admired each other.

Cameron had trouble hiding his feelings for Ida in front of Bosch, who was his boss and trusted him in all affairs.

Ida jumped back on the horse and rode through town that looked like a sandcastle being blown away by the western winds. The streets were filled with sand piling up. She stopped at the company store to get some groceries for the evening. A different clerk was behind the counter where the sand was reaching to one-third of the counter. She noticed outside that sand filled the space underneath the porch and formed mounds around the building. Mounds of sand were forming everywhere as the sand kept shifting and blowing in the winds coming from all different directions. The ghastly sand formations were engulfing the town, and the prickly sand grains were swirling all around her. The sand devils were dancing around the town.

"Where is our clerk?" she shouted.

The man behind the counter with a scarf around his mouth had fear in his eyes.

"He left the town when the sands started to move in," the short guy said.

Ida looked down at him and his fear, considering him useless in the battle against the sand. She could hear the grains of sand hitting the windows and getting stuck in the crevices. She picked up the paper at the counter, glancing over the headlines.

"I will take the newspaper, a bag of nails, ink, tea, bread and wine," she said while reading the paper.

On the front page, she saw a bizarre picture of the big sand hill with a sticking black rooftop of the warehouse with a chimney and a tree stump.

"Singapore: A Lost Town buried by sand."

She pulled out one of the old Singapore bank notes that people still used at the company store only. The clerk stared at the ornate note and the beautiful, strange woman.

"Where did you get one of these?" he gasped. "We don't accept them anymore."

"Well, that's all I have, and you will have to take it," she said. "I am the company's vice president."

The clerk took the defunct Singapore notes from the once vibrant "wildcat" bank in a thriving town.

"You can tell the president of the company that Ida is here in town," she said.

Grabbing her groceries, Ida rushed to the door that the wind blew open for her. All bundled up, she couldn't walk outside because of the wind. She stepped back into the store, and the door was banging. She was the only one in the store.

"I don't want to get buried alive in here," she shouted against the howling wind.

Ida tried again, fighting the blowing sand. She couldn't find her horse, but she felt for him and jumped in the saddle. The horse neighed, feeling her, and took her through the blowing sand to the Astor, only a few blocks away. Then the wind ceased to blow, and she could see the building all lit with candlelight during the day. Stimson was still there and stepped back when he saw her and gasped:

"Mrs. Ida, I thought you were dead," he stared at her. "You must be her ghost."

"Most people did," she said. "I am here alive, standing in front of you."

"I will give you any room you want," Stimson said. "They're all vacant. No one comes to Singapore anymore."

"Please give me the top corner room with a view of the town," she said.

Stimson handed Ida the keys and took her to her favorite large corner room. The room was untouched by time, including the library that she had developed for the hotel; all stood intact oblivious to the sand havoc. The ubiquitous grains of sand didn't get inside the Astor, standing witness to the glory of Singapore in its heydays.

"Do you still serve dinner?" she asked.

"Of course, Mrs. Ida," Stimson said. "At seven as usual. You still have your own company table."

Ida changed into her favorite blue evening dress with the bustle skirt. She tied her long hair in an updo with playful curls falling around her face. She put blue eyeshadow on her lids that complimented her deep blue eyes and deep red lipstick. All dressed up, she sat by the window and opened her leather-bound diary with the dedication from Art. This constant companion was a witness to her personal strife. She looked at the fiery garnet ring and kissed it. Then she heard the bell announcing that dinner was being served.

Astonished Ida walked through the long hallways with green painted walls decked with paintings, drawings and nautical items. She paused downstairs before entering the large dining room. The beautiful lobby was outfitted with Victorian furniture, and she sat down to read the Saugatuck paper.

"Who delivers the paper?" she asked Stimson.

"It's still the messenger boy," Stimson managed a smile. "He will bring the mail tomorrow."

"He must be older now," Ida said.

"Yes, he is," agreed Stimson.

Stimson showed Ida to her table decorated with red carnations. She heard someone behind her back, and she turned around.

"I knew you would come back," Bosch said. "Aiyanna told me, and so did the store clerk."

John sat next to her at the table. He was dressed up in a black suit with white shirt and handed her a bouquet of red carnations. He had the white cameo brooch pinned to the lapel of his jacket. Speechless Ida stared at his face with wrinkles framed by curly grey hair. He ordered a bottle of red Chassagne-Montrachet. His voice was deep and smooth, fueled with emotion.

"I had that brought for you from France," he said. "It came on a steamer from Europe two months ago before the sands started shifting and burying us alive."

While the sands shifted, the nouveau wine from Burgundy aged aboard the steamer palace known as the S/S *City of Paris*, arrived in Queenstown on its journey from Liverpool.

Stimson poured each a glass.

"To you my eternal love," John raised his glass looking through it at Ida.

And the musician was playing "Nearer, my God, To Thee" on a violin.

Shocked, Ida couldn't move to reach for her glass and then a bullet ricocheted through the room and John Bosch dropped dead with blood all over his face. The red blood trickled onto the white tablecloth and made a stream to the wine glass and joined the red carnations in the bloody reunion as someone knocked down the glass of red Chassagne-Montrachet to the tones of the violin.

Nearer, my God, to Thee,
  Nearer to Thee;
E'en though it be a cross
  That raiseth me,
Still all my song shall be
Nearer, my God, to Thee,
Nearer, my God, to Thee,
  Nearer to Thee.

Though, like a wanderer,
The sun gone down,
Darkness comes over me,
My rest a stone;
Yet in my dreams I'd be
Nearer, my God, to Thee,
Nearer, my God, to Thee,
Nearer to Thee.

47

Sand Castles

The company fleet, boasting the schooner *O. R. Johnson*, the tug *Flora* and the steam tug *Saugatuck,* sailed out of the Kalamazoo River carrying the Singapore mill and the machinery in the fall of 1875 to a new operation up north leaving behind depleted and barren sand dunes with sticking black stumps.

New lumber baron, Cameron, was heading the fleet standing at the helm of *O. R. Johnson,* with Stockbridge and Houghteling, the new owners of the Mackinac Lumber Co. at Point St. Ignace.

Disappearing in the distance were the shifting sands that covered Singapore along with big dreams of the founding father, Oshea Wilder. Cameron walked by himself to the back of the three-masted schooner to watch the dunes in the setting sun. The wind was in their sails carrying them away fast, but Cameron wanted to behold the fleeting moment, much like he wanted Ida. Elusive, like the wind in the ship's sails, Ida escaped him one last time, this time forever.

Back at the Astor, he saw her unpin the brooch from the coat of the dead man and watched her kiss his boss on the clean cheek. Ida gathered her bustle skirt and stood up giving him one last glance, and without a word, she left. Cameron heard the horse gallop into the night toward the lake. He walked outside in front of the Astor all lit up into the night as the wind stopped blowing the grains and sand devils around town. It was dead quiet. Silence surrounded him. He could have killed both Art and Ida a thousand times, but he never did. Cameron even found out about their hideout in Galena from a wise man in Chicago, who was friends with Uncle Thomas and took a train to the town. Upon his arrival in Galena, he spied on the couple, and followed Ida around disguised as the postman.

That afternoon when Ida was alone in the vineyards, he watched her shed tears not for him but for her torn love cursed by the Indians at that trail crossing in Singapore. He kept poison from Aiyanna, along with a gun and an Indian knife. A previous conversation with Bosch flashed through his head:

"I can't have her, and neither can you," Bosch sighed. "But I will make sure she's dead in the eyes of the world."

Cameron turned back to the train station in Galena and returned to Chicago.

Leaving the shifting sand dunes behind them, the schooner sailed north to Point St. Ignace where the waters of Lake Huron mixed with the waters of Lake Michigan and Lake Superior at Mackinaw Straits. The Mackinac Lumber Co. prospered under Cameron's hands who got married and stayed in St. Ignace.

The company bought several pieces of land on Mackinac Island with a grand vision of building a hotel there. In 1886, the Michigan Central Railroad, the Grand Rapids and Indiana Railroad, and the Detroit and Cleveland Steamship Navigation Company formed a new company called the Mackinac Island Hotel Company. They bought the land from Johnson & Stockbridge and constructed the Grand Hotel that opened in 1887. The Grand Hotel still stands on Mackinac Island, greeting visitors with the longest porch in the world.

The sands kept blowing over Singapore, until in the late 1870s they covered the pioneer town with its big dreams. There was a cemetery located east of the large sawmill at the end of the Dugout Road with markers. One marker claimed that Ida Bosch died in the great conflagration of 1871. The sand covered that as well, without mercy.

With Bosch dead, Ida and Art got married at the little chapel in the vineyards, back in Galena.

A Michigan Historic Site marker in front of the Saugatuck City Hall reads:

Beneath the sand near the mouth of the Kalamazoo River lies the site of Singapore, one of Michigan's most famous ghost towns. Founded in the 1830s, by New York land speculators, who hoped it would rival Chicago or Milwaukee as a lake port, Singapore was in fact, until the 1870s, a busy lumbering town. With three mills, two hotels, several general stores, and a renowned "Wild-cat" bank, it outshone its neighbor to the south, "The Flats," as Saugatuck was then called. When the supply of timber was exhausted the mills closed, the once bustling waterfront grew quiet. The people left, most of them settling here in Saugatuck. Gradually, Lake Michigan's shifting sands buried Singapore.

The marker was dedicated on July 13, 1958, and marks Registered State Historic Site No. 191. There is a yacht club named the "Singapore Yacht Club."

That is all that remains of Singapore that lies on private property north of the mouth of the Kalamazoo River. If you visit the area, you can take dune rides that will bring you the closest to what life was like in thriving Singapore surrounded by the sand hills. The wildcat bank building was moved to Butler Street, the main street in downtown Saugatuck. It has the bank cage for the teller and the Singapore Bookstore on the second story.

SINGAPORE, MICHIGAN

Beneath the sands near the mouth of the Kalamazoo River lies the site of Singapore, one of Michigan's most famous ghost towns. Founded in the 1830's by New York land speculators, who hoped it would rival Chicago or Milwaukee as a lake port, Singapore was in fact, until the 1870's, a busy lumbering town. With three mills, two hotels, several general stores, and a renowned "Wild-cat" bank, it outshone its neighbor to the south, "The Flats," as Saugatuck was then called. When the supply of timber was exhausted the mills closed, the once bustling waterfront grew quiet. The people left, most of them settling here in Saugatuck. Gradually, Lake Michigan's shifting sands buried Singapore.

REFERENCES & SOURCES

Saugatuck Douglas Historical Society
Research & Access to Online Collections

https://sdhistoricalsociety.org/collections/collections.php

https://hub.catalogit.app/4124

As an invaluable research tool, I used newspaper archives,
chicagology.com, www.allegancountyheritage.com,
www.loc.gov/item/today-in-history/october-08/
Library of Congress, Chicago Tribune, Chicago Evening Post,
Saugatuck Commercial Record

https://en.wikipedia.org/wiki/Great_Lakes_passenger_steamers

Made in the USA
Columbia, SC
06 August 2024

40080919R00131